love
Loyal and True

BOOK 2

MUST
LOVE
DIAMONDS

BY
STACEY JOY NETZEL

Love Loyal and True

Must Love Diamonds Series, book 2

Copyright © 2019, Stacey Joy Netzel

Love You, Baby – excerpt

Copyright © 2019, Stacey Joy Netzel

Evidence of Trust - excerpt

Copyright © 2014, Stacey Joy Netzel

Editor: Stacy D. Holmes

Cover Art: Cover Couture

ebook ISBN: 9781939143747

Print ISBN: 9781939143754

He had her nightgown fisted in his large hand, and the contrast of the delicate, light pink silk against his large, tanned hand made her stomach flutter.

"Is this yours?" he asked.

"One would assume—unless you have one exactly like it?" she quipped as she crossed the room to meet him.

His thick, dark brows hovered low over his whiskey-colored eyes. "Did your apartment building burn down?"

She'd only taken time to wash her underwear, so the pungent smoke odor that clung to the pink nightgown hadn't faded one bit. "I don't know that it burned *down*. The firefighters were still working when I left."

"Why the hell didn't you say so last night?"

She couldn't tell if the roughness in his voice was anger or guilt. *Loyal—feel a human emotion such as guilt? Hah. Right.*

"What does it matter?"

"You should've told me."

"Why?"

"I don't know." He shrugged his broad shoulders, his expression uncomfortable. "I'd have given you the bed."

"Yeah, right. More likely you would've mocked me and asked, *'If you're a real psychic, shouldn't you have known it was coming?'*"

His lashes lifted, his gaze meeting hers as he tilted his head. "Well, shouldn't you have?"

She narrowed her eyes at the cynical humor tugging at his lips. Yep. She wanted to hit him again. Hard.

"It doesn't work that way," she said through gritted teeth. Although, with her dream last night, it had come close.

His expression softened. "Are you okay?"

Annoyed that his question made her pulse leap, she reached to yank her nightgown from his hand. "Don't pretend like you care. You're an ass, Loyal. Always have been, always will be."

PRAISE FOR STACEY JOY NETZEL'S OTHER WORK

"**MUST LOVE FROSTING** is a fabulous contemporary romance; a well-written book loaded with a stellar cast of characters. The dialog is snappy, snarky and makes this book so much fun to read." ~ Deb D.

"The **Romancing Wisconsin Series** is fantastic...the characters are amazing and the plot makes you want to keep reading straight through." ~ Debbie

"**SPRING SERENDIPITY** is a sweet romantic book, that had me crying, smiling, mad and happy which is my kind of romance story." ~ Rhonda

"As usual, Stacey has an exceptional way of making her characters come alive both on the page and in the reader's heart that never misses leaving the reader satisfied and believing they are real."~ LovesToRead, for **SUMMER SCANDAL**

"This one had me biting my nails; the tension and anxiety were palpable. Stacey's characters are real, hot, sexy, and determined." ~ Bev, for **SUMMER SECRETS**

"Summer Bride has become my new favorite by this author. This book just seemed to hit it out of the park with its genuineness and real life situations and problems encountered by the couple." ~ Jan, for **SUMMER BRIDE**

OTHER TITLES BY STACEY JOY NETZEL

MUST LOVE DIAMONDS

Must Love Frosting

Love Loyal and True

Love You, Baby

To Love and Protect (2020)

ITALY INTRIGUE SERIES

Kidnapped*

Betrayed

Conned

*2012 Write Touch Readers' Award Winner as *Lost in Italy*

COLORADO TRUST SERIES

Evidence of Trust

Trust by Design

Trust in the Lawe

Shattered Trust

Dare to Trust

Vow of Trust

Illusion of Trust

WELCOME TO REDEMPTION SERIES

A Fair to Remember, Book 2

Grounds For Change, Book 4

The Heart of the Matter, Book 6

Hold On To Me, Book 8

Say You'll Marry Me, Book 10

(books 1,3,5,7,9 written by Donna Marie Rogers)

ROMANCING WISCONSIN SERIES

Mistletoe Mischief

Mistletoe Magic

Mistletoe Match-up

**Mistletoe Rules – short bonus story

Autumn Wish

Autumn Bliss

Autumn Kiss

**Autumn Glimmer – short bonus story

Spring Fling

Spring Serendipity

Spring Dreams

**Spring Spark – short bonus story

Summer Scandal

Summer Bride

Summer Secrets

**Summer Wager – short bonus story

STAND ALONE ROMANCE TITLES

More Than a Kiss, contemporary romance

Chasin' Mason, contemporary western romance

Ditched Again, high school reunion novella

Dragonfly Dreams, Christmas novella

Nina, Beach Brides sweet contemporary novella

PARANORMAL ROMANCE TITLES

If Tombstones Could Talk, paranormal novella

Beneath Still Waters (Part One), paranormal novella

Rising Above (Still Waters Part Two), paranormal novella

FREE READ

Holding Out For a Hero

PUZZLE BOOK

Passion & Puzzles

a Word Search and Crossword Puzzle Book of Stacey Joy Netzel Romance books

DEDICATION

To those for whom the hope for love springs eternal. May you find the one who brings your heart joy.

CHAPTER 1

*R*oxanna Kent shivered as a passing firefighter swirled the air up past the hem of her thin, satin nightgown. An EMS worker had given her a blanket, and a two-sizes-too-large pair of slippers for her bare feet, but they were no match for the chilly Colorado October night—even with the blaze raging through her apartment building across the street.

Strangely, she didn't feel the cold, even though she was aware of her body shivering and the occasional chatter of her teeth. Numbness had set in once the last of her neighbors escaped the smoke-filled halls. If she hadn't woken from her dream, heart pounding in terror, the phantom smell of smoke choking her despite the crystal clear air in her bedroom, would she have still made it out alive? Who would've been there to make sure?

No one.

Surrounded by firefighters, police, EMS workers, fellow homeless apartment residents, and a multitude of onlookers, she'd never felt more alone in her life.

"Excuse me?" A hand on her blanket-wrapped shoulder

1

drew her around to see a blond woman wearing a Red Cross jacket. "Do you have someone to call? Or can I call for you?"

"Um…" The one person—well, make that both persons— she would've called were out of town. Her best friend, Asher, and his fiancé, Honor, were in Hawaii on a photo shoot-slash-engagement trip. She turned her head back toward the fire. "My phone is still in there. I don't know the numbers."

She hadn't even thought of it when she woke from her dream. *Premonition*, she now realized. Even though she hadn't had one that strong since she was nine, it was a good thing she'd listened to her gut and gone out into the hall. She'd only wanted to reassure herself the phantom smoke was a figment of her imagination so she could get back to sleep. Instead, she'd discovered it was all too real and hurried to pull the fire alarm.

After that, everyone worked together to make sure no one was left behind as flames spread frighteningly quick. There had been no time to go back for anything, which meant her phone was likely melted on her nightstand by now.

The hand on her shoulder gave a gentle squeeze. "We're setting up a shelter at the community center for anyone who needs it. Volunteers are giving rides right over there."

Roxanna blinked and looked in the direction the woman pointed. She saw a few of the neighbors from her floor getting into cars. Some of them had managed to grab personal items, but she'd have to go see what she could find from her shop before she—

Ooh, the second floor apartment. Asher owned her retail building, and he'd always told her she could use it if she needed to. She'd never needed to—until now.

She managed a weak smile of something close to relief. "Thank you, but I have a place to stay."

2

The blond pressed a card into her hand. "Call if you need anything."

At her nod, the woman moved on to a family huddled together in blankets. Roxanna roused herself out of her stupor to take stock of what she needed to do. Get over to Lift Your Spirit, pick out some clothes from her inventory, then head upstairs for a hot shower. The smoke smell infused into her hair was strong enough to tighten her throat and make her eyes sting.

She searched for a way to get through the chaos to the back of the building where her Jeep was parked until she realized she didn't have her keys, either. A couple of shaky inhales kept her from bawling right there on the sidewalk and got her mind thinking. She kept a spare set at her shop, but she couldn't walk the two and a half miles in slippers and a satin nightgown, so she'd need to call a—

Nope. She had no money.

Damn. Now the sting in her eyes wasn't only from the smoke.

Swiping the tears from her face with one hand, she walked over to the volunteer staging area. A few minutes later, a black man named Leonard in his fifties, maybe early sixties, opened his passenger door for her.

"Thank you so much. I'm Roxanna." She slid in with a grateful smile, and once he was in his seat, she directed him to Lift Your Spirit.

About halfway into the ride, he said, "I think that's the psychic shop my granddaughter brings me cupcakes from every so often. Is that your place?"

She nodded as country music played softly on the radio. After barely two minutes of sitting, emotional and physical exhaustion were taking over.

"She brings me those chocolate covered cake balls, too," Leonard added. "They're very good."

"The cupcakes and the cake balls are Honor Hartman specialties." Her best friend's fiancé had started making the cake balls to use up her cake scraps, and customers had gone crazy for them. "Her cake shop next door to me will be opening in a few months."

"I'll make sure to watch for it." He turned off Aspen Street to drive around to the back of the building. It was almost three a.m. when he braked outside the back door of her shop.

"Thank you so much for the ride, Leonard," she said as she opened the passenger door.

"Are you sure it's okay for me to leave you here?" He ducked his head to look at the alley as a slight frown drew his gray eyebrows together. Other than a black SUV and an older, white, four-door car, the back parking lot was deserted at this time of night.

"There's an apartment upstairs. I promise, I'll be fine."

"I'll wait until you're safely inside," he advised.

Her heart warmed at his concern. "Thank you. You and your granddaughter are welcome to come by anytime for a free treat. Or even a reading."

"I don't do this to get paid back," he protested.

Her senses were way out of whack with everything that had happened, but a moment of focus revealed the orange tones of his aura, confirming his generosity and kindness was genuine. "I know. And I'm offering simply because I want to. Get home safely yourself."

They shared a brief smile before she turned to punch in the key code to unlock the back door. Thankfully, Asher had installed them on all the entrances when he first bought the building six years ago, so she didn't need a key.

The light blinked red, and she leaned her forehead against the cold metal of the door for a moment. She'd changed the code after a break-in attempt a few weeks ago, and it took a moment for her tired brain to recall the numbers.

4

47835

The light switched to solid green and the lock clicked. Energy saving motion lights came on in the outer hall as she stepped inside. With a final wave for Leonard, she shut the door and used the same code for the lockbox into her shop. From here in the back, she could see the soft, comforting illumination from the Himalayan salt lamps in her front windows and throughout the floor displays.

From one heartbeat to the next, the orange glow flashed her back to the fire, and her heart leapt into her throat with her sharp inhale. Smoke clung to her hair and clothes, filling her lungs as she tossed the blanket on a chair by the door of her reading room. Habit had her reaching out to graze her fingers over the stings of beads across the doorway when she spun around, and the comforting musical tinkle of sound followed her into her office-slash-storage room.

Thinking of her car keys, she frowned at the unorganized chaos on her desk and surrounding surfaces, not quite sure where to start looking. Folders and papers were piled all over the place, with one precarious stack reaching almost two feet high to the left of the computer monitor. After her accountant got married and moved out of state last month, she kept meaning to clean and organize, but with so many other things to get done, it was hard to find the time.

You don't make *the time.*

No, she didn't. The bills were depressing, she couldn't balance her profit and loss reports to save her life, and doing hours of paperwork in the back room was lonely. She was so damn tired of being lonely.

More tears burned her eyes, but a few determined blinks held them at bay.

"Now's not the time to clean the desk *or* have a pity party," she muttered. Since she didn't need the keys right at this moment, she turned away from her disaster area, toward the storage part of the room.

Her part-time employees, Tessa and Darcy, kept everything ship-shape over here. Once Roxanna verified new orders and made sure the inventory was correct, they didn't let her near their organized shelves.

Thankfully, though, she didn't have to dig through any boxes since there was a clothes rack off to one side with older clearance items that hadn't sold. A few select items she might try to cycle through the shop one last time, but most she planned to donate to a local women's shelter and take the tax write off.

She found a brown T-shirt, and a brown, gold, and black gauzy skirt, and then took a second, extra-large, orange tie-dyed T-shirt to sleep in. It would be a toss-up between lying awake the rest of the night or going comatose the moment her head hit the pillow.

Essential oils would help with the latter, so she made a quick trip out front for bottles of lavender and ylang-ylang, then grabbed socks and a pair of the fashionable new mid-calf, lace-up military boots she'd stocked for winter. With everything gathered in her arms, she made her way back out to the door in the hallway that led to the second floor.

After keying in the apartment code, she moved inside on auto-pilot. Light through the window from the outside street lamps guided her straight to the bathroom, where she shut the door and stripped down for a shower. A quick wash of her underwear in the sink ensured they'd be clean and dry when she woke up, then she stepped beneath the steamy spray.

After she scrubbed her hair and her body, she was in the middle of rinsing the suds away when the horror of the night replayed in her mind, and the tears she'd been fighting resurfaced yet again. She didn't need her psychic intuition to tell her releasing the emotion was the best thing to do right now. She turned her face up and let them flow as the water washed them down the drain.

Fatigue weighted her limbs when she finally shut off the water and dried from head to toe. She probably wouldn't need it, but dabbed a couple drops of the ylang-ylang oil on her temples, wrists, and the back of her neck anyway, then pulled the orange T-shirt over her head. With her five foot nine height, the extra-large barely covered her bare butt cheeks, but right about now all she cared about was getting to the bed.

She wrapped a towel around her wet hair, wishing she'd thought to look for a comb or brush in the shop. Now it would have to wait until morning, when she went down to open up. She grimaced as she remembered she was working alone tomorrow. At least it was Sunday, the one day she opened at eleven a.m. instead of nine.

When she shut off the bathroom light, the dark quiet helped soothe her frayed nerves. There was only one bedroom, and the door swung open easily. Room darkening shades kept out the light from the street, but the faint outline of the bed was enough to guide her silent footsteps.

She stripped back the corner of the comforter and slid between the cool sheets with exhausted relief. A deep inhale to ease the tension in her shoulders filled her nose with the faintest hint of distinctly male cologne. A tingle of unease raced down her spine at the same time the mattress suddenly rocked beneath her.

Roxanna froze as her heart surged up into her throat. Something warm and hairy brushed against her leg at the same time a muscled forearm snaked around her waist.

She screamed and swung wildly, kicking free of the sheets to scramble from the bed.

7

CHAPTER 2

$\mathcal{L}$oyal Diamond's dream went from sexy and promising to shockingly painful when a shriek nearly blew out his eardrums and a hand wacked him across the bridge of his nose.

"*Ow. God—what the fuck?*"

He jerked back against the pillow and wrestled his arms from the sheets as the bedside lamp clicked on. He blinked and shielded his eyes against the sudden brightness, then couldn't quite comprehend the astonished brown eyes staring back at him from a pale face framed by long, wet, brunette hair.

If he was still dreaming, it had become a nightmare. Pulse revving like a race car, he levered up on one elbow to face the woman standing beside the bed.

"What the fuck?" he repeated at the same time Roxanna Kent demanded, "What are you doing here?"

Wide awake now, he frowned at the accusation in her abnormally high voice and pushed up farther to lean against the headboard so she wasn't towering over him like Godzilla. "My brother gave me the key code."

8

When he lifted a hand to rub at the dull ache in his cheek and nose, she suddenly gave a sharp gasp. "Are you *naked?*"

He darted his gaze down as he grabbed for the covers. Heat climbed his neck when he saw lingering arousal from his dream. Pulling the sheet up over his hips to cover his exposed family jewels, he shot back, "Way to ask the obvious, psycho...I mean *psychic.*"

Her jaw clenched, and she started to frown, but then her eyes went wide before she whipped her head toward the door. "Oh, my God. Is there someone here with you?"

"Besides you?" he asked with derision. "No. And why is it that you *are* here?"

She turned back, eyebrows drawn together over her glare, her wet, tangled hair streaming down alongside her face and over her shoulders. "You didn't seem at all surprised when you grabbed me." Her gaze darted down for a split second, then jerked back up.

"I did not grab you—I was dreaming. Right now, I wish I still was." *No—that sounds bad.* "And *not* because *you* climbed in the damn bed with *me.*"

"I didn't know you were here," she snapped as she spun away.

For the first time his brain actually processed what she was wearing. Or more accurately, what she *wasn't* wearing. His heart started to pound faster when he saw bare ass cheeks peeking out from under the bottom of her orange tie-dyed T-shirt.

"Are *you* naked?" he asked.

Roxanna gasped and whirled back to face him, her hands going down to tug the hem of her shirt lower in both the front and the back while she stooped at the knees. He watched the neckline stretch down...and down some more.

His breath hitched as the material pulled taut against her chest and her pebbled nipples poked against the multi-

9

colored cotton. Her breasts were on the small side, but he'd bet they'd still fit his hands perfectly.

Blood rushed to his groin, and his erection hardened once more.

Fuck. He'd always hated his body's reaction to his brother's best friend. How the hell could he be so physically attracted to a woman he didn't respect and couldn't stand?

"I just took a shower and didn't have an extra pair of clean underwear," she explained, her cheeks bright red.

Explains the wet hair—and the bare ass. And whatever the hell smells like a spicy, tropical beach.

"How did you not hear me?" she accused with a frown. As if he was the one to blame for not stopping her from getting into bed with him.

"I was sleeping." And clearly, thoroughly exhausted after his twelve hour drive from Texas if he slept through her showering.

But he sure as hell was awake now. His traitorous mind conjured up an image of her tall, slim body all wet and soapy with those long, brunette curls of hers streaming down her spine to the dimples at the small of her back. Too bad he *hadn't* woken up for that.

His body throbbed hard in response, and annoyance surged right after. "Don't you have your own apartment?"

Her expression froze, then she bit her lip as her throat worked in a hard swallow. "I did."

When she didn't add more to make sense, he raised his eyebrows. "And now you don't?"

"Now I don't."

She looked like she might cry, and he wondered why she was being so damn cryptic at—he reached sideways to check his phone on the night stand—*three a.m.?*

"So, what the hell?" he prompted in exasperation. "Your boyfriend throw you out?"

"I don't have a boyfriend."

Good to know.

No! That's the last thing he cared about.

"Did you not pay your rent and get evicted in the middle of the night?" he asked with a sneer.

When he noticed her white knuckles against the backdrop of the orange T-shirt clenched in her fingers, his gut tightened with suspicion. Something wasn't right here.

"I didn't know you were here."

"Yeah, you said that already."

Which begged the question, if she really was the psychic she claimed to be, shouldn't she have 'seen' he was here? Sensed him, or a presence, at the very least?

It was too late—or early—to start that argument, but she didn't seem to be in a hurry to be going anywhere, so he swung his legs over the edge of the bed to swipe his briefs off the floor.

"What are you doing?"

Her shrill question made him pause. "I'm not going to sit here naked while you stand there staring at me." He paused and tilted his head slightly to the right. "Unless you want to strip and join me again?"

Her nose scrunched up. "Ew. *No.*"

The immediate response would have been a real ego blow, except her gaze dropped to his bare chest, and then tracked down to the sheet across his lap. Color bloomed in her cheeks, and she whirled toward the door.

"Stay here. Go back to sleep. I'll take the couch."

Apparently, his brother's apartment came with a roommate whether he wanted one or not.

As she hurried away, Loyal couldn't help but check out her gorgeous legs that went on for days. It was a crying shame she hid such glorious assets under those long skirts of hers.

He almost grinned at the sight of both her hands in a death grip on the back hem of her shirt. She'd pulled it down so hard to cover her ass, he imagined what was no longer covered in front. Another surge of lust hit hard.

The moment she disappeared from sight, he dropped back on the bed. He pressed his palm over his erection in an attempt to ease the ache. The increased pressure made him want to wrap his fingers around himself and stroke hard until he found release.

He groaned under his breath.

Fuck. Now he needed a shower—a cold one.

CHAPTER 3

*R*oxanna jerked awake with a gasp, her heart thumping in panic during the seconds it took to realize she'd been dreaming again. But this time there was not another fire. She was safe on the couch in Asher's empty apartment above her shop, with the sunrise of a new day shining through the sheer window curtains.

Relief was short-lived when she remembered the shock of coming face to face with his older brother at three o'clock in the morning. He'd warned her Loyal might use the place if he moved back to Colorado, but that had been months ago, and she'd completely forgotten about it until she ended up in bed with him—sans panties.

That was a scenario she'd dreamed about for years. Turned out, the reality had both exceeded and fallen short of her frustrating, oft-recurring secret fantasy.

Naked Loyal was *so* much better than she'd imagined— and, um, bigger, too. Eyes closed, she pictured his broad shoulders, trim abs, and the dark, sexy trail of chest hair leading her gaze down to the promise of something really

13

damn good. Her breath hitched in her throat as longing twinged in her core.

She shook her head and opened her eyes, because after that—or in spite of that?—it had become a nightmare. He'd been a jerk from the first day they'd met, and last night had proved no exception, starting with him calling her *psycho*, as if she'd planned the whole insane scenario. And then he'd suggested she strip and join him.

The guy hated her, so she knew it was nothing more than a shock-jock comment meant to ruffle her feathers, but a small part of her wanted to throw caution to the wind and call his bluff—and that pissed her off. Sometimes the loneliness made it hard to breathe, but she wasn't desperate enough to toss aside her self-respect for a quick roll in the sheets with a guy who didn't even like her.

At least, she hadn't thought she was until he was naked in front of her.

She'd hurried out the door before temptation overrode common sense, and went straight to the bathroom to find a blow dryer for her underwear so she wouldn't flash her ass again in the morning.

As for the fire, she hadn't told him because it would've gone one of two ways. He would've been the jerk he usually was, she'd have cried, and she would've wanted to hit him again. Or, he'd have felt sorry for her, she probably still would've cried, and she would've wanted to hit him again.

Same results either way, except this time, she would've been able to aim her swing for maximum pain. Especially since, more than likely, she would've been hitting him for the first reason. However, she didn't want to cry in front of him, so she'd kept her mouth shut.

A quick rub of her eyes did nothing to alleviate the dry, scratchy irritation lingering from the smoke. She rose to peer over the back of the couch at the clock on the kitchen wall, then dropped down onto the decorative throw pillow when she saw it was only a few minutes after seven a.m. Desperate for another hour or two of sleep, she adjusted her T-shirt back down over her panties and pulled the blanket she'd snagged from the recliner up to her chin.

Five long, exceedingly torturous minutes later, she flipped the covering aside with a huff of annoyance. No way she was going back to sleep now. Every time she closed her eyes, the sexy jerk in the other room was right there.

Invading her mind space.

Making her body way too hot.

She was better off getting dressed and heading downstairs for coffee and one of Honor's leftover cupcakes from yesterday. If she hurried, she could avoid running into Loyal again this morning, and start figuring out what to do.

First on the list? Call her rental insurance company to see about getting a hotel until she could locate a new apartment to rent. Because Asher *had* warned Loyal might use this place, she couldn't ask him to leave. Well, she could, but she'd have to play the pity card, and no way in hell she would do that with him.

Roxanna ran her fingers through her hair along her scalp and grimaced at the amount of finger-combing she'd have to do to detangle her long, still-damp curls if she didn't locate a brush. As she lowered her hands, she heard the sound of a door and jerked her head up to see the bathroom door was now closed.

Damn, Loyal was up already? She didn't want to have to speak to the unbearable jerk. And if she had to, couldn't she have been dressed first? Too late now, since she'd left her clean clothes folded on the bathroom counter.

She stood and wrapped the blanket around her waist while waiting impatiently for him to come out and go back to the bedroom. Sitting down to wait, she kept her head down in case he not only slept in the nude, but also walked around au natural. And then as she thought about it, she couldn't help sneaking a peek every couple seconds.

Uggh. Stop.

Silently lamenting about having to share space with him, she wondered what the hell had she done to karma that her apartment building caught fire on the exact night he decided to show up back in Colorado?

The door opened a few minutes later, and her pulse leapt as she shot a covert gaze under her lashes. He'd put pants on. Whew.

Or damn?

When he turned into the living room instead of going back to the bedroom, she lifted her head, and her breath caught all over again. Although he'd pulled on a pair of black dress pants, his mussed hair, dark stubble, and bare chest had her pulse tripping all over itself.

She noticed he had her nightgown fisted in his large hand as she stood. The contrast of the delicate, light pink silk against his large, tanned hand made her stomach flutter. Too bad he hadn't taken it off her instead of picking it up from the bathroom floor.

Stop thinking like that!

"Is this yours?" he asked.

"One would assume—unless you have one exactly like it?" she quipped as she crossed the room to meet him.

His thick, dark brows hovered low over his whiskey-colored eyes. "Did your apartment building burn down?"

She shifted her gaze to his hand. She'd only taken time to wash her underwear, so the pungent smoke odor that clung to the pink nightgown hadn't faded one bit. "I don't know that it burned *down*. The firefighters were still working when I left."

"Why the hell didn't you say so last night?"

16

She couldn't tell if the roughness in his voice was anger or guilt.

Loyal—feel a human emotion such as guilt? Hah. Right.

"What does it matter?"

"You should've told me."

"Why?"

"I don't know." He shrugged his broad shoulders, his expression uncomfortable. "I'd have given you the bed."

"Yeah, right. More likely you would've mocked me and asked, *'If you're a real psychic, shouldn't you have known it was coming?'*"

His lashes lifted, his gaze meeting hers as he tilted his head. "Well, shouldn't you have?"

She narrowed her eyes at the cynical humor tugging at his lips. Yep. She wanted to hit him again. Hard.

"It doesn't work that way," she said through gritted teeth. Although, with her dream last night, it had come close.

His expression softened. "Are you okay?"

Annoyed that his question made her pulse leap, she reached to yank her nightgown from his hand. "Don't pretend like you care. You're an ass, Loyal. Always have been, always will be."

With that, she brushed past him and shut the bathroom door before he could see the tears that had suddenly turned everything blurry. She was not a crier, and yet the past twelve hours she seemed to be leaking every damn five minutes. She splashed cold water on her face, then found an unopened toothbrush and a tube of travel-size toothpaste to brush her teeth.

While she dressed, she made a face at her reflection in the mirror. The brown T-shirt she'd picked to go with the skirt was soft and stretchy. Being tall and slim—willowy, her mother used to say—her breasts were on the smaller size, but the snug fit made it embarrassingly obvious she wasn't wearing a bra.

Second on her list—shopping for a bra.

As she pulled on socks and the mid-calf military-style boots, she knew it wasn't really second, but it would be up in the top five. In the meantime, she'd grab a sweatshirt or something from the shop.

Loyal wasn't in the living room when she exited the bathroom. With all her things gathered in her hands, she started for the door. A sudden urge to stop and turn back had her wondering *why*? It wasn't like they were friends and she needed to tell him where she was going, or even say goodbye, for that matter.

She kept going and quietly let herself out of the apartment. Down in her shop, she went through the motions of grinding beans for the fresh roast coffee, took a small bakery box of Honor's pre-made cupcakes from the freezer in the back so they'd be thawed by eleven for customers, then stood in the office and stared at her desk.

Why had she let it get this bad again? She needed to find her spare Jeep keys and her rental insurance info, but would she find it in time to make the necessary calls and walk over to pick up her vehicle before it was time to open? Probably not.

With a low groan of resignation, she put the cupcakes back in the freezer and grabbed a clean sheet of paper from the printer. She wrote and taped a *Closed for Personal Emergency* sign on her front door before returning to her mess of a desk.

A bump of her hand sent the teetering stack of papers, folders, and mail on the left side spilling to the floor. She cursed under her breath as she knelt to scrape everything back into a pile, then dug around in her desk drawers a good ten minutes before she found her spare keys. Karma was really bitch-slapping her with the need to get more organized.

"I'm listening, Universe," she muttered. "I promise. I've learned my lesson."

But first, she wanted to get her Jeep, and she really wanted to see what was left of the apartment building. She snagged a wool poncho sweater from the front, pulled some cash from the register for the much needed bra, then went to pour a cup of coffee for the two and a half mile walk.

After an odd moment of hesitation, she found herself turning back to add a dash of cream and sugar. She didn't usually add the extras, but black seemed too bracing this morning. Too much like the soot she was sure to find at the apartment. She gave the lighter liquid a brief stir, then skimmed her fingers over the beads strung across the door of her reading room as she headed out with her keys.

She was pulling the door closed behind her when Loyal came through the door from the second floor stairway.

"Hey," he said conversationally. "I wondered where you went to."

Since he had to wonder no more, she didn't bother to respond past a tight-lipped smile. His dark pants, white shirt, and a charcoal suit coat were tailored to perfection for his broad shoulders and tall, athletic build. He should've looked stuffy and uptight with the starched white collar and pressed lines in his pants, but he'd left the top button undone, and wore the clothes with an effortless confidence that made her pulse speed up.

He'd combed his stylishly cut dark hair, but he hadn't bothered to shave the stubble lining his strong jaw. The ruggedness only added to his sex appeal. You'd think his years-long animosity toward her would make her immune to his handsomeness, and yet the man's beauty still took her breath away every time.

His gaze dropped to the cup in her hand and his expression turned hopeful.

"Is there more where that came from?"

She wanted to say no. Be the jerk to him that he always was to her and tell him to take a hike to the coffee shop three blocks away. Instead, she sighed inwardly and stopped her door from latching. She *had* made a full pot in anticipation of serving customers who now wouldn't be drinking it, so no need to let it all go to waste just for spite.

"How do you take it?"

"A little sugar, a little cream."

The jolt of that reveal made her swallow hard as she extended her cup to him. "Take this one and I'll get myself another."

He accepted it with a curve to his mouth that made her pulse skip. She wasn't used to being on the receiving end of his genuine smiles. The mocking ones? Those she was all too familiar with.

"What do I owe you?"

"Don't worry about it."

He lifted the cup in salute. "Thank you."

"Yep." Before she got lost in that unexpected smile and the yummy scent of his cologne slowly infusing the hallway, she pushed the door open and slipped back into her shop.

"Roxanna—"

Nope.

She shut the door on whatever he was about to say. Her heart might be blind when it came to Loyal Diamond, but she wasn't stupid. She was too emotionally vulnerable to let herself get drawn in when all it would take was one caustic remark from him to slay her wide open. The man had a knack for saying just the right thing—or the exact wrong thing, as the case may be.

After pouring herself a cup of black coffee, she exited Lift

Your Spirit through the front door and turned east into the bright sunshine. While the afternoon temps usually climbed to around sixty degrees even in late October, the mornings were frosty, and the warmth on her face was welcome.

She'd fully expected to spend her walk mentally going over everything she needed to do after the fire, but instead, her thoughts stubbornly remained on Loyal.

When it came to him, Idiot was her middle name. She'd been pining for the guy from the first time Asher introduced her to his older brother—all because of a stupid vision she'd had when she was nine. These days, the details were fuzzy save for the distinct voice saying, *"The love of your life will be loyal and true."*

Hearing Loyal's name for the first time, foolish, twenty-two year old, stars-in-her-eyes Roxanna decided Fate had led her to her soul mate.

Her soul mate, however, hadn't quite felt the love. Far from it.

Granted, he'd been engaged and days from the altar at the time, but when Asher mentioned she was a psychic, his older brother had first laughed, then snorted with open disdain. She found out later his fiancé had been a frequent caller to the psychic hotline she used to work for. The woman had spent thousands, then left him on their wedding day. Asher told her one of the psychics convinced his fiancé he wasn't the right guy for her.

After that, Loyal's remarks became more direct. More scathing and hostile. The worst was four months ago, when he'd called her a whack-job in front of his entire family and guests at his parents' thirty-fifth anniversary party. Usually, she could shake the words off, but that night, he'd reawakened a whole host of insecurities she thought she'd managed to bury in her past.

That she wasn't normal. She wasn't good enough.

She wasn't lovable.

She knew she shouldn't let him get to her. Just because he was a jerk didn't mean she was any of those things. But, rational understanding didn't stand a chance against engrained emotions that had been set deep when her mother abandoned their family when she was nine, and then left her again at twenty-two. Add in a workaholic father, being raised by strict grandparents who complained daily she was too much like her mother, and she didn't need her Colorado State University psychology degree to tell her it was enough to screw up anyone's sense of self-worth.

Asher had been her rock for years. She'd never revealed the full extent of everything to him, but he'd been the one to get her through when her mother came back into her life after ten years of silence only to leave her again. Her mother claimed she wanted to reconnect, but in reality, she'd only wanted to use Roxanna and her abilities to help operate the hotline scam designed to rip off innocent people—like Loyal, and his fiancé.

She'd been so gullible, letting her inner child's desire for her mother's love and acceptance blind her to what was really going on. There were very few people she couldn't read, and her mother was one of them. Loyal was another.

That should tell you something right there.

Yeah, it should, but just like with her mother, her heart didn't listen—at first.

The moment her mother realized Roxanna figured out the scam and she'd milked their relationship for as much as she was going to get, she'd skipped town with her boss and every penny in Roxanna's bank account without so much as a goodbye.

Left flat broke and completely alone, old inadequacies had risen up with a vengeance. That was the night she'd met Asher at a college frat house poker party. She'd cleaned him out down to his last dollar, and for some inexplicable reason, they'd bonded. He'd been the first person to ever make her feel loved. Not in a man and woman sense, but as a friend.

The guy came from one of the richest families in the state, and he didn't care she was freakishly tall and dressed like a biker hippie. He didn't care she was broke. He didn't care she noticed and said strange things. He'd simply taken her for who she was and offered unconditional friendship and love that fed her inner craving for acceptance.

And then he'd taken her home to meet his father the governor, his mother, Janine, and all his siblings. There had been an instant connection with the Diamond family that warmed her soul in a way she'd never experienced before. He had saved her when she didn't even know she needed saving.

They'd gone through a lot together; heartbreak on each side. Her with her mother, him with his own stupid ex-fiancé who used him for his connection to the governor's office. For the past six years, they'd always been there for each other.

But now Asher had Honor, and Roxanna was alone again.

As she crossed a side street, she felt bad even thinking that, because she would never begrudge him his happiness. She was thrilled for her best friend and the love he'd found with his cake baker. Once they worked through their issues, the two of them couldn't be more perfect for each other. But Honor was the one he turned to now, not Roxanna. Five months ago, it had been Honor who helped him deal with the shock of learning he had a half-brother from his father's one-night-stand thirty-one years ago.

And damn it all anyway, those lonely feelings of inadequacy had reared up again. It wasn't his fault, or Honor's. It wasn't even her mother's fault, horrible as she was, or her father's, or her grandparents'.

It was something she needed to work on for herself.

23

Roxanna straightened her spine as she walked, squared her shoulders, and lifted her chin.

She didn't have to be what others considered *normal*.

She *was* good enough—no—she was good, *period*.

And like Asher, she *would* find someone worthy of all the love she had to give. Someone who would love her back, just as she was.

CHAPTER 4

"*You're an ass, Loyal. Always have been, always will be.*"

Well, she wasn't wrong.

Normally Loyal didn't care. Normally, he felt completely justified in whatever asshole thing he said to the woman. But realizing he'd been a jerk right after Roxanna's apartment had burned in a fire left him feeling a little like he'd kicked a puppy. Or a kitten.

A very beautiful, sexy kitten.

He sent Asher a quick heads up to let him know he'd find a different place to stay so Roxanna could use the apartment, then sipped his coffee—with the exact right amount of sugar and cream—as he searched online and found a report of the fire. Seeing it wasn't far away, he started his Range Rover and navigated out from behind the building.

He made a left turn onto Aspen Street, and a couple blocks later, the back and forth sway of Roxanna's long, brunette curls caught his attention up ahead.

She strode along the sidewalk with her earth-toned skirt swishing around her legs and boots. His usual type tended to wear Louboutins, or Manolo Blahniks, but there was something about Roxanna's lace-up military boots that were oddly kick-ass sexy.

Loyal slowed the SUV, darting his gaze back and forth between her tall form and the road. Her purposeful stride made it clear she had a destination in mind, and yet she moved on those long, killer legs with a lithe grace that would've served her well had she chosen to be a dancer. Or a model.

Instead, she called herself a psychic.

His lip curled in distaste. They were nothing but a bunch of cons, preying on people's emotions and insecurities and hopes and dreams all while swindling them out of their money.

For him, it was the principle of it all. The dishonesty of the profession. The group that had reeled Lisa in hook, line, and sinker had been well-organized and very smooth. They'd even convinced her if he wouldn't keep paying to support her "spiritual journey," marrying him would be a mistake—and boy, had she followed their advice.

In hindsight, they'd probably done him a favor, but he sure as hell wasn't about to thank the money-grubbing crooks. The money Lisa had racked up was chump change to him, but he assumed many of their other victims couldn't afford to cover thousands of dollars like he'd had to for her. How many other lives had they ruined? How many were they still ruining?

That right there was why he couldn't stand so-called psychics.

As far as Roxanna was concerned, he sometimes wrestled with the rationale his brother wouldn't be friends with a thief. Not knowingly, anyway. It made him question if she was that good at fooling Asher and the rest of his family—

26

who also loved her—or could she possibly be on the up and up?

If he believed the latter, he'd have to admit she could be the real deal. But a woman who could read his mind and know what he was thinking and feeling? No way in hell he was going to open himself up to believing in that creepy shit.

As he drew even with Roxanna, he gave a tap on the horn. She startled and glanced over. When she spotted him behind the wheel, her brows drew down into a frown, and she kept walking while staring straight ahead. An impatient beep from a driver behind had him gunning the gas to make a left turn at the next intersection to intercept her. Cross traffic was dead at eight a.m. on a Sunday morning, so he rolled down the window and took a casual drink of his coffee while he waited.

Roxanna's step slowed mid-block, her narrowed brown eyes glaring at him. Finally, she moved forward once more and walked up to his window. "What?"

"Are you going to your building?"

"My Jeep is there. I couldn't drive it last night because my keys were in my apartment, and my spare keys were at the shop."

Had she walked all the way here last night in that thin nightgown? The idea was absurd, yet he wouldn't put it past her. He felt bad again, though he knew it had nothing to do with him.

The chill of the morning had put color in her cheeks during the few blocks she'd been walking, so he offered, "I can give you a ride."

A toss of her head sent a ripple through her shiny, sun-kissed hair. "I prefer the fresh air."

He cocked his eyebrow and took a sip of coffee while giving her a moment to change her mind. She remained silent and stubbornly still.

"Suit yourself," he said as he reached to put his coffee in the cup holder. "But you can't say I'm *always* an ass anymore."

Her gaze narrowed, and she opened her mouth to reply, but he took his foot off the brake and drove away. Like her shutting the door in his face.

Two right turns and a left put him back on track to her apartment building, and five minutes later, he slowed to a stop across the street from the brick building that still had a couple of fire trucks around the perimeter.

It hadn't burned to the ground, though his gut tightened as he took in the black soot around the blown out windows on the top two floors, and the collapsed roof on the far end. The thought of her being trapped inside the burning building made his heart beat faster and shortened his breath.

He frowned at the unexpected reaction and slid his gaze toward the small groups of people clustered beyond the yellow caution tape. They watched the remaining firefighters making sure the fire was completely out. The expressions of despair on their faces told him they were likely tenants, too, and he recalled the flash of emotion on Roxanna's face last night when he'd been all snarky about her having her own apartment.

He considered parking and waiting for her to arrive, but suspected she wouldn't welcome any comfort or moral support he would offer. The thought of pulling her into his arms sped up his pulse all over again.

Fuck.

He shifted his foot from brake to gas and got the hell out of there. He was an idiot for even considering being nice to her. Last thing he needed was to complicate his life with sympathy for a con artist like Roxanna Kent.

By eleven a.m., he'd grabbed his stuff from the apartment above her shop, booked a room at a hotel a few minutes away, and now made the turn into the driveway of his parents' estate. His cell dinged for an incoming text, and he picked it up as he parked behind the multitude of family cars filling the driveway.

His brother was four hours behind on his Hawaiian trip, and was probably still in bed with his new fiancé, so he wasn't surprised he was just replying now.

Asher: *What the hell is going on? Why is Rox staying at the apartment with YOU?*

Loyal: *There was a fire at her apartment building last night.*

Asher: *Holy shit. Is she okay?*

He started typing a reply, but his phone rang before he could finish. "Yes, she's okay," he answered.

"Honor's here," Asher advised. "I got you on speaker."

"Hey, Loyal," she greeted. "Do you know what happened?"

"Not really. Just that she showed up at the apartment at three o'clock in the morning because of the fire. She's not exactly chatty with me, you know."

"Whose fault is that?" his brother accused.

He ignored the flash of guilt the question sparked. "Whatever. I drove past the building earlier. There won't be much to salvage, if anything."

"I can't believe this. I have to call her."

"I don't think she has a phone," Loyal advised. "I didn't see one last night, or this morning."

"Then tell her to call us as soon as she gets it replaced."

"I'm not going to see her. I told you I won't be staying there. I already booked a hotel."

"We can call the shop," Honor said.

"Yeah, that'll work," Asher agreed. "I'll let her know she can stay in the apartment as long as she needs. Or hell, she can even just move in."

"That would make sense," his fiancé said. "How come she never did that before? Seems like that would be ideal with her shop right below."

"I offer every so often, but she's funny about that stuff. She doesn't want anyone to think she's taking advantage of our friendship."

Loyal shifted impatiently in his seat. He didn't want to hear how noble and good Roxanna was. It clashed with his inner narrative and made him feel...kind of like an ass.

Frowning now, he asked, "Do you two need me for this conversation?"

"Not really," Asher replied.

"Then I'm gonna go. I just got to the house for brunch."

He waited for, *Talk to you later,* but instead he got silence.

Then Asher asked, "You're going to brunch?" in a voice that was equally surprised and cautious.

Loyal frowned at his screen. "I always go to Sunday brunch when I'm home. Why wouldn't I?"

No more than the question was out of his mouth, a rusty, red pick-up truck turned into the driveway behind his Land Rover. He glared at the rearview mirror as a flash of white-hot heat was followed by icy cold.

"Are you kidding me? What the fuck is he doing here?"

CHAPTER 5

*L*oyal slammed his door as Grayson Cole opened the one to his Ford F-250 truck. The red hunk of junk was an eyesore, like his half-brother. He hadn't seen the guy since the day he and Asher had gone to meet him after the whole secret son/brother scandal erupted at the start of his father's senatorial campaign five months ago in May.

After the DNA test their family had done confirmed he was indeed the result of his father's one night stand thirty-one years ago, Loyal stayed in Texas except for Celia's wedding in August. Thankfully, Grayson hadn't gone to the wedding, because Loyal hadn't wanted to see the guy then any more than he did now.

And yet, here they were.

When Grayson got out of his truck, his big female German Shepherd, Remy, leapt to the ground beside him. Loyal recalled the dog from their visit to his house and kept his distance. The animal sported an olive-green vest with an American flag patch on the left side, and second patch on the

31

right proclaiming *Service Dog.* He didn't remember her wearing that the last time.

Remy remained at Grayson's side, and Loyal shifted his gaze to his half-brother. Looking at the guy was like looking at himself in a cheap mirror. He wore old jeans, scuffed army boots, and a tan T-shirt under an unbuttoned black and blue plaid flannel shirt.

Loyal adjusted the cuffs of his dress shirt under his custom tailored sport coat as he growled, "What the hell are you doing here?"

Grayson shut his truck door and murmured a command that brought the dog up against his leg as he faced him squarely. "The same thing as you, I imagine."

Last time they met the guy was all, *"Get the fuck off my property before I call the cops."* Animosity still rang in his voice, but now they were on Loyal's home turf. Much as he'd like to return the favor, more so he wanted to find out what was going on.

He crossed his arms and braced his feet shoulder width apart. "I'm here to eat brunch and enjoy time with *my* family." The guy's eyes narrowed the slightest bit at his emphasis on *my,* and he tilted his head slightly. "I thought you didn't want anything to do with us pretentious pricks?"

"Your father is setting up a foundation for veterans. We're going over some of the details today."

Your father, not *our.* Loyal lifted his eyebrows at that distinction as well as the news he'd revealed. "So much for not wanting our money."

"If it helps *my* brothers who fought for your freedom to sit here on your privileged high horse in your gilded little castle, yeah, I'll take the fucking money."

"You don't know shit about me," he ground out.

Grayson simply shrugged as if he didn't care one way or the other. They stood in silence for a long moment, until a light whine from the dog drew Loyal's gaze down. When he looked up again, his half-brother arched his brow.

"So, what's the deal here?" Grayson asked. "You gonna try to keep me from going in or what?"

He clenched his fingers on his biceps at the word *try*. Of course the asshole could be cocky with a guard dog at his side. He'd love to lay him out right here in the driveway, but even if he managed to get one good swing in, he doubted the dog would let him get any further than that.

Much as Loyal would prefer to walk ahead of him and show him this was *his* territory, the idea of that damn dog at his back made the hair on the nape of his neck tingle. He stepped back and to the side for Grayson to go first, then followed him and the German Shepherd.

They stopped at the formal entrance, and Loyal shouldered by on the opposite side of the dog to open the door. He stood aside, and Remy swept through to do a swift recon of the foyer, then circled around to his half-brother's side as the guy stepped inside.

Grayson murmured, "Good girl," the dog nudged his hand, and then the two of them went through to the family dining room where everyone was likely waiting, leaving Loyal to close the door.

His jaw clenched with the realization they'd been there before. But the guy didn't belong here, that much was obvious just by looking at him. Did his dad realize he was only there for the money?

Their family gave generously to support the veterans in any way they could, but much of it was done anonymously. His dad always said he wanted the political work he did to benefit the people to stand on its own merit. He didn't seek out big donation photo ops, because he didn't need or want to buy his way into the hearts of the voters.

But all of a sudden he was going to set up a foundation

for veterans? What the hell was that all about? He didn't want to buy votes, but he was okay with buying his son?

And why in the hell is this the first I'm hearing about any *of this?*

He hung back at the dining room entrance and watched his mom and dad greet his unwanted half-brother without a word about the dog at his side. Dogs weren't allowed in the house when they were growing up—or now. They stayed in their luxury kennels in the stables and enjoyed the run of the grounds.

Father and son exchanged a very brief, businesslike handshake, while his mom pulled him close with a tight hug, giving the guy the same treatment she'd give any of her own children currently sitting silently at the table. Loyal was amazed at her capacity to forgive. Back in May, he'd been convinced his parents would divorce over Grayson, and here she was five months later, embracing him and welcoming him into the family with a warm smile.

Her eyes widened when he caught her gaze over the guy's shoulder.

"Loyal!" She stepped around the German Shepherd and hurried across the room. "I didn't know you were home."

He met her halfway. "I got in late last night."

As she hugged him, he noted with some surprise she was wearing jeans. Granted, he hadn't been around much the past six years, but all his life, his mother dressed in the latest fashions that did not include denim, especially for Sunday brunch. He stepped back and turned to face his dad—also in jeans instead of his customary business casual.

What the hell?

There was a strange pause before he and his father moved in for a one second half-hug and back slap. His chest tightened at the awkwardness. Why the caution on his dad's face?

Did he feel bad about showing his usual affection in front of Grayson after their formal greeting?

After they stepped apart, he made his way around the room to hug Grandpa Ira and Grandma Irene. His sister, Celia, also got a hug, but he shook hands with her husband, Robert. They were newlyweds after first postponing the wedding because of the family scandal, then rushing to rebook everything.

His baby sister, Shelby, added a kiss on his cheek with her hug, while his youngest brother, Merit, stood to offer a hand clasp, shoulder bump, and slap on the back.

"Loyal." He uttered his name like an insult, even as he grinned his welcome.

"Mooch."

For as many times as he'd used the nickname with animosity, today he injected a note of genuine affection. The Diamond siblings—*true* Diamond siblings—had to stick together.

As he pulled out the empty chair at his usual spot, he noticed his dad carrying a chair over from the corner of the room while his mom hurried to get another place setting from the side china hutch. She directed Grayson to the new seat just as the weekend staffers carried in brunch dishes from the kitchen. Remy lay down beside her owner's chair when he sat.

Brunch was always served after the last person arrived, and it appeared they'd been waiting for Grayson—who would've sat in *his* spot if he hadn't shown up.

A spurt of jealousy flared at the thought of the guy taking over his seat at the table. In the family. The guy was older than him by about three months, so he'd already taken that position by default.

Loyal's jaw clenched with irritation. It was childish to let any of it bother him. He didn't doubt his parents' love, and he didn't want for anything financially, both because of a generous trust fund and his own hard work, so it wasn't like Grayson could actually take anything away from him. Feeling insecure while not understanding why was extremely unsettling and annoying.

All along, he'd told himself he didn't give a fuck, and yet here he was...discovering he gave a fuck.

And that pissed him off, because he didn't *want* to give a fuck.

His father quieted the side conversations for a quick prayer to bless the meal and those eating it, and then his mother officially started brunch by passing the first dish—to Grayson.

"Why didn't you stay here last night, Loyal?" His mom caught his eye as she lifted a second plate piled high with bacon and sausage. "You know I hate the thought of you in a hotel."

"I'm using Asher's apartment," he fibbed. He *had* used it last night, he just wasn't going to use it anymore. Which meant he'd be looking for his own place sooner than later, so when his mom found out he'd moved to a hotel, she wouldn't badger the heck out of him. She didn't understand his aversion to moving back into the family home at thirty years old, but it wasn't going to happen.

"Is this it then?" Shelby asked. "No more Texas?"

"Yeah. Uncle Matt's audit is all wrapped up, and I wanted to come back before election night. As soon as I find my own place, I'll have my things shipped back."

He thought he heard a snort from Grayson's corner of the table, and when he cut his gaze to the guy, he was shaking his head with a smirk. Loyal ignored him. A person didn't have to be rich or privileged to pay a moving company. He was providing someone with a job, and they were earning a damn good wage for their work. Same as he did for his own job.

"We're thrilled you're finally home," his mom said.

"What are you doing for a job?" Grandpa Ira asked gruffly. "Don't forget, idle hands are the devil's workshop."

Loyal gave a soft snort and arched his brows at his brother next to him.

"Don't look at me," Merit brushed him off. "I keep my hands plenty busy."

His emphasis on *plenty* made Robert choke on a laugh. Celia elbowed him in the ribs as Grandpa guffawed, Dad frowned, and Mom sighed.

Well, his youngest brother did keep his hands busy—with a different girl each week. Or so he'd heard.

When he noticed the others watching him, Merit huffed out a sigh. "Why do you guys always try and turn this on me? Grandpa asked *Loyal* the question."

Noticing Grayson's judgmental gaze taking everything in, Loyal took pity on his youngest brother and turned it back on himself. "I'm not sure what I'm going to do yet, Grandpa. I've been kicking around the idea of starting my own accounting firm. After the last couple of years, though, I'm going to take it easy at first. Maybe start with a select few clients."

Across the table on the corner, his half-brother's knuckles turned white as his hand gripped his fork. His glare was full of resentment, and Loyal could guess why. He'd hired a private investigator to look into the guy back in May, and knew since getting out of the military, Grayson worked odd jobs and barely scraped by most months.

But that wasn't his fault, was it?

At the head of the table, his dad cleared his throat. "You know, this move of yours has come at a very opportune time."

His muscles tensed, and he fought to keep his expression impassive as he warned, "I have my own plan, Dad, and poli-

37

tics don't figure into it. I'm going to register to vote so I can get my ballot in, and that's it."

"Don't worry, Loyal. I gave up on my sons following in my footsteps a long time ago."

His shoulders relaxed, until he noticed the sideways glance his dad cast toward Grayson. He narrowed his gaze as his pulse ticked up with a resurgence of resentment. Wouldn't that just take the cake if his new son decided to step up to the political plate where he, Asher, and Merit had refused.

His dad set his silverware down on the edge of his plate, then sat up straighter as he wiped his mouth with his napkin. "Grayson and I have been discussing starting up a foundation for our veterans."

"So he said outside," Loyal commented tightly.

"I think that's awesome," Shelby chimed in.

Loyal noticed their mom lay her hand on his baby sister's arm and give a light squeeze. His sister pressed her lips together and sat back in her chair.

What the hell was that about?

"With my campaign ramping up these next nine days before the election," their dad continued, "I can't devote the time I'd like to get it up and running with him."

He looked back to find his dad's gaze locked on him.

"And if the vote goes in my favor, God-willing, I'll be in Washington quite a bit, and still won't have time."

He did not like the sound of where this was going. "What's your point, Dad?"

"I'd like you to take a seat on the board with Grayson."

"*What?*" Grayson stiffened so fast, Remy leapt to her feet beside him with a soft growl. His hand on the Shepherd's head immediately quieted her.

"You want me to work with *him?*" His astonished laugh contained no humor. "That's not gonna fucking happen."

"Loyal," Grandma Irene admonished from his left. "Watch your language."

He cringed, but kept his focus on the right end of the table.

"That was not part of the deal." Grayson seemed equally shocked at the unexpected offer. And pissed off, too.

"No, it wasn't, but it is now," his dad said in a firm voice. His father glanced at his mom, who gave a subtle nod. They were back to making decisions together, like they had ninety-nine-point-nine-percent of their married life—Grayson being the result of the point-o-one-percent they hadn't.

"You will still be head of the foundation," his dad assured him. "You'll make the main decisions of where and how to focus the charity, but Loyal will be the CFO and oversee the money."

"You don't trust me?" he bristled.

"No offense, son, but I don't know you well enough yet."

"Offense taken, *Mr. Diamond.*" He tossed his napkin on his plate. "A month ago you tried to give me a million dollars. No strings, you said, and *I said no.*"

Loyal barely kept his mouth from gaping open even as he registered a soft gasp from one or more of his siblings. His dad had tried to give the guy a million dollars?

And he turned it down?

"But I come to you about an honest charity to help veterans in need and suddenly I have to have a fucking babysitter for your fucking money?" He snorted with disgust. "I'll take the million instead."

"That is no longer on the table. *This* is what I'm offering. Take it or leave it."

Grayson's jaw clenched tight as he switched his glare from their dad, to Loyal. Then he shoved away from the table and headed for the door with Remy trotting dutifully at his side. Halfway to the door, he came to an abrupt halt and half-turned toward the table.

"Thank you for the meal, Janine." He shifted his gaze to Grandma Irene. "I apologize for my language, ma'am."

With that, he continued out of the room and slammed from the house. Loyal actually understood and wouldn't mind following suit.

"He didn't actually say no." His mom broke the silence.

"Oh, my God, that was *such* a no, Mom," Shelby exclaimed.

Merit, Celia, and Shelby all started talking at once, but their dad held up a quieting hand as he caught Loyal's gaze. "He just needs to calm down and think about it. Like someone else I know."

"I'm perfectly calm, Dad. The answer is still no." He let his gaze convey his commitment to his answer, then dropped his attention to the eggs on his plate, lifted his fork, and said, "Did you guys know Roxanna's apartment building burned down last night?"

As expected, the news elicited shocked exclamations.

"Oh my God, is she okay?" Mom asked.

"She is. No one was hurt," he assured them as his father recognized his distraction tactic and sat back in his chair with resignation.

"Did she lose everything? Where is she staying?"

Shit. He hadn't thought about that when he'd said earlier he was staying at Asher's apartment.

"You let her know she's welcome to come stay here with us for as long as she needs," Mom declared.

He frowned at the assumption everyone kept making that he would relay their messages. "You let her know. I'm not going to talk to her."

"Because you're a jerk," Merit chimed in.

"I don't know why you don't like her," Celia said as she

40

lifted her juice for a drink. "It's not her fault Lisa turned out to be such a flake."

And just like that, his distraction shifted in a direction he hadn't expected. It wasn't anything he hadn't heard before. The family got on Merit for his lack of ambition. They got on Loyal for his dislike of Roxanna. He didn't care—not much, anyway. Besides, it didn't take long for the conversation to morph in a different direction, so he kept quiet and rode it out.

With Grayson and Remy gone, the meal settled into their regular family rhythm and ended with a lengthy discussion of the upcoming Halloween fundraiser for the Children's Hospital on the thirty-first.

His mom was hoping to top last year's totals, and since it would be one of the last big events before election night, she was going all out. Loyal had been able to get away with a large monetary donation in the past, but now that he was home, she made a point of letting them all know they'd be expected to attend for the sake of the children and their father's campaign.

Which meant in addition to a place to live, he'd also be looking for a costume that would keep him incognito from the rest of the crowd after he put in the obligatory appearance with Mom.

As was customary, the staff had gone home after serving, and the kids were in charge of cleanup as their parents and grandparents shared one last cup of coffee. And, as was usual, Merit carried his plate into the kitchen, but quickly disappeared, leaving the rest of them to pick up his slack.

A half hour later, Loyal wiped off the kitchen island counter and tossed the washcloth to Robert at the sink. His brother-in-law had stepped up in cleaning duties from the first brunch he'd attended over seven years ago.

"I'm gonna take off," Loyal said. "See you guys around."

"I'm so glad it'll be more often now," Shelby said with a grin.

"Like you'll even notice with your nose stuck in your books all the time, Bells," he teased with a tug on her dark ponytail.

She side-ducked out of his reach. "I'm just following my plan, like everyone else."

"Like everyone else? And what's Mooch's plan?"

"To not have a plan."

"Can't argue that he's not following it," Robert pointed out.

"No," Loyal agreed. "Definitely not."

"You'll have to come over for dinner soon," Celia urged. "I want you to see the new house."

"Text me and let me know when," he said as he backed out of the kitchen. "I gotta go before Dad corners me about that CFO crap again."

"You know, Grayson's not *so* bad," Shelby said. "And Remy is a sweetheart."

Of course she'd say that. Their soon-to-be veterinarian loved any animal, no matter what.

"That dog doesn't like me anymore than he does," Loyal said. "Feeling's mutual," he added over his shoulder before moving out of sight.

He almost made it to the front door when his dad's voice stopped him in the foyer. "Loyal. Your mom wants to talk to you before you sneak out."

Crap.

He halted and turned back. "I wasn't sneaking."

"No? Then where's my goodbye?"

He rolled his eyes and stepped up to give the old man a hug. Despite the eye roll, he didn't actually mind one bit—as long as he didn't bring up working with Grayson again.

This time, his dad gave him a tight squeeze before easing

back. He kept a hand clasped on his shoulder as they shared a smiled, but then his dad sighed.

Here it comes.

"I know you don't want to talk about it, but I'm going to ask you again to consider the board position for the foundation."

He started to shake his head as his mom hurried toward them with a huge, square, linen-lined basket.

"I'd really like you to do this for me," his dad insisted. "For the family."

Nothing like laying on some family guilt. It hadn't worked back when he wanted him to get into politics, and it wasn't going to work now. His dad would just have to accept that, too.

Loyal didn't say yes or no, or even that he'd think about it as he backed out from under his dad's hand and his mom pushed the basket into his arms. It was heavier than he expected, with a number of competing scents wafting up from the items piled inside.

"What is this for?"

"I want you to take it to Roxanna."

Sonofabitch.

Neither one of them would give him any peace, would they? He grit his teeth as he inhaled. "Mom—"

"It's a care package I threw together to replace some things after the fire, and a couple of gift cards I keep on hand. Your dad and I are leaving for Grand Junction in an hour for the final campaign tour, and we won't be home until Thursday. I don't want it to wait that long, so don't be an ass about it and get going. Please."

That last word was supposed to soften the *ass,* but it also added guilt, especially when she raised her perfectly sculpted eyebrows. "It will not kill you to be nice to her for the one second it'll take you to drop it off."

No, it wouldn't kill him. Yes, he was being an ass about it.

It just annoyed the shit out of him that he was being guilted into dealing with the two people he most wanted to avoid. One, he didn't quite know why his resentment was so damn strong.

The other he knew exactly why, and needed to stay the hell away from her.

CHAPTER 6

Seeing her burned apartment building in the daylight was worse than when she'd watched the flames shooting toward the sky. Roxanna realized she'd been in shock last night, and even during her walk, a small part of her kept hoping it had all been a bad dream.

Unfortunately, it was all too real. She commiserated with a few of her neighbors on the scene where the firefighters were still working, and they thanked her for the early warning. Most of them knew what she did for a living, and not one of them asked her how come she hadn't been able to stop it. And even though she had helped get people out in time, she wished her gift gave her the ability to keep bad things from happening.

But as she'd told Loyal, it didn't work that way. If it did, none of her neighbors would be homeless right now. *She* wouldn't be homeless. And she wouldn't have had to pay cash for the cheapest phone available because her cell, license, and other ID had gone up in flames with her purse.

When she returned to her shop after making one addi-

45

tional stop for underwear, bras, and socks, she tossed the smoky blanket from last night out into the back hall and put her purchases down on the chair. The coolness of the hanging beads against her fingers offered physical grounding as the musical harmony of them clinking together soothed her spirit.

A blinking light on the phone near the cash register indicated a message, and when she moved over to listen, the concern in Asher and Honor's voices made her chest tight with renewed emotion.

She dialed them on her new phone, but because she'd been able to transfer her number, Asher didn't bother with preliminaries when he answered. "Thank God you're okay."

"Hey, Rox." Honor's voice told her they had her on speaker. "How are you doing?"

"A little overwhelmed, but otherwise I'm hanging in there."

"I wish we could give you a hug right now."

The warmth of their concern came over the line and she smiled in appreciation. "I'd take it."

"Loyal told us you stayed at the apartment last night," Asher said. "He wasn't a jerk, was he?"

If that was the first thing her best friend asked about, then he didn't know she'd climbed into bed with his naked brother when she was practically naked herself. Loyal must not have told them about *that* part.

Thank God.

"No more than usual. It was fine. I was only there a few hours. As soon as I can find the info for my insurance policy, I'll see how much they cover for a hotel and get one booked."

Then she wouldn't have to deal with him again. If she was being honest, the naked part hadn't been such a hardship, but then he'd opened his mouth.

"Actually, Loyal said he'd go to a hotel. He's already booked and moved."

She blinked in surprise. "Really?"

"Yep. So the apartment is all yours as long as you need it."

He'd actually done something nice? Guess she *really* couldn't say Loyal was *always* an ass anymore.

Or, more likely, he'd only moved to avoid having to see or talk to her again.

She ignored the discontent that thought spawned, because she knew damn well not seeing or talking to him again should make her happy, not sad.

"You know, Rox, I've been telling you all along you're welcome to move in there, so there's no reason to even go looking any further for a different place to stay. It's furnished already, it's above the shop, and it's *free.*"

"And after the fire, no one will think you're taking advantage of anything," Honor added.

Roxanna swallowed hard. She'd never taken the offer for exactly that reason, but now… "Maybe."

"I don't want to hear maybe," Asher said firmly. "I'll charge you some rent if it makes you feel better, but you just need to move in. This way you don't have so many things to replace all at once."

That was a really good point.

"Did you go by your building yet this morning?" Honor asked. "We looked it up after talking to Loyal earlier. It's amazing no one was hurt. It looked like the fire went through the whole building."

"Yeah, I had to go get my Jeep earlier. It is bad. Doesn't look like there'll be much of anything left, but I won't know for sure until they let us in to look around. *If* they even do. When I asked when that might be, the guy I talked to said they have to wait until the inspector gives the all clear that

47

it's structurally sound before anyone can go inside. That could take a couple of days, or up to a couple of weeks."

And in the meantime, it was crazy how many things a person didn't realize they took for granted until they weren't there at hand. Simple little things. In the couple hours between picking up her Jeep and coming back to the shop, she'd reached for her purse a half-dozen times. For lip balm, her sunglasses, gum, one of her oils, a pen.

"If you need anything at all, please let us know, okay? I can transfer some money, or you can use anything from my house. Anything you need."

"Also," Honor chimed in, "there's a spare key for my house in that birch basket on Asher's counter. Help yourself to my closet if you want. Obviously, most of my pants will be too short, but maybe some of my tops will fit."

"I appreciate the offer, but I've been able to find some stuff off my clearance rack in the shop. I might go over to do some laundry in a day or two, though."

"Go for it," Asher said. "Mi casa es su casa. Help yourself."

"Thanks, guys. I really appreciate it. Now, enough about depressing stuff, tell me how your trip is going." When they didn't answer right away, she said, "Seriously, give me something positive to think about. Please."

"It's going great." A happy smile brightened Honor's voice. "I climbed a cliff with my bare hands and a rope yesterday. It was awesome."

"She's a natural," Asher added. "And, I'm beginning to think, an adrenaline junkie."

"If I am it's because you made me one," she argued. "We're going again today."

"Go figure. She doesn't want to lay on the beach. Our secluded, private beach."

"Tomorrow," Honor promised.

Roxanna smiled at the two. She was very happy for them, even if it made her feel lonelier than ever. "I'm glad you're having fun."

"We are. But we'll be home on Thursday to make sure we don't miss the Halloween party on Saturday."

The reminder brought a frown and took her right back to the fire. Her usual gypsy get-up for telling fortunes to raise money for the kids had probably gone up in smoke. "I'll have to come up with a new costume."

"Mae and I are picking ours up Thursday afternoon after we get back. Why don't you come with us and look for something then?" Honor suggested.

Mae Lockhart was Honor's best friend, and Roxanna had hit it off with the bubbly blond construction company owner right off the bat. "That sounds like a plan. Listen, I'm going to let you guys go climb your cliffs, and I'm going to tackle my desk."

"Oh no," Asher said gravely, his voice low and ominous. "You're taking on The Desk?"

"Yeah. Or more accurately, the whole office area. My insurance info is in there somewhere. Wish me luck."

"Text me when you're done so we know you made it out alive."

"Ha ha." Her smile as she hung up turned to a grimace when she eyed the mountain of crap on her desk and nearby surfaces. She had her own mountain to climb, though even with her fear of heights, Honor's Hawaiian cliffs sounded like tons more fun.

Knowing she couldn't put it off any longer, she scooped up an armload of paper from the desk and set it in the middle of the empty space on the floor. After adding another pile from the extra chair, and everything from the top of the file cabinets, she sat pretzel-leg to start sorting. She was halfway through the first pile when she came across a bundle of unopened mail. She remembered tossing it on the desk a couple of weeks ago, intending to sort it later, but she'd gotten distracted with a delivery, and then it had gotten buried and forgotten.

It was mostly junk, but as she reached the bottom, there was an envelope with the name of her insurance company in the return address window. She smiled with relief. Exactly what she needed.

She slid her finger under the sealed flap, but the moment she pulled out the enclosed letter, a foreboding sensation zigzagged down her spine. When she unfolded the letter, one specific line jumped out at her.

Please be advised if we do not receive payment in the next seven days, your policy will be cancelled and your coverage will lapse.

Seven days. Her hand shook as she darted her gaze to the date at the top.

October 7.

Twenty-three days ago.

White-hot waves of nausea rolled through her stomach with the confirmation she had no insurance. None. Nada. Zilch. Worse, since she'd bundled the renter's coverage with her business insurance, she was totally vulnerable at the moment.

How in the world was she going to replace all her things?

Panic and despair welled up in a dizzying whirl until she forced herself to take deep breaths to calm down.

She was alive. She had her shop. She'd be okay.

The mental litany allowed another calming breath. Thanks to Asher, she had a place to stay, and also she had a little in her savings. She'd get by okay.

"It's your own damn fault, anyway," she muttered to herself, angry she'd buried her head in the sand after her accountant left. Although, Mirela should've had this bill paid before she left. She'd assured her everything was up to date that last day.

Don't go blaming someone else for your stupidity.

True, she should've double-checked everything, now she had to deal with the consequences. Starting with, no more putting off the crap stuff just because she hated doing it. She knew it was more than that—when it was hard to understand, it made her feel stupid and inadequate, but she had to stop with the excuses and grow a damn spine.

As that truth sank in, she eyed the chaos spilled all around her.

Starting right now.

The next envelope she opened contained a personal check made out to her for twelve hundred dollars from a woman in Colorado Springs. She didn't recognize the name, so she tucked it back into the envelope to ask the girls about it on Tuesday. Maybe one of them had taken a deposit for a weekend Lift Your Spirit seminar? Nothing was on the books that she could recall, and it was dated a few weeks ago, but Tessa might have forgotten to write it down with her pregnancy brain.

It would be a surprise she'd welcome right now. The income would be nice, and the weekend seminars were always rewarding.

The crap she was doing today was not, but she forced herself to sit her ass on the floor and keep working until the last paper was sorted and every single piece of mail was opened. Unlike Honor scaling her cliff, there was no sense of accomplishment for Roxanna as she counted the three unpaid invoices on one pile, and a second late notice for the shop's electric bill.

She needed to take care of that before they contacted her

building owner—Asher. She was still making payments to him for the business loan he'd given her to open the shop six years ago. She didn't want him to know she'd fallen behind on other things.

"You're just like your mother."

Her grandmother's shrill, disapproving voice made her cringe. She hadn't heard that voice in real life *or* in her head for years.

Denial rose up as Roxanna pressed her fingers to her temples and straightened her spine. She was not like her namesake. The elder Roxanna Kent was more cunning than stupid.

More of a thief than an irresponsible idiot about finances.

And she, daughter Roxanna Kent, was going to *stop* being a financially irresponsible idiot.

First things on her list for tomorrow...get her business insurance reinstated, pay her electric bill, get herself in good standing with her suppliers, and then see if Tessa or Darcy could cover for her while she went to the DMV for her driver's license, and the courthouse for a new social security card.

In the meantime...she stacked all her sorted piles together and stood so she could file as needed. When that was done, the final stack with her profit and loss reports mocked her. They were the one thing she hated the absolute most about her business. But balancing her accounts so she knew exactly where she stood and what cash she might be able to use to replace some of her belongings was currently her top priority. Even if she'd much rather take a bottle of wine upstairs to drown her sorrows for a night.

"Just frickin' get it done," she muttered as she sat at the desk and turned on the computer so she could log into the program with her password taped on the underside of the mouse pad.

Two hours later, each beat of her heart was followed by an answering throb in her head that even peppermint oil couldn't relieve. She was no closer to making sense of her P&L than when she started, and the frustrating math only strengthened her craving for a large glass of wine. She stared at the mocking, red negative number on her screen and amended that to *huge* glass of wine.

When her stomach growled, she glanced at the clock. A double take confirmed the hour hand creeping past six p.m. She'd been stuck in the office for hours. But clearly, she wasn't going to get any further with a headache and an empty stomach, so she shut the computer down.

Taking another twenty from the register to order herself some dinner, she tucked it in her pocket, and went to select a leftover cupcake and a bottle of her favorite Riesling from the Whitewater Hill Vineyards in Grand Junction display in her shop.

With her newly purchased bag of lingerie hooked on her wrist, she pulled the door closed and headed upstairs. It was quiet when she keyed in the code to enter the apartment, though why she thought it might be otherwise, she had no idea.

She was used to being alone, and Loyal being gone was a good thing—a *really* good thing.

Ignoring the contradictory heavy sensation in her chest, she set her things on the counter and found a wine key in the drawer to open her bottle. Then she poured herself a full-to-the-tippy-top glass and took a big swallow. Notes of tangerine and lime lingered on her tongue as the liquid slid down her throat to warm her empty belly. Her gaze strayed toward the bedroom with her next drink, and her pulsed ticked up.

Wine in hand, she slowly walked through the living room, glanced into the bathroom, and then moved into the bedroom. After last night, it seemed prudent to make sure she was indeed alone—but then she gulped a swallow to drown out the ridiculous surge of disappointment when she saw the empty bed.

She tilted her head slightly when she noticed the uneven comforter tossed over the pillows, and the edge of the sheet hanging down crookedly along the mattress instead of neatly tucked in. Loyal had made the bed, kind of, but she'd bet her whole bottle of wine he hadn't bothered to change the sheets.

"Probably doesn't even know how to do such a menial task," she groused to the empty room. The guy had grown up with maid service. He'd probably had one in Texas, too.

She sat on the bed, set her glass on the nightstand, and fisted a hand in one of the pillows to bring it up to her face.

A deep inhale flooded her senses with the scent of the cologne she'd noticed last night, right before he scared the shit out of her. Her lashes drifted closed as she savored the seductive, manly notes of sandalwood and pine, and maybe a hint of...cinnamon?

She breathed in again, sighed, then snapped her eyes open and stiffened her spine when she realized what she was doing. Tossing the pillow aside, she reached for her glass and took two deep swallows in quick succession.

And one more on her way back to the living room.

Her headache was starting to ease as she sat on the couch and turned on the TV. She pulled out her phone to call for pizza, only to become distracted by the movie on the screen when the guy playing the main character reminded her of Loyal.

Tall. Handsome. Nice body. Sexy stubble.

As she studied the actor's face, she wondered why she couldn't be attracted to Merit? He was just as pretty, plus he was always nice to her. Or Grayson? The Diamonds' half-brother looked eerily like Loyal, but the two times she'd met him, there hadn't been a single spark of awareness, no slow spread of tingling heat, no excited leap of her pulse.

"Nope. Stupid me. Gotta go and fall for the jerkiest Diamond of all."

She gave a longing whimper, finished off the rest of her glass, then decided she needed a refill.

CHAPTER 7

$\mathcal{L}$oyal parked his Land Rover next to Roxanna's old green Jeep and muttered under his breath as he pulled the basket from his back seat. If he'd been smart, he would've come right over after brunch and left it in the apartment on the table. Then he wouldn't have to see her or talk to her. Instead, he'd been annoyed with the task and procrastinated.

Now he was annoyed all over again.

He stomped up the stairs and gave a sharp rap on the door. After a full minute, he considered leaving it in the hall, but his mom would have his head if she found out. So he knocked again, then started punching the code into the lockbox.

The door suddenly swung open, and he shifted the basket back to both arms as he looked up.

"Speak of the devil." Roxanna held the edge of the door with one hand and a half-full glass of wine in the other. "I was jus' talkin' 'bout you."

Loyal leaned sideways to see behind her, his gut clenching

at the idea of her having some guy in there with her. "I didn't realize you had company."

"I don't."

He shifted his narrowed gaze back to her as she took a drink. Maybe she'd been on the phone before he knocked.

Or talking to spirits.

Who the hell knows with people like her.

"Mom heard about the fire and made you a care package." A little jerk of the basket drew her gaze down to his arms.

"Aww." She smiled suddenly, and stepped forward to grasp the edge and look inside. "Your mom's the *best*."

"Easy," he warned when the weight of her hand threatened to topple everything to the floor. "This thing is heavy. Let me put it on the table."

She stepped aside, and he walked inside to set it down. He expected her to follow, but turned to find her topping off her glass. When she set the wine bottle down, it was half-empty, and her fingers gripped the neck of the bottle to steady herself.

"How many glasses of that have you had?" he asked.

"This is number two—and a half. Cheers." She raised the nearly over-flowing glass in salute before putting it to her lips.

"Wow. You're a lightweight if you're drunk off two glasses."

She scrunched up her nose. "I'm not drunk. I'm just...tippy."

His gaze lingered on her mouth, her bottom lip wet and shiny from her last drink. "You mean *tipsy?*"

"That's what I said. Tippy. I didn't eat dinner, but I'm not hungry anymore anyway."

She leaned against the counter, then changed her mind and pushed off to come check out the basket. He noticed she still wore those boots and the earth-toned skirt, but on the way back to her face, his gaze caught on her shirt and held. Brown, V-neck, and clinging tight enough to her torso and chest to reveal she wasn't wearing a bra again.

The sight of her nipples poking through the thin fabric had his dick paying swift attention.

"Ooh, chocolate." She moved closer, her shoulder brushing against his as she dug into the goodies. "And wine. Candles." She lifted one to her nose. "*Mmm.* They smell nice."

She smelled nice. Peppermint teased his senses, a completely different scent from last night, yet equally appealing.

Roxanna kept going, taking more basic essential items out one by one, exclaiming over each of them like a kid opening a Christmas present. Shampoo and conditioner, a brush, makeup, deodorant, a toothbrush and toothpaste, towels and washcloths. Toward the bottom, she pulled out a square package.

"Sheets! And a fuzzy robe? She thought of everything." She slid her hand over the plush, white material. "Ooh, it's *so* soft."

He should move away from the warmth of her body seeping through the sleeve of his shirt, yet he was entranced watching her rub her palm back and forth across the fuzzy robe. He imagined her doing the same to his chest, and his stomach, and lower.

A sharp jolt of lust made him suck in a breath.

"I love these towels. And there's a gift card—no, *two* gift cards! This is so nice. Your mom is the *best.*"

He grit his teeth. "You said that already."

She shot him a belligerent frown through her long, sooty lashes. "Well, she is. Unlike *you.*"

There we go. Thank you.

He gave her a tight smile and finally stepped back from

her heat. "On that note, you have a good night. Maybe stop drinking and eat something."

She raised her glass and took a deep swallow, her gaze defiant.

"Or not," he murmured sarcastically.

When she lowered the glass and licked at the wine on her wet lips, he fisted his hands against the urge to grab her and kiss her. Would she taste as good as she smelled?

Whoa. No way. Time to get the fuck out.

He spun around and headed for the door.

"Hey!"

Her exclamation brought him back around to find her watching him with an intensity that made his heart thud hard. *She knows.* She'd read his mind and knew he wanted to kiss her and taste her and touch her until—

Fuck, man, stop thinking!

"You're an accountant, right?"

He blinked at the unexpected question. "Uh...yeah."

"I can't get my numbers to add up."

Confusion creased his brow as lust still revved his pulse. "What?"

"My numbers." She waved her hand as if he would magically understand. "Downstairs on my computer. I can't get the numbers to work, and it's driving me crazy." She lifted her glass. "Driving me to drink *cra-zee*."

He moved closer again, and braced one palm on the kitchen counter. "Are you talking about your business?"

"Ye-es." She nodded while drawing out the word as if he was an idiot.

"Don't you have an accountant to manage your books for you?"

"She left me." After another sip, she lowered the glass and pouted. "She got married and left, and now everything's all messed up. What am I doing wrong?"

"First off, it sounds like you should've gotten another accountant," he said wryly. "Second, I'd have to actually look at the numbers to tell you what you're doing wrong."

Not that he would, though.

Her head tilted, those pretty brown eyes of hers full of surprising curiosity. "Do you actually like numbers?"

"I do."

"Why? They're so annoying when they don't add up."

A reluctant smile tugged at his mouth. "But they're perfect when they do."

She squinted as if trying to make sense of that in her head. "But why do you like them?"

And the wine wins.

"One plus one equals two. The answer is either right or wrong, there are no gray areas. They can't say *yes* one minute and change their mind the next."

Her confused frown was almost comical.

"Numbers don't lie like people do," he explained simply. "What you see is what you get." Unlike *both* of his ex-fiancés.

Now her eyebrows lifted as she gave a sage nod. "I can see people."

The simple statement started his pulse racing again, even though her words told him she still didn't grasp his meaning.

"I can see if they're happy or sad or mad. Sometimes, if they're good, or bad." Her brow wrinkled. "If they hurt and need help."

Then again, maybe she did grasp his meaning just fine. What she saw is what she got.

Or what she thought *she saw*, he corrected in his mind.

What she *pretended* to see?

It dawned on him this could be the perfect opportunity to put her to the test. With her guard down and her loose tongue, he could prove she was a fraud like all the people at that damn psychic hotline. He'd called the cops to report their fraud on his non-wedding day, but they'd already skipped town, so he never got his justice.

"What do you see when you look at *me?*" he asked.

She stared at him with that eerie intensity brightening her eyes again.

He suppressed a shiver. He didn't believe she was a real psychic, and yet his heart pounded high in his throat at the possibility she would see something he didn't want her to see —something he didn't want anyone to see.

For the first time ever, he noticed her thick-lashed eyes weren't a plain, chocolate brown. There were intriguing, subtle variations of dark and light that could apparently mesmerize a guy into letting her look deep into his soul.

Holy fuck, he was in trouble.

And yet, he couldn't look away.

After a long moment, *she* looked away and reached for her glass. "I can't read you. I've never been able to read you."

Relief released his trapped breath, followed by the oddest sense of disappointment.

Then again, *how convenient.* "Why not?"

"I don't know." That note of belligerence crept back into her voice. "Some people I can't read. It's not that big a deal. I can't read my mother, either." She took a gulp from her glass, then muttered into her wine, "Don't need to read her to know she's no good."

He frowned at that comment. It didn't sound like she had a good relationship with her mother.

"Don't need to read you either," she added as she pushed to her feet.

To know I'm no good?

He had no time to ponder that question as she swayed hard. Loyal lunged forward and caught her before she fell flat on her face. When she was somewhat steady on her feet, he

61

took her almost-empty glass with his free hand and transferred it to the kitchen counter.

"Hey. Gimmie that back."

"Nope. You're done for the night."

"You're not the boss of me." She tried to shake him off, but her inebriated efforts were laughable at best.

"Come on." He got a firm grip on her arms and turned her around so he could march her ahead of him. "It's time for bed."

"Ooooh." She did drunken jazz hands as she stumbled back against him. "Loyal's going to bed with the whack-job."

He snorted even as the brush of her ass against the front of his pants got his blood flowing fast and furious. Steady pressure on her arms put a few inches between them and started her moving forward. "I'm not going to bed *with* you, Roxanna, I'm putting you to bed to sleep it off."

"I need to sleep *you* off," she muttered under her breath.

His pulse skipped a beat, and he gave her a sideways glance as they reached the bedroom. "What does *that* mean?"

"It means you're no good for me."

Well, that actually might be true, but why was *she* saying it? Why would she even think it?

He steered her to the bed and turned her again to sit her down. After a moment of scrutiny, he kneeled and started untying her girly combat boots. She braced her hands on the edge of the mattress and leaned forward. He caught a stronger whiff of peppermint as those long, wavy locks of hers spilled down to bracket both sides of his head, the tips brushing against his forearms. The thought of her hair brushing other parts of his body made his erection throb and had him biting back a groan.

A swift upward glance caught her watching him, her brown eyes shadowed with an emotion he couldn't identify. Or maybe didn't want to identify.

"What did I ever do to you that you gotta be so mean to me all the time?" she asked.

He swallowed hard and dropped his attention back to her boots. That's what he hadn't wanted to put a name to. She looked hurt—*sounded* hurt. As if the things he'd said to her over the years had mattered to her. But she always got so defensive, and in his mind, her fierce anger only confirmed the guilt of her profession and justified each accusation and insult he'd uttered.

But what if he'd just been hurting her all this time? Every thing he'd said, like a slice with a knife he couldn't take back.

Guilt swirled with shame as he pulled off her unlaced boot and moved to the other.

"Loyal."

The plea in her voice tripped his pulse and drew his head up like a magnet.

"Why do you hate me?"

"I don't hate you, Roxanna." The denial was self-defensive and automatic, and yet with his next breath, he realized it was true. He didn't hate *her*, he hated what his mind said she represented.

He pulled off her other boot and set it next to the first, then avoided her gaze as he rose and dragged the covers back. "Come on. Get in bed."

"Kiss me."

He jerked his gaze to hers, his fingers clenching on the comforter. "What?"

"Kiss me." She reached up to grab a handful of his shirt. "Just once."

His body screamed *yes,* but somehow he managed to shake his head. "You're drunk. You don't know what you're asking."

"I'm asking you to kiss me. Come on, it won't kill you."

No, but her begging might.

"You'd hate yourself in the morning," he predicted as he resisted her pull on his shirt. "You'd hate *me* in the morning."

"I hate you now."

The words stung more than he ever would've thought possible, and yet something in her eyes weakened his resistance.

"Help me sleep you off, Loyal. Please."

Geezus fuck. He'd never heard the word *please* used so effectively before in his life. When she arched her eyebrows and tucked the corner of her bottom lip between her teeth as those beautiful brown eyes beseeched him, he was toast.

He sidestepped and leaned down to cover her mouth with his in one smooth motion. Her lips were soft, and a swipe of his tongue gave him a citrusy taste of wine and Roxanna.

It was so wrong, but he wanted more. From one heartbeat to the next, he *needed* more.

Her lips parted with a soft sigh, and he tilted his head to dip his tongue inside her mouth. She brought her free hand up to the back of his head, spearing her fingers into his hair as her other hand held tight to his shirt. His heart thudded hard as desire surged through him, urging him to stroke deep and explore all she offered.

As her tongue tangled with his, she leaned back, pulling him with her. He caught himself from falling on top of her with his hands braced beside her shoulders. The urge to climb up onto the bed and cover her body with his almost overrode the little voice in his head telling him to stop.

She's too drunk. She really will hate me in the morning—and herself.

Loyal reluctantly broke the kiss and eased back. Roxanna made a sound of protest, her hand still fisted in his shirt.

"We can't," he said as he tried to pry her fingers from the material.

"Why not?" she asked with a frown. "Cuz you don't like me?"

"You don't like *me*," he countered. "And you're drunk. You don't know what you're doing."

"I'm not that drunk."

He scoffed. "Yes you are, otherwise you would have tossed me out the moment I set the basket down." Especially if she'd been able to read his mind on what he wanted to do to her. With her. It would shock the hell out of her...like it did him.

"You think I'm so drunk and lonely, I'd have dragged any man who showed up at my door with presents into the bedroom?"

Would she have?

He was astonished all over again to realize it disturbed him that she might have. It bothered him she might be lonely enough that any man would do.

And yet the alternative wasn't any better, was it? She hadn't dragged him to the bedroom, but she had practically begged him to stay.

What was it she'd said...*help me sleep* you *off.*

As if she needed to get over him like she needed to get over being drunk. But that couldn't be. She hated him. She'd even said so before he kissed her. The alcohol should make her more truthful, right?

Confusion swirled as his body urged him to do one thing while his mind emphatically ordered the opposite.

Before he could decide, Roxanna went from holding him close to shoving him away.

"Get out." Then she rolled over and crawled up to the pillows at the head of the bed. As she fumbled to get beneath the covers, she grumbled, "I don't need a jerk like you in my life. No one does—which is probably why both your fiancés left you. The second one wised up just in the nick of time."

Her words struck a raw nerve deep inside. His jaw clenched as he glared at her from beside the bed. "You don't have a fucking clue what you're talking about."

"Oh, but I do. I know all about you, Loyal Diamond." She smirked at him as she dragged the second pillow into her arms. "Maybe if you weren't so uptight and judgmental, a woman might actually like you."

He'd dated since his last fiancé. In Texas—and here—there were more than enough women who wanted him. Like Merit, he never lacked for female companionship when he wanted it, he just didn't flaunt it like his younger brother.

"Plenty of women like me, Roxanna."

"If you're any good in bed, I'm sure they do."

If?

"But looks and sex and money'll only get you so far." Lying on her side, she hugged the pillow to her chest and closed her eyes. "You gotta be worthy of what the other person gives you, and you aren't worthy of much."

She was getting awfully deep for a person who hadn't been able to get her numbers to add up when she was sober. Problem was, she was hitting a little too close to home, making him leery of that psychic shit again.

He took a breath to argue, but then pressed his lips together when he realized she was out cold, just that fast. Damn woman hit him with a poison-tipped barb and then went right to sleep without a care in the world.

As he spun on his heel and strode from the room, he justified *that right there* was part of why he'd been mean to her over the years. Because she was so damn good at being mean right back.

CHAPTER 8

*R*oxanna rolled over, then let out a low moan as her head protested the movement. God, her mouth felt like it was stuffed with cotton, and she was all hot and sweaty. She listlessly pushed the covers down and pulled out her arm to rest over her aching forehead. Last thing she clearly recalled was her frustration with her accounting program before coming upstairs with a bottle of wine.

Then things got fuzzy.

She had a vague memory of Loyal inside the apartment, but that didn't make sense, because she'd specifically checked to make sure he'd left.

Her mind strayed back to the word *accounting*, and her eyes popped open. She had to open the shop.

"Shit!"

Panic had her scrambling to get out of bed, but her legs tangled in the sheets. As pain hammered at her head, she realized part of the problem was she was still wearing her long skirt. Man, she must've really been out of it to crawl into bed with *all* her clothes on.

The struggle to free herself only magnified her headache,

so she took a breath to calm down and squinted at the digital clock on the night stand. Relief eased her alarm when she saw it was twenty minutes after eight a.m. She didn't open until nine, so she had time—even if it wasn't much considering she needed to shower and pick out clean clothes off her clearance rack downstairs.

Moving more slowly, she managed to untangle her legs and sat on the edge of the bed. Her boots were set side by side in front of the nightstand, and she had a flash image of Loyal kneeling at her feet to take them off.

Oh, boy, that's a new fantasy.

Wine on an empty stomach was officially a bad idea.

Actually, Loyal on his knees looks pretty good.

Apparently, the wine was still messing with her head.

And the rest of her, considering it still felt like it was a hundred degrees in the room even without the covers. She stripped off her skirt before heading straight for the bathroom to pee and gulp handfuls of water to wet her dry mouth.

As she leaned against the counter and tried to will her piercing headache away, she amended her earlier thought to —*wine on an empty stomach is a* horrible, no-good, stupid *idea.*

A hot shower helped some, but as a few more snippets of her alcohol-fueled dreams surfaced, she acknowledged she was going to need ibuprofen to assist with her oils this morning.

Extra strength—and fast.

She shut off the water and grabbed a towel to dry off. The idea of putting her dirty, sweaty clothes back on to go down to her shop made her wince. Then she noticed a fluffy white robe hanging on a hook on the back of the door.

That hadn't been there yesterday, had it?

She must've missed it, but who cared? It was a godsend right now, because even though the back entrance to her

68

shop and upstairs was private, going down there in a towel would have been weird. She slipped into the super soft robe and tied the sash as she stepped out of the bathroom to go get her bag of new underwear and bras off the counter in the kitchen.

"You doing okay this morning?"

Roxanna jumped and screamed at the sound of the gravelly voice from the couch. When the man of her dreams sat up, she sagged against the wall, head and heart pounding hard.

"Damn it, Loyal. You scared the shit out of me."

"Sorry. I thought you saw me this time."

No, but she was seeing him now. Acutely aware she was naked beneath the robe, her fingers clutched the material together at her throat as her gaze raked over his bare chest. She darted a glance to his clothes laid neatly across the arm of the neighboring recliner and wondered if he'd slept in the nude again or left his briefs on.

Stiffening her spine against the desire to find out, she demanded, "What the hell are you doing here? Asher said you moved to a hotel."

"I did, but you were really drunk last night. I figured I'd better stay to make sure you were okay."

Wow. That actually sounded nice, but confusion swirled as parts of her dream floated in and out of focus.

Loyal at the door with a basket.

Taking away her wine glass because she'd had too much.

On his knees untying her boots.

Her begging him to kiss her.

Him actually kissing her.

That was a dream...wasn't it?

She shifted her gaze and spotted the big square gift basket on the kitchen table. A care package from Janine. Her fingers tightened on the fuzzy robe.

69

Oh, God. Not *a dream.*

A dizzying combination of humiliation and dread whirled in her belly as the devil took an ice pick to her brain.

"I need ibuprofen," she muttered.

"There isn't any. I checked."

She bit back a whimper and headed for the door. There was some downstairs in her desk, and she needed clean clothes to get dressed for work.

But a couple steps past the couch, she knew she'd go crazy if she didn't know exactly what happened the night before, so she turned around to ask. She froze when she caught sight of Loyal's sculpted ass as he stood and reached for his pants. Thankfully—or not—he was wearing a pair of black boxer briefs.

She enjoyed the smooth slide of muscle under skin as he stepped into his dress pants, but when he straightened and turned toward her while zipping up, she averted her gaze toward the windows. "Um...nothing happened last night, did it?"

"Like what?"

A quick glance caught his raised eyebrows as he leaned to scoop up his shirt. "I don't know exactly."

"I don't have sex with drunk women who can't consent," he stated.

"I didn't think *that,*" she scoffed, heat burning her cheeks.

It had been so long, she was positive she'd know if she'd had sex last night, whether she remembered it or not. And, if she *had* had sex with Loyal when she was too drunk to remember every single detail, she'd never forgive herself. Even in this moment, she was angry the kiss was only a blurry memory.

No. Damn it. She had to stop thinking that way. The rare nice gesture from him was not enough to make up for all the years he'd been a jerk. Besides, the basket was from his mom, not him.

But he slept on that uncomfortable couch to make sure you were okay when you were too drunk to know better.

So what? He wasn't a nice guy. She was moving on. She was done with him taking up unearned space in her heart.

"What did you think?" he prompted.

"I…" She couldn't say it out loud to his face. Especially when he was standing there all bare-chested and sexy with his shirt dangling from his fingers.

"You don't remember, do you?" As soon as he asked the question, a smirk tugged at his mouth. "Ah…no, you *do* remember. That's the problem."

"I was drunk." she rationalized with a lift of her chin. "People do stupid things when they're drunk. *Really* stupid things."

"Like beg a guy they supposedly hate to kiss them?" he asked as he finally shrugged into his shirt.

Exactly like that.

Humiliation set her face on fire, and she spun around for the door again. "There's no supposedly about it—I do hate you."

"Where are you going in that robe?"

His voice was closer than expected, and she cast an alarmed glance over her shoulder to see he'd grabbed his socks and shoes to follow her. Her heart lurched with him being close enough for her to catch a faint whiff of male mixed with lingering cologne. He hadn't taken time to button his shirt yet, and she tightened her hand on the door handle to resist the urge to reach out and touch his chest. To trail her hand down over his ripped abs, follow the happy trail of hair—

Geezus! Hadn't she just reiterated she hated him?

"I don't have clothes up here, so I have to get dressed

71

down in my shop," she explained impatiently. "I have to open in twenty minutes."

He backed up a step and swiped her bag of underwear and bras off the counter. "Don't forget these."

Heat flooded her face as she snatched the bag from his hand and yanked open the door. Her head still hurt, and he was making it worse.

"What did you mean last night when you said you needed to *sleep me off?*"

His question made Roxanna's stomach bottom out, but she refused to look at him. "How would I know?"

She did know, but if he hadn't already figured it out, she sure as hell wasn't going to explain it to him.

"You are the one that said it."

"We've already established drunk people do and say stupid things," she argued as she moved into the hall. She tried to pull the apartment door shut in his face, but he caught it and stepped out after her. "Clearly, I didn't know what I was saying."

His footsteps dogged hers on the stairs. "Last night you assured me you knew exactly what you were doing."

"And you believed me when I was that drunk?" She shot him a frown over her shoulder. "Shame on you."

He looked guilty for a brief moment, but then he shook his head. "That's not going to work. You can try to turn this back on me, but I had plenty of time to think after you passed out."

She faced forward, her heart thumping madly in panic. "Hope you didn't hurt yourself."

"Aw, look at that." Amusement filled his voice. "Using weak insults to avoid the truth."

Roxanna was at her shop door now, and desperate to get inside as he crowded close enough for her to once again inhale the goodness of him. He wouldn't follow her in there to keep up with the interrogation, would he? Clearly he *had* figured it out, so why the hell was he so intent on pushing this damn point, anyway?

To humiliate me even more.

Okay, then, how could she convince him the truth was not really the truth?

"You can admit you want me, Roxanna," he taunted in a husky voice as she keyed in the lockbox code. "That's the first step in getting over addiction."

"Rein in the ego, jackass." The light turned green, and she opened the door only enough to slip partially inside before meeting his gaze. "I was pretending you were your brother."

He drew back in surprise. "Asher? I thought you two—"

"No, God, not Asher."

"Merit?"

She tilted her head and raised her eyebrows. The moment it dawned on him exactly whom she was talking about, his whole body tensed. His face flushed, his nostrils flared, and his eyes went dark as his eyebrows slammed together.

"You said *my* name," he said in a tight voice. "You said *Loyal* last night."

"Of course I did," she bluffed past the guilt that was making it hard to breathe. "Because you wouldn't have kissed me if I'd called you Grayson."

CHAPTER 9

*L*oyal's fists clenched as he stared at the door after Roxanna shut it in his face. Again.

"You wouldn't have kissed me if I'd called you Grayson."

She was fucking right about that.

He forced his hands to relax against the urge to punch something. And just why the fuck did the thought of her and his half-brother make him crazy? He shouldn't care if she liked Grayson.

He *didn't* care. She could like whomever she wanted, because he didn't even like *her*.

Liar.

No. Lust did not equal like.

He finished dressing right there in the hall, then stalked out to his Land Rover and drove back to his hotel for a shower and clean clothes.

As he dried off, he concluded he needed to go back to avoiding Roxanna. That had worked for years.

Mostly.

Once he'd put on a pair of tan khaki's and a navy vest

over a crisp, white button up, he spent a couple hours on his laptop checking out houses online. There were plenty to choose from, but nothing caught his attention, leaving him restless and annoyed. His thoughts kept turning back to Roxanna, but iron determination shut them down each time.

When his stomach reminded him he hadn't eaten, he shut his laptop with a grimace. Room service didn't appeal, but neither did going out to sit somewhere alone. Spur of the moment, he texted the one person he guessed would be wide open for an early Monday lunch. The response came back a few minutes later.

Merit: *Lunch? You and me? Why?*

Loyal: *To eat food. Why else?*

Merit: *Are you dying?*

He frowned at his phone and gave a grunt of annoyance.

Loyal: *No, dipshit. Can't two brothers go to lunch?*

Merit: *Asher and I have done lunch. You and Asher have done lunch. Me and you? We don't do lunch.*

Loyal: *We do today.*

Merit: *Seriously. How many months you got left? Is it a brain tumor? An aneurism about to burst? Testicular cancer?*

Loyal seriously second-guessed his offer even as he replied: *Shut the fuck up and meet me at Nick's in half an hour.*

Merit: *That's the Loyal I know. C ya in a few.*

He rolled his eyes and grabbed his keys.

His youngest brother strolled into the pub five minutes late, looking like he'd rolled out of bed and tossed on the first pair of ripped jeans and sweatshirt he picked up off the floor.

Loyal raised his glass of Black Maple Hill from the table he'd snagged in the corner. Merit shrugged out of his leather jacket and took a seat as their red-headed waitress paused on her way by to ask his drink order. He requested a beer, and she promised to return shortly before moving on to the next table with her tray of food. Merit turned his head to watch her go, his gaze locked on the skin-tight fit of denim across her curvy backside.

"Hey," Loyal greeted wryly as he lifted his bourbon for a sip.

"Hey," he returned as he twisted back around. "You notice if she's wearing a ring?"

"Can this not be about you picking up a chick?"

"I just want to know if I can flirt or not."

"She's going to flirt either way for a good tip, so ease up man."

Merit picked up his menu with a muttered, "And this is why we don't do lunch."

Loyal grit his teeth, then forced his jaw to relax while his brother perused the options. By the time he set the menu aside, their waitress—Carly—returned with Merit's beer and a big, bright smile. She was not wearing a ring, and the two flirted their asses off as she took their order. On her way back to the kitchen, she tossed his younger brother a saucy grin over her shoulder.

While Loyal had no problem finding women to spend time with, he much preferred a more sophisticated approach. Some real conversation added to the whole process and at least gave the illusion of something more than a hook-up.

That realization was somewhat startling, and he frowned slightly. After his two broken engagements, he'd sworn off anything resembling—or that could turn into—a committed relationship. As long as both parties consented, it didn't have to be anything more than mutual fun, so why the hell would he feel the need to disguise sex as something more than sex?

That was a little too deep of a question to ponder on an empty stomach before noon on a Monday, so he lifted his glass and asked, "What's new?"

"I'm on a lunch date with my big brother," Merit deadpanned. "You tell me."

A wry grin curved his lips as he swirled the amber liquid in his glass. "It's been brought to my attention recently that I can be a bit of an ass, and I—"

Merit nearly choked on his beer, then had to wipe a dribble off his chin. "A *bit* of an ass? Who uttered that massive understatement?"

"I was going to ask if I'm really that bad, but no need now." He avoided revealing who made the accusation. "I don't mean to be."

Not all the time, anyway.

"Only since Lisa." His brother's brown gaze narrowed as he rested his forearms on the table while twisting his beer round and round with the tips of his fingers. "But then again, I imagine it sucks having been engaged twice and still never been married."

"It does," he agreed. It was humiliating, too.

"But still, you know, you can lighten up. Quit being so damn buttoned up and uptight." He gestured toward Loyal's vest and sport coat as he practically parroted Roxanna's drunken words.

"What, I should be more like you?"

"I'm not so bad."

"You're not so good, either," Loyal countered without any real judgment.

His brother made a face and shrugged, but he also avoided his gaze as he raised his bottle for a long drink.

Genuinely curious as to what his brother wanted to do with his life, he said, "You know, the other day after brunch, we were all talking about what we have going on. What about you? You're twenty-five and still no job, so what exactly is your plan these days?"

Merit set his beer down with a thunk. "Fucking A, man, not the infamous Diamond family plan. Why do we all have to have a plan?"

"Because otherwise, where is your life going, and how are you going to get there?"

"It's going wherever I feel like it at the moment, and however I get there is how *I* get there."

"Doesn't that bother you, not knowing what to expect?"

He hadn't expected his growing attraction to Roxanna, and it was driving him crazy. Not so much the physical aspect of it, that had already been bothering him for years, but the staying last night to make sure she was okay, and the excited—fucking *excited*—leap of his pulse when he came to the conclusion that maybe she had a thing for him, too.

And the fucking worst that he still couldn't shake off no matter how much rationalizing he did, had been her saying she'd imagined him as Grayson. He sure as fuck hadn't expected *that* when trying to ruffle her feathers this morning.

"Why should I bother to plan if I don't have to?" Merit reasoned as he relaxed back in his chair. "It's not like I need the money. If I went out and got myself a job, aren't I just taking it away from someone who might actually need it?"

Loyal blinked in astonishment. That explanation wasn't nearly as self-centered as he would've expected from Mooch. Guilt twinged in a way that was becoming all too familiar recently, and had him looking at his youngest sibling in a new light.

"You don't have to work for money, I guess."

Though that sounded weird to him—he'd always measured his steps to success by the increasing numbers in his bank account. He'd learned that from Grandpa Ira and their dad, though these days it seemed his dad measured success in the next highest office. He would not be surprised if he ran for president some day.

Merit narrowed his gaze. "All you guys do is rag on me to get a job."

"We all just want you to do something with your life."

"Yeah, well, it's *my* life, isn't it?" He fiddled with the corner of the label on his bottle, eyebrows heavy over his lowered gaze, his jaw set tight.

Yeah, it was his life, and what he decided to do with it was on his shoulders, not anyone else's. Loyal realized it was time he quit hounding his brother—quit making little digs that might be hurting someone he loved.

That reminded him of Roxanna again, and he raised his glass to down the last of his whiskey in one bracing swallow.

Suddenly, Merit sat forward and fixed him with a mutinous glare. "You know, just once I'd like to be asked instead of told, or, not even considered at all."

"What does that mean?"

"Dad hasn't asked me even once to work on his campaign."

Loyal frowned. "But you have helped."

"Of course I have. In fact, I'm heading over to headquarters to work with Shelby when she's done with class, like we've done almost every afternoon for the past couple of months."

"I don't understand what you're getting at then?"

"Dad never asked for *my* help, but he asked for Shelby's."

"He never really asked me, either."

"Until two days ago, you lived in Texas. Why would he ask you? Except, wait...the *moment* you *do* show up in town, he asks you to join the board of the new foundation he and Grayson are starting."

"Hey, you're welcome to it. I want nothing to do with that."

"Except he asked you, and you know damn well that means you take the job or no one gets it."

Loyal shook his head. "Dad isn't going to scrap the foundation simply because I won't be the CFO. Why don't you talk to him? Tell him you're interested."

"Dad doesn't listen to me. He's too busy with the campaign. When he's not doing that, he's pointing out everything the rest of you are doing. Or he's offering Grayson millions of dollars to open a veteran's foundation."

"You want me to talk to him?"

Merit gave a huff of frustration. "I don't want to be the damn CFO, Loyal. I just want to be *asked* for once."

Before he could reply, Carly arrived with their burger baskets. As if a switch had been flipped, his brother sat back and flashed the curvy redhead a charming smile.

"Can I get you guys anything else?" she asked.

"I'll take another beer and your phone number," Merit said smoothly.

She laughed and tilted her head toward Loyal in silent inquiry.

"Water, please. And an empty dish for ketchup."

"Coming right up."

Merit pushed his fries aside and squirted ketchup into the space he'd created in his basket. Then he set the bottle on the table between them and laughed at Loyal's grimace. "You're going to dip them in the ketchup anyway, so why so anal?"

"I don't like soggy fries."

"It all tastes the same."

Loyal waited for his empty dish.

He debated returning to their conversation about the CFO position and the foundation, but he wasn't so sure he wanted to get into that subject any deeper. Besides, his brother was busy digging in, and then Carly came back. She gave Loyal his dish and Merit her number.

"Enjoy," she said before heading to another table.

His brother gave him a triumphant grin as he pocketed the slip of paper, then took a big bite of his burger and spoke with a full mouth. "You never did say who said you're an ass. Was it Roxanna?"

That was not a subject he wished to return to, either, so he chewed one of his crispy French fries without answering.

His brother laughed. "Good for her. You deserve it."

Yeah, in hindsight, he did.

After he washed his food down with a drink of water, he asked, "Do you really think she's psychic?"

Merit shrugged. "I've never had her give me an official reading, but Celia did, and she said the stuff she told her was spot on."

"She probably got information from Asher."

"Nope. Cece said it was stuff no one knew. And there's the fact we've all seen Rox read Asher to a tee."

"They do call themselves best friends," he pointed out before taking a bite of his burger.

"She had Honor pegged with the whole not believing in love thing."

Loyal scoffed and swallowed. "Which is why she's now engaged to our brother."

"It was Asher who taught her to believe," Merit countered.

"You believe in that soulmate crap, too?"

His brother shrugged. "Yeah, why not?"

"That's rich coming from the guy who has a different woman every week."

"You telling me you've been celibate since your last engagement ended?"

Loyal's turn to shrug as he continued eating.

"Yeah, didn't think so. We're all searching, aren't we? Some of us just look at more options than others."

He laughed and shook his head.

"Listen, you asked what I thought about Roxanna and I told you. If you want proof one way or the other, have her do a reading for you."

"Who's to say she won't just make shit up? That's exactly what they do on those hotlines."

"*You* say. You'll know. She's not a hotline, and you'd be face to face."

Yeah, which is why she told me she can't read me. She knows I'll know it's bullshit.

"Look, I know you got majorly screwed over with Lisa, but she was definitely not the woman for you. She was way too self-centered."

Loyal pondered that truth as he munched more fries.

"What?" Merit feigned surprise. "No smartass *takes one to know one* comment?"

"Nope. I'm letting that one slide. Especially since I know you're right about Lisa. Last I heard, she married Jeff Richmond. I don't know who I feel more sorry for."

"I heard about that, too. They're actually quite perfect for each other. Richmond got his trophy wife, and she'll get to do whatever she wants while he screws around on the side."

Loyal dropped the last bite of his burger down into the basket, his appetite suddenly gone. "How the fuck did I end up engaged to her?"

"You were climbing the ladder of success." Merit gave him a grim grin around another mouthful of burger. "Workin' on The Plan."

"I guess I was." He'd reworked his plan the day he hadn't gotten married, only right now, he wasn't so sure he liked where burying himself in work had gotten him. Burned out. Missing family. Taking out his unhappiness on people who may or may not deserve it.

Well, he was home now, and he could change some of what he didn't like about the past six years.

Roxanna was a whole other matter. He wanted her out of his head, but he couldn't help returning to her words last night. It bothered him that he may have hurt her over the years, and yet with his next breath, he'd remind himself of her drunken dig about his fiancés, him not being worthy, and her sober punch to the gut this morning about Grayson.

Most disturbing was the urge to find her and kiss any thoughts of his half-brother right out of her head. When he was done, his name would be the only one she spoke from those wine-flavored lips of hers.

His pulse picked up, and he grimaced while grabbing a napkin to wipe his mouth and hands as Merit finished his food. He paid their bill with a generous tip, then Loyal followed his brother out the door as he pulled his keys from his pocket.

"Hey. You and Bells want help at headquarters this afternoon?"

"We'll be making personal phone calls to connect with the base, so do you really have to ask?"

"Apparently, you *like* to be asked."

Merit shot him a sideways glance. "I bare my soul to you and you mock me. Fuck you, man."

"What time?" When his brother's face screwed up into an exaggerated expression of horror, Loyal backhanded him on the arm. "Gross. What time are you meeting Bells, dipshit."

Merit chuckled as he headed for his vehicle. "One-forty-five."

"I'll see you there."

If he was lucky, talking to potential voters for his dad's campaign would keep his mind off his simmering resentment about Roxanna using him as a stand-in for the half-brother he hated.

CHAPTER 10

"Honor and Mae are here," Tessa called from the register on Thursday afternoon.

Roxanna slammed the file cabinet with a frustrated huff and walked over to her already messy desk to swipe up her new purse. It had been a shitty week, and not just because of the fire. Ever since she'd lied to Loyal about why she'd asked him to kiss her drunk self, she'd felt sick to her stomach. She still couldn't get her accounts to balance out, and the check she'd found on Sunday night had gone missing.

Karma was seriously pissed off at her, and her gut told her it was all because of her mean-spirited lie. She'd wanted to throw him completely off track, and considering she hadn't seen him since Monday morning, it appeared to have worked. Too bad she couldn't enjoy the peace and quiet.

When she turned around, the redheaded cake baker engaged to her best friend stood in the doorway, her blond bestie beside her still wearing her red Lockhart Construction logo shirt, jeans, and tan work boots.

"What's got you all riled up?" Honor asked.

"I'm missing a check. I think it got mixed in with the

84

mountains of paperwork I filed Sunday night, but I haven't been able to find it."

"Need some help?" Mae offered.

"Thanks, but I've had enough of the file cabinets today. I'll look again tomorrow."

"Any word on your apartment?"

That was another thing. She answered Honor's question with a shake of her head as they headed out. "They're still investigating what started the fire. No one's cleared to enter the building until that's finalized."

She switched the subject to Honor and Asher's trip as they got in the car, and on the way to the costume shop it morphed to their wedding set for May. Loyal would be the best man, and Mae the matron of honor. Roxanna was to be paired with Merit, and Honor's sister Glory would've been with Grayson, but the Diamond's new sibling had firmly declined the request to be a groomsman, so they were looking for someone else.

"But it's months away," Mae said. "Surely he'll be more comfortable with the family by then?"

"Asher didn't want to push it." Honor turned into the store lot and parked her car. "We're just hoping he comes."

"You really think he'd skip the wedding?"

"Maybe. There's still a lot of tension with the way he and Loyal seem hell bent on hating each other."

And you knew that when you threw Grayson's name in his face.

Roxanna winced in shame as they started inside.

"Asher said something about seeing if his friend Dev can stand up."

Dev Torrez. Now there was another guy she could've decided to like besides Loyal. Tall, devilishly handsome, muscled, and *nice.* If only the oldest son of the Diamond's housekeeper wasn't gone on classified missions for the military ninety-nine percent of the time. Well, that and the one time she'd met him five years ago, she'd noticed young Shelby mooning over him from the wings.

"I'm really going to need to meet all these guys soon," Mae said.

"You haven't met them yet?" Roxanna asked with surprise.

"Only Asher. Ian had a busy summer with soccer, and everyone and their brother seems to be remodeling these days. I've been so busy, it's crazy. I was supposed to meet Merit at that cookout a couple weeks ago, but Ian was sick."

And for Mae, her six-year-old son came first—as he should.

"Now that Loyal's back, we should plan a dinner for the wedding party," Honor mused. "Sometime after the election is over."

Mae nodded. "Sounds good."

A whole evening in the same room as Loyal sounded like hell to Roxanna, but she kept quiet as they paused at the register for Honor to give the sales lady the name for their reserved costumes.

"I'm going to go start looking," she said a moment later. It would be a miracle if she found something decent a mere two days before Halloween. With the way her week was going, if the party wasn't also a fundraiser for the children's hospital, she'd be tempted to skip it altogether.

Mae walked with her and commented, "I think I need to book a reading with you. I need to know if love like Honor and Asher's is in my future. Things are looking pretty bleak these days."

She glanced over at the pretty pixie blond in the middle of browsing a rack of costumes. "I can't always give a definitive answer during a reading, but at the very least, we can examine your aura, and clear your energy flows of anything blocking your path to finding love."

"Well, single motherhood is one big energy block," she said wryly.

"Plenty of single parents find love," Roxanna argued with a smile.

"I know. And I swear, I wouldn't trade Ian for any guy, but someday the woman in me wants more. She wants to *feel* like a woman again, not just an overworked mommy CEO."

"That same woman in me totally gets you," she murmured while swiping past the French Maid, the Sexy Cheerleader, and the Slutty Nurse. The high end rental shop meant the costumes were top of the line, but she still needed a skirt that covered past her ass, or she'd end up feeling as exposed as she had that night she'd climbed into bed with Loyal.

Was that only a week ago?

Not even, and yet it seemed so far in the past already.

"Do you ever see stuff for yourself," Mae asked with curiosity. "Like, would you sense if the guy of your dreams was in the same room?"

She gave a soft snort as Honor joined them.

"They're holding our stuff at the front." The redhead raised her eyebrows and pinned Roxanna with her green gaze. "Guy of your dreams? Do tell."

She shrugged as she felt the soft, supple leather of a black Catwoman suit, then flipped it to the left. "There's nothing to tell. I mean, back when I was nine, I did have a dream that the love of my life would be loyal and true, but I've discovered I have as much of a chance of finding a guy like that as I do finding a unicorn. He doesn't exist for me."

Mae's eyes widened. "Ooh—maybe it's Asher's brother, Loyal. Like, literally, he's *Loyal* and true. That would make perfect sense."

Oh, man, why had she even said that out loud? She'd never told anyone about that stupid dream before. Roxanna shot a quick glance of alarm at Honor, because the last thing

87

she needed was her telling Asher, but the cake baker's attention was focused on the rack of costumes.

"Rox and Loyal mix like oil and water," she contradicted while pulling the Catwoman suit off the rack. She held it up in front of Roxanna as if eyeing the fit. "But this, right here, is like cake and frosting."

"Oh, please. No way I'm wearing that."

"Come on, at least try it on."

"I can't give readings in leather," she protested when Honor completely ignored her and headed across the store with the suit.

"Says who?" Mae tugged on her arm and dragged her along. "Catwoman can be psychic for one Halloween. I bet it'll look great on you."

"It's never going to fit right off the rack."

"Then we'll ask the sales lady to find you the right size in the back."

She took the costume into the dressing room, determined to show them it didn't fit and get on with finding something more appropriate. Except when she pulled the suit on and zipped up the front, she was absolutely floored. At her five-foot-nine, the odds of it fitting off the rack were crazy astronomical, and yet it did.

Even more astonishing, the form-fitting leather was comfortable without being constricting. It felt...right—an odd sensation after everything had been so wrong for the past week.

"Let's see it," Honor called.

She put on the mask and opened the fitting room curtain.

"Perfect," Mae said with a pleased grin. "Look at that. You look awesome."

Honor was smiling, too. "Mae and I are too short to ever wear something like that, but she's right, it's great."

"I don't hate it," she said with a casual shrug. If she was

being honest, she even felt a little sexy. She wasn't going to be honest enough to say that out loud though.

"I'll go tell the lady to add it to my bill," Honor said as she turned toward the front. "Asher said he's covering yours since you always donate the readings."

"Thanks."

While Roxanna changed, Mae spoke through the curtain. "I kinda wish I could go, now."

"You're not coming?"

"Ian and I are trick-or-treating earlier with Honor, her sister, and her twin nieces, but then Ian and I have a tradition of sorting through all his candy and watching a scary movie. I can't break that."

"It sounds like fun." Though it made her feel a bit lonely. Mae had her son. Honor had Asher. She was still alone.

"I wouldn't miss it, but I'd still love to see you at the party. If your *loyal* and true love is there, he won't be able to take his eyes off you. Add in the mystery of your mask and it could be a romantic evening."

He wouldn't be there, and yet she couldn't deny her pulse sped up at the thought of seeing Loyal again.

Until her stomach knotted.

She ignored the guilt—or tried to.

She'd had to feed him that lie, even if it went against the very fiber of her being. She couldn't waste her life any longer pining for someone who didn't like or respect her and her work. Since she couldn't avoid him completely, she needed to make sure he didn't think he had one over on her because she was head over heels in love with him.

Head over heels?

Oh no. She was attracted to him, and she could admit—to herself—she wanted to run her hands all over his firm, sexy muscles, but *love*?

No.

Which was precisely why she had to find someone else to lust after, so she could move on.

Late Saturday morning, Roxanna finally pulled the missing check from her file cabinet with a shout of triumph for Darcy in the front.

"You found it?"

"Yes." She carried it out to the register. "Take a look at the name. Does it ring a bell? I can't find any paperwork to go with it. Did Tessa say anything about booking a weekend seminar?"

Darcy's twin blond pigtails to go with her cheerleader costume swayed back and forth as she shook her head. "Not that I can remember, but doesn't mean she didn't."

Three months pregnant Tessa forgetting to add a weekend to the calendar was the only logical explanation. "Let's check with her when she gets here," Roxanna said as her phone buzzed in her skirt pocket.

She pulled it out to answer as she set the check on the counter. Her pulse skipped when the caller identified himself from the police department and let her know her apartment had been cleared for her to sort through her belongings—or what was left of them.

"I would suggest you bring a couple of boxes to put things in, and be sure to wear old clothes. You're going to get very dirty."

Old clothes. It was a good tip, if not for the fact all she had was new clothes because everything else she owned had been burned in the fire. But, of course, the officer was only trying to be helpful.

"Thank you for letting me know." She stared at the screen after she hung up, a little surge of hope lighting in her chest even as she tried to caution herself there was probably nothing left.

"Everything okay?" Darcy asked with concern.

"Yeah...that was the police. I can go into my apartment."

"Oh, good. You should go now. I'll be fine here until Tessa comes in."

"Are you sure? It gets really busy with the trick-or-treaters in the afternoon."

"One hundred percent sure. Tessa and I can handle it. Go."

"All right. Thanks." She turned to leave, then turned back. "About the check."

"I'll check with Tessa and take care of it. Don't worry about it."

"Thank you," she said, her mind already back to the apartment.

As she grabbed a box and looked to see what she could use for old clothes, her chest tightened at the thought of having to go alone. Asher would go if she asked, but she knew he was at his parents' house, helping his mom direct their hired crew with last minute party setup, and she didn't want to take him away from his family.

Out of the blue, Loyal's surprisingly concerned *"Are you okay?"* the morning after the fire popped into her head. It had been her first non-hostile experience with him, and shortly after, he'd offered her a ride to her building so she didn't have to walk. She had a fleeting urge to ask for his support now, but it was quickly doused with the memory of his expression when she'd thrown his half-brother in his face.

If she called Loyal—which she couldn't because she didn't even have his number—he'd probably tell her to go to hell. And justifiably so.

She was well and truly on her own.

Roxanna found an old smock she'd used for painting a

year or so ago, grabbed a medium sized box for whatever she could salvage, threw in a couple garbage bags for good measure, and headed out.

When she parked her old Jeep behind the blackened building, she saw a couple of her fellow tenants milling about. Her heart thumped hard as she gathered her things from the passenger seat, checked in with the building manager, and cautiously made her way inside. The smoke smell lingering in the air outside was twenty-times stronger inside, and she pressed the back of her hand up to her nose as her stomach churned.

Grim hellos and subdued smiles were exchanged with anyone she met in the hall, and then she slowly climbed the stairs to the second floor. Shock halted her steps when she saw the extent of the damage. Walls were burned down to the studs, and what was left resembled charred prison bars. She could see into every room thanks to no walls and the burned out windows allowing outside light into the power-less building.

When she moved to the doorway of her apartment, any hope of salvage was snuffed out in one stomach-sinking glance. Footsteps and voices drew her shell-shocked gaze as two fireman in half their gear—boots, pants, T-shirt, and suspenders—appeared at the top of the stairs.

"We have gloves and a mask that we recommend you wear."

She accepted the supplies the taller, dark-haired guy handed over. "Thank you."

"If you need anything lifted out of the way, or carried out to your vehicle, let us know, okay?"

She nodded, and they moved on to check the other apartments.

Finally, Roxanna took a deep breath and stepped into the only space she'd called home since the day she'd packed her things in Wisconsin and moved to Colorado. She hadn't looked back—there wasn't much to look at—but this loss here, pretty much a *total* loss, was a nauseating gut punch.

Not a total loss.

The reminder was swift and true. She needed to always consider first that she was alive. All her neighbors were alive. What she had lost were only material items that could be replaced. For as long as she'd been practicing life affirmations at Lift Your Spirit, that should always be her first thought.

It *would* always be her first thought from now on.

With that in mind, she squared her shoulders, fit the mask over her nose and mouth, and pulled on a pair of gloves to start picking through the ashes of her belongings.

Almost two hours later, her efforts resulted in half a box of blackened items she might be able to clean up back at the shop. Soot darkened her skirt, arms, gloves, and probably her cheeks from when she'd swiped stray hairs away from her face. Somehow she must've breathed ashes or dust particles in, because her eyes and throat were itchy, her lungs were tight, and she was so stuffed up it was almost impossible to breathe out of her nose.

But all she had left to go through was her bedroom—or what used to be her bedroom—so she kept at it. She didn't plan on coming back again.

Her phone was right there, melted to the charred remains of her nightstand. Moving aside the burnt pieces of what was left, a sudden memory made her pulse skip. Then her stomach dropped with dismay and she frantically dug into the debris.

She swallowed hard when she finally lifted a gold chain enmeshed in a melted puddle of plastic from the ashes. The amulet from a grocery store vending machine had been worthless from the start, but her mom had made it something special when she took her into a jewelry store to buy the chain.

Tears stung Roxanna's eyes, sparking anguish and anger. She shouldn't care about losing something so trivial from the woman who had betrayed her time and again, and yet the necklace represented that one perfect memory she'd cherished of her mom. That one perfect day they'd spent together when she was nine, when she knew her mother loved her.

Before the selfish woman abandoned their family. Before she'd betrayed her husband and daughter, and before she came back to do it all over again ten years later.

CHAPTER 11

"*B*atman returns."

Loyal offered his brother's fiancé a grim smile as he joined the group congregated off to the side of the haunted house that had been constructed in the lower, detached garage. His mom always went all out to raise as much money as possible for the kids.

Asher and Honor made a striking couple as Zorro and his wife from that nineties *The Mask of Zorro* movie. Merit was unsurprisingly a one-eyed pirate—he wouldn't want a full mask obscuring his pretty mug from the ladies. Bells had gone all out as Beauty from *Beauty and the Beast* in her golden ball gown, and Reyes, the youngest of the Torrez siblings, had opted for the classic Grim Reaper with a scythe.

Loyal scowled as he adjusted the string securing his black cape around his neck. Batman had seemed ideal to hide behind the mask, but he hadn't counted on the cape choking him—or the skin-tight spandex pants showcasing the family jewels. He kept fighting the urge to cup his hands in front of his crotch and hoped hooking his thumbs in the utility belt while holding his long-neck beer bottle was cover enough.

95

Then again, whether he was in a Batman suit or a tux with a bowtie around his neck, he hated these events. There were too many people, with their cars lining not only the driveway, but up and down the street as well. It was his own damned house and he'd had to park all the way down by the stables.

Hundreds of costumed guests milled inside, out on the patio, and between the main house and the haunted house. He knew the money raised for the children's hospital was essential; he just didn't want to deal with the noisy crowd. There was a good reason he liked numbers better than people.

Earlier, he'd made his sizeable donation, so now all he had to do was make sure his mother saw him, and hang out for another half-hour or so while lying to himself he wasn't keeping an eye out for a certain leggy, long-haired brunette. After that, he was going to answer an emergency call from Gotham City.

"You've certainly got the brooding intensity down pat," Reyes Torrez observed.

Loyal hadn't seen the guy since he'd gotten out of the Army last month. He switched his beer to his left hand, then reached to shake the younger man's hand and pulled him in for a half-hug. "Hey, Rey, nice to have you back home, man."

"You, too, I hear."

"Yeah, I finally had enough of Texas. Too hot and too far away. How's it going? Your mom said you're working with your dad at the stables again."

"The horses have always been my thing. Though, if the Army still had the Calvary, I would've stayed in for the best of both worlds."

"I thought they did?" Shelby asked.

"For ceremonial purposes only," Reyes advised. "That

wasn't something I was going to be able to get into, so I'm back with you guys."

Asher clapped him on the shoulder. "Glad to have at least one of you around, seeing as how Dev and Solana don't appear like they'll be back anytime soon."

"I know. Dev always seems to be on a mission somewhere. Solana's working a big case in Washington State. They are both hoping to be home for Christmas this year, though. If they do, it'll be the first time we've all been together for the holidays in over five years."

"Your mom and dad will love that," Loyal said.

Merit raised his glass. "Man, if that happens, I'm calling a party down at the guest house."

"Like old times," Reyes toasted with his beer.

"Almost," Asher corrected as he hugged Honor to his side. "Now Celia has a husband and I have a fiancé to join in."

"And another brother," Shelby added.

An instant flash of annoyance brought Loyal's scowl back. His baby sister shot him a quick glance, but looked away when she saw his glare.

Oblivious to the tense undercurrents, Reyes gave an enthusiastic, "The more the merrier."

"Keep us posted," Merit ordered as Celia flew up with her broom, her pointed, black hat three feet wide, and her green face makeup and warts professionally applied.

"Hey, guys, looking great." After an exchange of mutual admiration, she turned to Asher. "Is everything okay with Rox? Mom said she's not doing readings this year."

At the mention of the psychic's name, Loyal went on instant alert and his heartbeat sped up.

"She texted earlier that she cleaned out her apartment today and wasn't feeling well after, so she was going to stay home."

97

"Was she able to save anything?" he asked before he could help himself.

His brother shook his head. "Not much. I'd have gone to help, but she didn't even let me know until she was done."

Her independence was admirable until it was foolish.

Dare you to tell her that to her face. Oh, she'd tell him right where to go for sure.

"I can't even imagine losing everything like that," Shelby said. She looked from Celia to Honor. "I know Mom sent over a care package, but we should see if she wants to go shopping. We can get her a whole new wardrobe."

"Asher and I already tried offering," Honor said. "She insists she's good with what she has for now and will replace things a little at a time."

Loyal recalled her complaining her numbers didn't add up last weekend when she was drunk. Made him wonder if she was having money problems. He also wondered if she'd bothered to hire herself a new accountant yet.

Maybe he could offer—

No you cannot.

Suddenly restless, he said, "Listen, I'm going to find Mom for the obligatory appearance, then I'm slipping out. You guys have fun."

He gave a backward wave to the chorus of, "Night, Batman," "Later, Batman," and a "See ya, old man," from Merit and rounded the corner of the house to make his way up the steps onto the patio as he drained the last of his beer.

A vampire couple blocked the top stair, so he angled to slip past them, then had to immediately dodge sideways to avoid knocking over a patio heater. The move slammed his shoulder into the back of another guest wearing a hooded cloak and a quiver of arrows.

Loyal instinctively reached out a hand to Robin Hood's shoulder as he stepped back. "Sorry, man."

The guy turned around, and any sense of apology flew right out the window when Grayson's hard gaze met his.

"Watch what the fu—" He broke off and darted a look around. "Watch where you're going."

Judging by the dark glare, he'd recognized him past the Batman mask. So much for being incognito. Loyal dropped his gaze to fully take in his half-brother's get-up. If he didn't hate the guy so much, he might have found it funny.

Without another word, he turned to leave. Loyal hadn't made it two steps before the obvious costume statement had him thumping his empty bottle on a table as he turned back around. Aware of the other guests within earshot, he moved in close and lowered his voice.

"Why didn't you take the money my dad offered you?"

Grayson's brown eyes appeared almost black in the shadows. "Because it was fucking guilt money," he ground out in an equally low voice. "He wasn't trying to help me. He just wanted to make himself feel better for not being in my life."

Loyal considered that, then surprised himself by asking, "Couldn't it be both? Or maybe it truly was him trying to help, because does he really have anything to feel guilty about when he didn't even know you existed?"

Grayson's gaze narrowed. "I don't need Diamond charity."

"You came to our house and *asked* for it."

He leaned in and jabbed his finger into Loyal's chest. "You know why I asked for the foundation money, so don't go acting like *I'm* a charity case."

"No, you're just a noble sonofabitch, aren't you?" Loyal shook his head, backed up a step, and spun around to leave back down the stairs so he could go straight to his vehicle at the stables. He was done. He wasn't even going to attempt the crowd inside the house, and if Mom asked, the others would vouch for him.

"Are you going to do it?"

Grayson's question made him pause, but he didn't turn back. Something in his voice made Loyal's automatic *no* stick in his throat.

"I don't like this any more than you do," his half-brother stated. "But we don't have to like each other to help people who need it. The veterans deserve it—they've *earned* it."

There was a rough emotion in the guy's voice that over-rode the resentment between them. It dug in deep and triggered a fresh wave of guilt and obligation that hit Loyal dead center in the chest.

"I'm still thinking about it," he ground out before almost flying down the steps without looking back.

Mr. Torrez kept the outside stable lights dimmed during events to discourage anyone from exploring where they didn't belong, but Loyal didn't need light to find his spot. So many times over the years he'd escaped down to the worn, wooden bench along the side of the building. The tall, cone-shaped Arborvitaes on either side cast long shadows to ensure anonymity.

He skipped the dimly lit bench and leaned back against the brick wall in the dark. With the solid support at his back, slowly, he became aware the noise of the Halloween party had faded into the background. The peace and quiet away from the crowd soothed his raw nerves, eased the pressure in his chest, and finally allowed him to draw in a deep, settling breath of the cool October air.

Seconds later, movement on his left caught his eye and drew his head up. A slim figure in a black suit and mask walked slowly past the stables, then stopped. In the dim light, Loyal identified a Catwoman costume skimming the curves of the tall woman. After one swift appraisal, he let his gaze take a longer lingering look.

Leather covered her from neck to toe, but damn, that ass, those legs in those boots…her whole body was sexy as hell.

All of a sudden, his heart skipped a beat as he darted his gaze from the military-style boots to the dark curls streaming down the middle of her back. A moment later, she sat on the bench, pulled off the mask, and raked her hair back with her hands.

Roxanna.

His heart pounded with anticipation, though he wasn't sure why after her parting shot a week ago. When she remained silent while staring toward the main house, he realized she didn't even know he stood there in the shadows.

Now what? Should he reveal himself, or wait for her to head up to the party?

He knew the moment he opened his mouth he'd scare the hell out of her, and yet after hearing she'd cleaned out her burned out apartment earlier, he wanted to make sure she was okay. Ask if she needed anything, like someone to talk to, or a shoulder to cry on.

A mouth to kiss.

Loyal shook his head at the ridiculous direction of his thoughts and hooked his thumbs in the utility belt of his costume as he forced himself to wait.

But soon it became clear by her slumped shoulders and absolute stillness, she wasn't in a hurry to get up to the main house. He let out a silent sigh of resignation, then couldn't help the upward tug of his lips as he shouldered away from the building.

"We have to stop meeting like this."

CHAPTER 12

*R*oxanna's heart jammed into her throat to strangle her surprised squeak. She jerked toward Loyal's deep voice so hard she nearly fell off the bench. When she saw him lurking in the shadows in a Batman costume with a smirk on his mouth, anger spiked hot and hard.

"God, you're such an ass. Stop doing that!"

"Hey, two out of three were not my fault. Actually, neither was this third one. I waited for you to leave, but it's like your butt is glued to the wood there."

She growled her annoyance and spun her leather-clad butt around on the bench so she wasn't facing him. One glimpse of his strong, stubbled jaw and his damn kissable lips beneath that scowling half-mask and it wasn't the scare that made it hard to catch her breath.

"What are you doing down here anyway? Shouldn't you be up there?" She waved the cat-ear mask in her hand toward the Halloween party.

"Too many people up there."

The comment brought back a fuzzy memory of his voice in her head. *"Numbers don't lie like people do."*

102

Both statements indicated he wasn't much of a people person.

Big shocker there.

"Asher said you were staying home," he commented as he moved closer.

The blackened remains of her apartment flashed in her mind.

"I don't have a home," she muttered before she realized how pitiful it sounded. Annoyed with herself, she stiffened her spine and squared her shoulders.

Loyal swung his leg over to straddle the bench, his cape billowing around him as he sat down facing her profile, a mere two feet away. It was crazy how the simple proximity of his knees front and behind made her heartbeat rev up all over again. When she shot him a sideways glance, her breath caught at the concern in the dark eyes shining through his mask.

"You okay, Roxanna?"

The uncharacteristic sympathy in his soft voice breached her defenses, and the emotions from earlier swept forward in a dizzying rush.

She lifted a shoulder, blinking fast as she turned her gaze toward the party lights across the grass. "I've been sitting in my Jeep for the past twenty minutes trying to work up the energy to go up there, but…"

"Why do you have to go?"

"The fire is nothing compared to what so many of those kids face every day at the hospital."

"Maybe so, but that doesn't mean it's any less to you. You're allowed to take time to process everything without feeling bad."

She swiveled her head toward him in astonishment. Maybe she'd been transported to an alternate universe on the drive over. "Who are you, and what did you do with the real

Loyal Diamond?"

His smile of acknowledgement was subdued. "He took the night off."

Her heart skipped as she dipped her gaze down his chest, past his belt, to the spandex covering his muscled thighs. Black leather boots encased his calves and feet, and she had to admit, he wore the costume well.

So *very* well.

Realizing she was staring and in danger of drooling, she murmured, "The goodness of the suit is getting to you."

"Actually, there is a debate as to whether Batman is good, or if he's really a villain."

"Seeing you in that costume a week ago, I'd have said villain." Her lips quirked as she lifted her gaze back to his. "Now, I'm not so sure."

"The same argument is had for Catwoman."

Roxanna tilted her head in surprise. "I would not have pegged you for a comics guy."

"Not so much now, but I read the hell out of them when I was a kid. I don't imagine the argument has changed much in fifteen or twenty years."

A trio of loud party-goers walking to a nearby vehicle drew their attention. In the silence between them, she was hyper-aware of the man beside her, and marveled at their civil—almost friendly—exchange. She wasn't quite sure what to make of it considering how they'd parted Monday morning. Recalling the moment she'd shut the door in his face triggered a wave of remorse.

He reached up to pull his mask off and dropped it on the bench. Lifting both hands, he scrubbed his fingers through his flattened hair, then did one casual swipe to smooth it into his regular style. Kind of. After sneaking a sideways peek beneath her lashes, it took everything she had not to reach over to arrange the remaining errant strands just so.

"There is good and bad in all of us," she said, referring back to whether the characters they'd dressed as were heroes or villains.

"True."

He shifted slightly while rubbing his palms up and down on his thighs. Almost as if he was nervous—which was a very odd look for the oldest Diamond sibling. One of the things she'd always admired about him—secretly, of course—was his self-assurance. Even if most times he was an ass about it.

She realized how messed up that was, but ignored it anyway as she monitored his movements from the corner of her eye.

When his hands went still and he took a deep breath, she bit back a mystified smile. Definitely nervous—but why?

"I know I've been somewhat…ah…cynical of what you do. And I—"

Her snort of disbelief cut him off. "*Somewhat?*"

"Okay, a lot," he conceded. "I've been a *lot* cynical of your profession, and—"

"Cynical isn't the right word, either."

He frowned. "May I talk?"

"Go for it. Just get it right."

"I'm trying to apologize here."

That should've shut her up, but the words kept coming. "Mocking is the word you're looking for. Contemptuous. Disparaging. Hostile. Any of those would do, too."

"Or, I don't have to apologize at all."

"I just want to make sure you understand how you've come across the past six years."

"I *do* understand." Exasperation stiffened his tone. "Why the hell do you think I'm apologizing? Or *trying* to."

Her neck ached from having her head turned to look at him, so she swiveled her body to face him while drawing her leg up to rest sideways on the bench. With her own mask grasped between her linked fingers, she met his gaze. "Go ahead."

"I have not been very..." With the hesitation, his gaze lowered as he clearly searched for his words. Then he sighed, and the corner of his mouth quirked in resignation when he shifted his gaze once more. "Yeah, okay, I've been *hostile* to you when I should not have been. I know you didn't have anything to do with that psychic hotline that blew up my last engagement, but I still blamed you for it."

Guilt dropped her gaze to her lap. Even if she hadn't knowingly contributed to the scam, did she carry culpability?

"Are you still in love with her?" Her heart skipped at the question, dreading his answer.

"With Lisa? God no. Truth be told, those thieves probably saved me years of unhappiness and a ton of money in alimony. I was with her for all the wrong reasons, but I had blinders on. I was too focused on the career ladder I was climbing to realize it."

Her guilt eased, and she arched her brows with a smile. "So, you could say a psychic helped you out."

"I wouldn't go that far," he scoffed. "Those people are still con-artists, and if I found them, I'd do everything I could to make them pay."

Her stomach pitched. They were having a real conversation for the first time ever. Even though she knew *she'd* done nothing wrong, what would he say if he knew she'd worked with the scammers? That one of them was her mother? Would it matter to him that she hadn't seen hide nor hair of the woman since the thief cleaned out her own daughter's bank account and skipped town, or would he still want to make her pay?

Loyal flipped his mask end over end on the bench a couple times. "Here's the thing. Nothing personal, but I still don't believe in what you claim to do. It's just..." His shoulders lifted beneath his cape. "I won't be an ass about it anymore. And I'm sorry if what I've said in the past has hurt you or...I don't know...made you feel bad."

So, he was done being a jerk but still thought she was a fraud?

That apology didn't make her feel any better.

However, she couldn't control what he believed, and he was being honest. *Honest*, not *mean*. Could she really fault him for that?

Probably not.

Definitely not if she was keeping her mouth shut about the hotline.

She forced a slight smile with her nod. "I appreciate the honesty. In that spirit, I need to apologize as well."

"For that shot about Grayson, or the one about both my fiancés leaving me?"

"Oh, no." She covered her mouth as if she could keep in whatever it was she'd said a week ago. "What did I say about your fiancés?"

"That if I wasn't so...gimmie a sec—let me make sure I get it right..." He glanced skyward, one eye squinted a tad more than the other. "*Uptight and judgmental*, a woman might actually like me."

The self-mocking humor in his voice let her relax as she lowered her hand. "Well, *that* is true, so I guess I'm not all that sorry."

His slight grin faded. "And the other?"

She winced. "Yeah. I am sorry for that. I've felt bad about it all week."

"For pretending I was him, or for saying it?"

She knew what that question was really asking, and the memory of his voice echoed in her head.

Numbers don't lie like people do.

She couldn't lie again. "For saying it. I wasn't really pretending you were Grayson."

Relief flashed in his eyes, though it was gone so quickly, she wondered if she'd read it correctly or only imagined it. And then he gave her a cocky grin that made her stomach flip over.

"I knew you wanted me."

No sense denying it when she'd let the cat out of the bag while she was stupid drunk. "I want plenty of things that aren't good for me."

"I might not be good for you, but I could be very good *to* you."

Good Lord, her heart was going to beat right out of her chest.

"Stop it." Her laugh came out high and breathless, and his grin was way too knowing. "We've only just called a truce. Don't push it."

He lifted his hands, palms up. "You're right." He scooted back a good six inches as he scooped up his mask. "It's not like we could have more than one night anyway."

I'll take it!

No. That idea was way too hazardous to her heart. She already knew from Asher that his brother hadn't been in a single serious relationship since his last fiancé. He didn't want to be, and he was being completely honest with her again, so she needed to heed the warning.

Moving on, remember?

She forced another smile. "Which is exactly why you're no good for me."

His gaze locked with hers, and from one breath to the next, time stood still.

One night.

Just one, and then *I can move on.*

The heat rising in her body made the cat suit nearly

unbearable. Her fingers twitched with the urge to unzip and let the cool night air in.

Approaching voices shattered the moment. As they both looked away, Loyal rose to his feet and stepped over the bench in a fluid motion.

"Come on. I'll walk you up to the house."

Roxanna rose as well, and the heels of her boots put her almost at eye level with his six-foot-two frame. "I think I'm going to go home. If I go up there now, I'll feel obligated to do readings, and I'm not up for it emotionally."

She half-expected a snide comment, or even a mocking glance at the very least.

But he made good on his promise by simply nodding. "I'll walk you to your car then. I'm leaving, too."

Nice Loyal was dangerous on a whole new level. She couldn't use defensive anger to keep him at a distance. Physically, or emotionally.

As they walked, she kept circling back to his one night comment. Wanton energy built deep in her core with each step. When the two of them reached her Jeep, she turned around to find him right behind her. Not so close that he invaded her personal space, but enough for her to consider closing the distance to plaster her leather against his spandex.

The thought almost made her laugh. Never in a million years would she have expected to see *him* in spandex and a cape. He was usually way too buttoned up in his suits and vests.

Lo and behold, he wasn't uptight or judgmental tonight, and she liked the hell out of him.

That did make her smile.

He smiled back as he said, "I'm glad we ran into each other tonight."

"Me, too."

His attention flicked down to her mouth before those dark eyes met hers for a heart-stopping moment. Her smile faded at the same time as his.

A frown creased his brow for a millisecond, and then he backed up a step and cleared his throat. "Drive safely."

Roxanna swallowed hard when he started to turn away, her heart racing as she impulsively called him back. "Loyal."

He swung back immediately, but didn't speak. His heated gaze raked down the length of her cat suit, leaving her breathless all over again.

"I think I remember something else from the other night."

"What's that?"

She stared at his full bottom lip. God, she wanted his mouth on hers again. So bad. Bad enough to say something that would probably make her sound like an idiot. "You're a good kisser."

One corner of his mouth tugged up with his soft snort. "Hate to tell you, but you would have thought a horse was a good kisser that night."

At the reminder of how drunk she'd been, she lifted her gaze to quip, "Or a horse's ass." His low, rich laugh sent another wave of heat coursing through her while she tilted her head. "Are you saying I only imagined it was good?"

"No, I'm good." He cut the distance between them in half. "In fact, I'm exceptionally good, but you were so tippy I don't think your memory of *that* kiss should be what you base your judgment on."

There was that self-confidence she found so darn sexy even as she corrected, "You mean tipsy."

He grinned. "You assured me the word was *tippy*. I believed you when you almost fell on your face."

The heat making her so very uncomfortable was no longer strictly from sexual longing. "Oh, God. That's embarrassing."

"It was cute. At least, when you weren't being mean to me, you were cute."

She bit the corner of her lip and arched her brows in apology. "Sorry."

"I deserved it."

As the seconds ticked by, she gathered enough courage to say, "So...if I shouldn't use *that* kiss to judge..."

Why aren't you already kissing me?

As if he'd read her mind, he stayed right where he was and said, "You told me not to push it."

Roxanna frowned in disbelief. "Yeah, but then I brought up the kiss I apparently begged for when I was drunk."

"And?"

"Well, I thought I was being pretty obvious, but if you need me to print out a formal invitation..."

She trailed off when his wide-ass smirk told her he was teasing.

"God," she muttered past a reluctant grin. "You're still an ass."

Damn man was as exasperating as his brother. Difference was, she'd never once wanted to kiss Asher more than she wanted her next breath.

CHAPTER 13

*R*oxana's lungs constricted when Loyal reached his arm out from under his cape to slip a hand around her waist and tug her close. Hip to hip, his hard thighs branded hers through the soft, supple leather of her suit.

"You sure about this?" he asked.

Be cool. "Yeah. And if you're not as good as I *imagined*, we can go back to hating each other."

His lips quirked at her flippant challenge. "I don't think I can ever go back to hating you, Roxanna."

She loved the way he said her name, especially when he got all serious. His tone dropped an octave, turning his voice slightly raspy. It gave her stomach a little flutter every time.

He threaded his other hand through her hair to the nape of her neck, his warm touch sending a cascade of anticipation tingles down her spine. She slid her hands up to his shoulders, her lashes drifting closed as he leaned in.

She had one moment to drink in the pure yummy masculine scent of him before the press of his mouth on hers jolted her already frantic heartbeat. She sucked in a quick breath, her hold tightening on his shoulders while his lips moved over hers. Firm yet gentle. Purposeful yet patient.

So much more patient than she want—

He licked at the seam of her lips, and she opened to him eagerly. The slide of his tongue against hers made her stomach wobble. As he angled his head to deepen the kiss, the dark stubble on his chin scraped against her skin. Her soft moan of approval made his arm band tighter, pressing her against him from thigh to chest.

He took his time with the seductive kiss, his exploring strokes deep and sensual, then shallow and teasing, and back to tummy-tumbling, tingle-inducing, core-clenchingly sexy. He proved her fuzzy memory was not an adequate judge of his skills, and her fully sober self acknowledged his self-confidence was one hundred percent justified.

Loyal Diamond wasn't merely a good kisser, he was indeed exceptional.

If he's this talented with his lips, imagine what he could do with the rest of his body.

She did, and another soft moan crawled up her throat as she wound her arms around his neck to thread her fingers into his thick, soft hair.

His mouth moved more urgently, stoking her hunger. He slid both hands down to palm her ass, the strength of his grip pressing her against his very rapidly growing erection. Those Batman pants weren't going to conceal anything, and she felt the full effect of him through the thin, soft leather of her costume.

When she rubbed her leg against his, hooking her boot along the back of his calf, he grasped behind her knee and dragged her thigh up toward his hip. The move ground his hard length against her pelvis, setting off a deep, primal throb that weakened her knees. His splayed fingers skimmed back along the underside of her thigh, his pinky so close to her core her inner muscles clenched hard.

She was nearly panting when he dragged his mouth from hers at the same time he wound her long hair around his wrist to tug her head back. His breath rasped hot and heavy against her cheek, then under her jaw, and down along her neck. He nipped and licked and sucked at her skin, leaving a damp trail along the collar of her costume that instantly chilled in the October air. The contrast only heightened the fiery desire sweeping through her from head to toe.

We could only have one night.

It wasn't such a bad idea, was it? She could purge him from her system.

Or more likely, she'd end up with one amazing night to tuck away in her heart for years to come. Something was better than nothing.

His fingers flexed on her thigh as he buried his face in the crook of her neck. A deep inhale scraped his scruff against her skin, followed by a low growl from the back of his throat. "God, you smell so damn good. What is that?"

"Peace and Calming. It's an essential oil blend to get me through the party."

With him, though, and her struggling to catch her breath, the oils had zero chance of being effective.

His body tensed against hers, and for a second, she feared he was going to pull away. But then he gave a rough sigh and nuzzled his way back to her mouth to claim her lips for another mind-muddling kiss.

Just as her mind fully surrendered to her decision, his roaming hands settled at the small of her back, and slowly, the kiss went from passionate, to sensual, to gentle and almost...apologetic.

Confusion swirled when he eased back and put distance between them. He reached up to gently pull her arms from around his neck and pressed them to her sides. "I shouldn't have done that."

"I asked you to," she reminded. "Both times."

His grip tightened, holding her back when she tried to move closer. "And both times you were vulnerable. The other night you were drunk. Now you're still dealing with the emotional aftermath of the fire."

She frowned at his words. "I'm one hundred percent sober right now, Loyal. I know what I want. *Who* I want."

His nostrils flared and his fingers flexed, as if he was fighting hard to keep from pulling her close again. "Damn it, Roxanna, I don't do relationships. And I'm not stupid enough to have a one night stand with my brother's best friend."

No matter how much he wanted to. Even though she couldn't read him psychically, she could see the hunger in his eyes. She felt it in his grip preventing her from moving close to press against his chest. It was clear he wanted her, but short of getting down on her knees to beg—

She flicked a glance at the bulge below his belt.

No. No begging.

She wasn't that desperate for love.

Her stomach bottomed out. She wasn't that desperate for *sex.* No one was talking love here.

Sex is off the table, too, so...

Feeling like a pathetic idiot, Roxanna held her chin up as she backed away. His hands clung for a moment before he let go.

"You're right," she said stiffly. "You've barely been civil for five minutes, so clearly, I'm not thinking straight."

She turned away to open her door and fumbled for the handle as a burning sensation pricked her eyelids.

Don't you dare cry.

Loyal caught her arm and spun her back around. She

115

gasped in surprise when he braced a hand on either side of her, trapping her against the Jeep as he leaned close.

"I told you I wasn't going to be a jerk anymore, so don't make it sound like I'm being one now."

Chest tight with remorse, she stared at his chin. "I know. I'm sorry."

"You know why I said no," he accused.

She nodded, the force of her pounding heart making it impossible to speak.

As they stood there, his heat burned through her leather suit from head to toe. She lifted her lashes, and her breath caught in her chest when his fiery gaze locked with hers. Time suspended as a whirlwind of conflicting emotions seethed between them.

His body pressed hers against the vehicle, hot and hard as his breathing grew shallow.

"One night."

Those two rough words were a question, a warning, and a promise all in one.

She should say no. She should be smart like he'd tried to be. But she'd never felt more alive in her life, more *wanted*, than this moment with him.

"One night," she managed to whisper in agreement.

Roxanna expected him to kiss her then—ached for him to kiss her—but he grabbed her hand and pulled her with him. She was suddenly too nervous to ask where they were going, and moments later they reached his Land Rover. He opened the passenger door, but instead of stepping aside for her to slide onto the seat, he leaned inside, grabbed something from the glove box, then slammed it shut, and then the door.

He took her hand again and they were halfway to the stables when it dawned on her he'd grabbed a condom. Her stomach flipped over. She hadn't had to think about protection in a very long time. She was on birth control, but that wasn't the only consideration.

At least *he* was prepared.

At the stables, he reached behind a bush growing close to the brick wall, and a moment later he'd unlocked the side door. After he put the key back, he held the door open and arched his brow at her.

"Still want to do this?"

She fought a confused frown at the challenge in his rough voice. Was he trying to scare her off? Get her to change her mind by offering an offensive quick roll in the hay?

One look into his eyes and she saw that's exactly what he was doing.

Because it was a misguided attempt to save her from herself, she overlooked the potential jerkiness of the move.

Roxanna held her head high as she strode past him into the dimly lit stable. Over the years, she'd come down with Asher to see the horses a few times, and like always, she was grounded by the earthy scent of horses, hay, and oiled leather. The stable manager, Estefan Torrez, was a stickler for keeping everything neat and clean, so it had never smelled like she'd expected a barn to smell.

The click of the lock behind her made her nerves flinch, and she drew in another deep breath of the soothing scents. This night was hers. She was going to make the most of it.

A moment later, Loyal brushed past her with a blanket in his hands. Her heart kept a fast rhythm in her chest as she followed silently. He entered an open stall with hay stacked inside, and studied the layout for a second.

"This should work." He pressed both palms on a couple of bales stacked nearly waist-high against the wall of the neighboring stall and gave them a few crude, hard shoves. "Perfect."

After tossing the blanket over the bales, and dropping the

condom on the edge of the blanket, he reached up to untie his costume cape. Not once did he turn to look at her, and Roxanna narrowed her gaze at his calculated, matter of fact approach.

Time to turn the tables.

CHAPTER 14

$\mathcal{L}$oyal knew there was a very high probability when he turned around Roxanna would slap him across the face.

He'd deserve it, too. Hoped for it.

His heart thumped so damn hard as he tossed his cape on the hay beside the blanket. He was scared right now. Of wanting her too much. Of *liking* her too much. The damn woman kept rising to his challenges, shocking him again and again while turning him on in a way that threw him wholly off balance. He felt out of control and needy around her, and he didn't like it one bit.

Instinct urged him to run as fast as he could in any direction away from the brunette witch behind him. His dick kept his feet planted firmly in the stall.

After a final deep breath to prepare, he turned around so she could smack him and storm out and he could get on with his life.

But one look at Roxanna, and his breath seized in his lungs. He was fucked.

Well and truly fucked.

She stood about three feet away, the front of her suit unzipped from throat to navel. The open material revealed the swell of her small breasts and his body throbbed when he realized she wore no bra underneath that leather. It immediately had him dying to know about her underwear.

Without meeting his gaze, she shouldered past him, then boosted herself onto the hay to sit facing him. His mouth went dry when the top of her suit gaped open, giving him a teasing glimpse of her dusky, pebbled nipples.

When she finally did lift those long, sooty lashes to meet his gaze, she arched an imperious eyebrow, as if to say, *"Well? Let's get on with it."*

He took a step forward, his gaze on her while he fumbled with the buckle of his belt.

She raised a foot and came within an inch of kicking him in the groin. When he lurched back in alarm, she grinned. He narrowed his gaze.

Keeping her foot raised, she said, "This suit can't come off unless my boots come off."

The husky pitch to her voice made his blood sizzle. He finished undoing his belt, dropped it at his feet, then took a firm hold of her ankle so *he* could guide the sole of her foot to his thigh. As he undid the laces, he glanced up and nearly swallowed his tongue when she reclined on her elbows. The move made her top gape wide open to expose her bare breasts. His trembling fingers fumbled to get her boots off as fast as possible.

She watched him, a smile playing on her lips that had him silently vowing to make her pay for teasing him—in the best possible way. As soon as he tossed her first boot over his shoulder, she lifted her other foot.

While he worked those laces, he slowly slid his gaze up her long legs, past the dip of her belly button to her bare chest, and finally reached her flushed face. His heart was still thudding crazy hard, and his erection throbbed with every beat.

"Every man who's ever fantasized about Catwoman hates me right now."

Her gaze narrowed in warning. "No one better ever hear about this."

"What happens in the stable stays in the stable," he promised. "I'm just saying, this is a fantasy held by guys the world over."

"Is it one of yours?"

"I live in the world, don't I? And you make one hell of a fine Catwoman, Roxanna."

With that said, he tossed her second boot over his shoulder, took off her demure white ankle socks, and then hooked his hands behind her knees to tug her closer at the same time he stepped up between her thighs. A soft gasp parted her lips, and he was torn between kissing and touching.

He leaned forward and braced one hand on the hay beside her ribs, then flattened his other palm over her navel. Her stomach quivered under his touch, and he slowly slid his hand up, lifted to drag his knuckles through the valley between her breasts, then flattened again to wrap his hand around the back of her neck.

Her chest moved up and down with her quick, shallow breaths, the rise and fall of her pert mounds beckoning him to lick and suck. One hand clenched the blanket, the other her hair as he lowered himself down to flick one of her nipples with the tip of his tongue.

"Loyal." She breathed his name as a plea, her back arching, pushing her breast up to his mouth.

He wanted his name on her lips again and again.

Bringing his hand back down to cup one breast, he swirled his tongue around the tip of the other, then sucked her into his mouth. Her moan triggered an urgency in his own body, but he forced himself to take his time, to wring as many sounds of pleasure from her as possible.

Finally, he urged her to sit and captured her mouth with his while stripping her bare to her waist. Her hands were busy, too, tugging at his costume top, stripping it off, then going straight for his pants as their mouths collided again. He angled his hips back with a soft sound of denial, then laid her back so he could take her suit all the way off.

She lifted her hips, and he groaned at the feel of her bare ass cheeks against his palms. As he dragged the supple leather farther down, a sexy little black thong was revealed. He kept going, relishing the toned muscles of her thighs and calves, until he stripped the suit past the delicate arch of one foot, and then the other.

He raised his gaze slowly. "All these years...all those skirts."

"You don't like my skirts?"

"I had no idea what they hid."

Her cheeks pinkened in the most charming way, and he skimmed his hands up to hook his fingers in her thong. As he pulled it off, she moved to sit up. He sensed a sudden tension in her body and paused when he read the anxious look on her face. It was a marked difference from the seductive siren a few minutes ago.

He stepped between her legs once more and reached out to cup her cheek. "What? You change your mind?"

Please don't let that be it.

She flattened her palm on his abs and lightly stroked up his chest. Fire trailed behind her touch, and her other hand joined the first, her gaze following their path. "It's, um, been a very long time for me. And there's only ever been one guy before...now."

His heart kicked hard beneath her palm. Shit. She might as well be a virgin.

One night suddenly seemed wrong—and in the fucking hay to boot. He really was an ass.

"It's fine, Roxanna." Somehow he managed to force the rest of the words from his lips. "We don't have to do this."

"I want to," she blurted when he started to step back. She grabbed the waistband of his pants to keep him right where he was. "I just—kiss me. I stop thinking when you kiss me."

He knew he should say no, but with her gorgeous body naked before him, he couldn't have if he wanted to—and he damn sure didn't want to. The idea that he was only the second man to ever touch her so intimately triggered a primal feeling of possession that left him shaken to his core.

"Loyal."

That whispered plea had him dipping his head to cover her mouth with his again. He slid his tongue against hers as he ran his hands all over her body. Her soft skin and womanly curves were heaven.

As soon as she was good and worked up again, he eased her back and kissed his way down her throat to her breasts. After a minute, he moved to her ribs, and lower across her belly.

When she tensed again, he said, "Trust me."

It wasn't a question, and yet, not a command, either. He placed a light kiss on her navel, then glanced up without lifting his head. Her darkened gaze met his, and she nodded.

"Close your eyes, and just feel. It's even better than a kiss. Promise."

Her throat muscles worked in a hard swallow, and then she closed her eyes and leaned her head back. The beautiful sight of her laid out before him seared into his memory before he shifted lower and got his first exquisite taste of her.

Roxanna's surprised intake of breath turned into a low moan of pleasure that had him wanting to strip off his pants and seat himself deep in her heat. Instead, he used his mouth and hands to take her to the peak. She reached one hand behind and up to hold onto one of the iron bars separating the stalls, and the other threaded in his hair.

Another image he'd never forget.

Her grip had his scalp tingling, and as one last swirl of his tongue detonated her climax, she cried out his name. He nearly came with her right then.

He kissed his way back up her body and felt for the condom as she caught her breath. He buried his face in her hair for a moment, breathing her in. She always seemed to have a different scent, and yet every time he smelled her, there was an underlying note that was achingly familiar. Her own unique scent that reached out to him no matter what else she dabbed on her skin.

She wrapped her arms around him, and slid her hands up to lightly rake her short nails through his hair. "That was a first," she whispered.

"Oral?" he asked as his searching fingers closed around the condom.

"And orgasm."

CHAPTER 15

*R*oxanna winced when Loyal stilled and lifted his head to look at her. Why in the world did she have to go and admit *that* to him?

"Are you serious?"

"Of course not," she bluffed, totally unconvincingly. Suddenly, she wished she had something to cover up with.

He leaned down and pressed a kiss to her collar bone. "I don't believe you."

She shrugged.

His lips trailed up her neck to her mouth, and he efficiently wiped any self-conscious thoughts away with a kiss that had her wanting his fingers and tongue to work more magic.

"Knowing that was your first makes me want to give you a second," he murmured against her mouth.

Who's the psychic here?

He seemed to be reading her mind with uncanny accuracy tonight. But hey, if the second was as good as the first, *hell yeah.*

"Okay," she agreed softly.

He grinned against her lips until she slid a hand down his chest, over his stomach, to the waistband of his Batman pants. The first brush of her hand against his erection triggered a groan from deep in his throat. He suddenly pushed off the hay, and she lifted her head to see him stripping off his boots, pants, and briefs.

The size and length of his erection shortened her breath, and her core muscles clenched as she watched him roll on the condom. His gaze locked with hers when he climbed up onto the hay bales with her and settled his weight between her thighs.

The unexpected intimacy of his gaze made her stomach flutter. Afraid he might see more than she wanted him to, she closed her eyes. Needing him inside her like she'd never needed anything else before, she drew up her knees on either side of his hips to urge him forward.

His biceps bunched and flexed beneath her palms as he held his weight off her while easing inside with slow strokes that went deeper each time. Finally, he gave one last thrust that buried him to the hilt and locked their hips together.

"You good?" he asked, his voice tight.

Bottom lip caught between her teeth, she concentrated on the amazing sensation of their joined bodies and nodded. Then she quickly opened her eyes. "You?"

"Yeah." The white of his teeth flashed with his smile as he withdrew his hips and then drove home again. "I'm definitely good."

She smiled back and lifted her hips to meet his next thrust. His low grunt conveyed his approval when she matched the rhythm he set. He bent his head to capture her lips, and a tingle started deep inside as his tongue mimicked the steady pistoning of his hips.

Inarticulate sounds of pleasure that she had no control over fell from her lips. Sensation built again, moving her hips faster, urging him faster. She reached with both hands to grasp the iron bars behind her head for an anchor while he moved over her, each thrust deep and hard, hitting just the right spot inside.

He pushed up higher on his arms and reached one of his hands to cover hers on the bar. The new angle had her seeing stars a half-dozen strokes later. As waves of pleasure crashed over her, his fast rhythm faltered before his whole body tensed and he climaxed with one final thrust.

He collapsed on top of her with a low groan of satisfaction.

"Holy shit," he muttered into her hair moments later.

Yeah. Holy shit is right.

The weight of his body on hers was a pleasure she hadn't expected. Arms wrapped around him, she lightly stroked her fingers up and down his back. Her couple of times with a boyfriend back in college couldn't hold a candle to what she'd just experienced.

What she'd shared with Loyal.

He shifted and rolled to the side, bringing her with him before reaching down to flip his cape over them like a blanket. She laid her head on his chest as his fingers threaded through the length of her hair. Until he hit a snarl, then he started back up at her scalp, and moved down again.

Hay bales weren't the most comfortable mattress even with a blanket, and still the strong, steady beat of his heart beneath her ear had her drowsy lashes drifting down.

Your true love will be Loyal and true.

The voice from her vision echoed in her mind, only this time *Loyal* flashed in her head as a name, not a word.

She snapped her eyes open. Her heart skipped and then raced with panic.

What was she doing? She couldn't lay there listening to his heartbeat, feeling his chest move up and down with each breath, fall asleep wrapped up in the warmth of his strong arms.

First of all, they were in the stables!

Second of all, she wanted a forever love like Asher and Honor's, and he couldn't give her that—*wouldn't* give her that.

Pain constricted her chest, but she couldn't blame him. He'd been totally up front with her—even tried to walk away. She'd pulled him back and agreed to the stipulations.

One night. No more. Now she had to honor the agreement.

Roxanna counted ten more beats of his heart before she forced herself to push up and lean over to place a kiss on his lips. She fought the urge to linger, pulling back before he could use his tongue to make her lose her mind and her will to leave.

"Thank you," she said as she scooted off the blanket covering the hay and looked for her thong.

"Thank you?"

Bewildered surprise colored his voice as he sat up. She snuck a glance at his raised eyebrows while she pulled on her underwear and swiped up her cat suit. With him watching her every move, she'd never felt more exposed physically or emotionally.

Drawing on whatever inner dignity she could muster, she stepped into the legs of her suit and pulled it up her body. "Yes, thank you. That was amazing." Her voice came out formal and stilted, the words sticking like sawdust in her dry mouth. "Not only are you exceptional at kissing, but everything else as well."

She zipped up and bent for her socks, then tugged on her boots. That was everything—no, wait, her mask. A frantic glance yielded nothing, but she didn't have time to care as Loyal clutched the cape at his waist and slid off the hay.

"I'll see you around," she said.

"Are you serious right now?" he asked with a dark glower. "Thank you and you're *leaving?*"

"One night," she murmured. "We agreed *one* night."

"That wasn't even an hour," he retorted.

Tears burned her eyes as she turned and fled the stall, nearly tripping on her boot laces.

"Roxanna—wait."

She flipped the lock on the outside door and yanked it open, praying he wouldn't follow her. If he did, he'd need to get dressed first. That should hopefully buy her enough time to escape.

She was almost to her Jeep when a voice behind her made her heart stutter.

"Rox?" Asher called out.

Nooo.

Her churning stomach twisted up tight. She fumbled with her keys to unlock the door, then yanked it open as he and Honor walked up.

"Hey. I thought you weren't coming?"

"I wasn't, but then I did. I thought I would try, you know, for the kids, but I'm still not feeling up to it, so I'm going home." She was babbling like an idiot. Asher would know something was wrong, so she avoided looking at them and slipped into the driver's seat.

Honor stepped forward before she could shut the door. She reached in and pulled a piece of hay from Roxanna's dark curls.

Her breath hitched as she met Honor's green gaze.

"Are you okay?" her friend asked softly.

"I am." Skepticism laced the redhead's expression, so she insisted, "I swear. I just...need to go home. Right now."

"I'm going to check on you tomorrow."

She nodded, knowing the cake baker wouldn't take no for

an answer. Finally, Honor moved back and Roxanna shut the door. She saw Asher frown when Honor backed him away from the Jeep. She'd have to talk to him tomorrow, too.

Good Lord. She was going to have to tell him she'd slept with his brother. Hopefully he wouldn't hate her. If she lost his friendship...the friendship of his whole family...

As she drove away from the Diamond mansion, the tears that had been burning her eyes trailed down her cheeks. She dashed them away and cursed the stupidity of her heart.

She hadn't been emotionally strong enough to give readings, what the hell had made her think she could handle the repercussions of sex with Loyal?

Exceptional, mind-blowing, life-altering sex.

CHAPTER 16

$\mathcal{A}$nger eclipsed Loyal's stunned confusion when Roxanna disappeared out the door.

"Thank you."

"You were exceptional."

"I'll see you around."

What. The. Fuck?

And why was his chest so damn tight he couldn't draw in a fucking breath of air?

He yanked on his stupid costume and swiped up the cape and blanket as the stable door opened. His heart leapt that she'd come back, and he lunged from the stall into the aisle. The sight of Asher and Honor sent a sharp stab of disappointment through his chest.

Fucking A. What the hell was wrong with him?

"You have got to be kidding me." Asher strode forward with a dark frown. "Tell me what I think just happened in here did *not* happen."

Sonofabitch.

He knew he'd screwed up, and yet his hackles still rose at

131

his younger brother's angry tone. "It's none of your damn business."

"Come *on*, man. You and Roxanna? The two of you can't even stand the sight of each other."

"We called a truce."

"So this was mutual?"

His jaw went slack in offended shock as he darted his gaze between his brother and his sober-faced fiancé. "*Of course it was mutual,*" he bit out. "I can't believe you would even ask that."

"I think what Asher meant was, Rox seemed upset when she left," Honor murmured.

He jerked his head up. What was *she* upset about?

"Did you two argue or something?"

"No." She hadn't given him a chance to argue anything. *And what, exactly, would you have argued?*

His jaw clenched. He had no clue.

"I don't know what the hell is going on, but you'd better not hurt her," his brother warned.

"Me hurt *her*?" Resentment surged forward again. "She's the one who just fucked me and left."

Honor's eyes widened, and Asher's fists clenched at his sides. "Don't be so crude."

"Well, she did. But whatever. Like I said, it's none of your damn business."

He brushed past the both of them and left exactly as Roxanna had such a short time ago.

When he got to his vehicle, he sat in the driver's seat and stewed. Why was he so angry? And why was his chest still so tight every breath hurt? He should be relieved the virtual virgin hadn't turned into a clinging vine begging him to love her.

Dramatic much?

He growled his frustration at the voice in his head and

started the engine to drive to his hotel. Family obligations or not, he never should've come to the damn party. The numbers he wrote on his checks had never screwed him over and left him wanting to punch something.

By late Monday afternoon, Loyal was going out of his ever-loving mind—because he couldn't get Roxanna out of his mind. With his father's campaign in hyper-drive for the election the next day, he should have been able to keep his thoughts occupied with something other than the smell of her, the taste of her, the sexy sounds she made when he made her come.

Should have, but failed. In fact, he'd gotten hard twice at headquarters and had to think about his fucking half-brother to calm himself the hell down. How pathetic was that?

Now, he found himself parked in front of Lift Your Spirit two minutes before closing. One glimpse of Roxanna under the store lights as she wove gracefully amongst the inside displays and his spirits *were* lifted.

So was his dick.

Obviously, one night with her—one *time* with her—hadn't been enough. But maybe a few more would work her out of his system, and they could both be on their merry way.

He was out of the Land Rover and pushing the door of her shop open before he could debate the wisdom of his plan.

Really? That's a plan? Sleep with her a few more times?

It was as good a plan as any.

The chimes that announced a customer's entrance mixed with the musical notes of a set of wind chimes Roxanna lifted toward a hook on one of her displays. She shot an absent glance over her shoulder as she said, "Sorry, but it's closing—oh."

133

Her surprised gasp was punctuated by the discordant clanging of metal as the chimes fell from her hand. Her gaze held his for a heart-stopping moment, then she quickly stooped to pick up the fallen merchandise.

Loyal flipped the *Open* sign to *Closed*, turned the lock, and slowly wound through the shop displays toward her.

"Hi," he said.

She hung up the chimes before moving to the register counter, her dark brows furrowed with her sideways glance. "What are you doing here?"

The breathless tone of her voice sparked hot, vivid, replay snippets of the stables, and sent blood rushing below the waistband of his khakis. She was wearing that earth-toned skirt from last weekend, the one that covered her from waist to ankle. Thing was, now that he knew what she hid underneath, he wanted to sit her up on that counter, lift the material to her waist, and bury himself in her heat. Then he'd take her upstairs so he could take his time and taste every inch of her body while she breathed his name over and over.

Shit. Now he was hard again. And, unfortunately, the moment he'd entered the shop, he realized *"let's do it a few more times until this thing between us fizzles out"* wasn't really a plan after all.

Honor's comment had come back to plague him the past couple of days. Had Roxanna really been upset when she left the other night, and if so, why?

She moved to stand behind the register and shot him quick little glances as he stopped with the counter between them. Something akin to relief flickered across her expression.

He narrowed his gaze at that glimpse of emotion. Is that why she'd been upset—was she afraid of him? The idea that she might be turned his stomach. He hadn't done anything to frighten her, had he?

"Did you hire a new accountant yet?"

Her head jerked up, and she gaped at him. "What? How did you know I—"

"That night you were drunk. You complained your accountant got married and left, and now your numbers don't add up."

Color infused her cheeks. "Oh."

He pulled a newly printed card from his pocket and held it out to her. "If you haven't hired someone yet, I'd like to offer my services."

She stared at the charcoal, gold-foil embossed card as if he were handing her a snake. Or maybe a rat, because maybe she liked snakes. He suddenly wanted to discover everything she liked and didn't like.

She huffed out a breath as she lifted her anxious gaze to his to repeat, "Seriously, what do you want?"

I want you to say my name again.

He wiggled the card between his thumb and forefinger, and finally she reached to swipe it from his grasp. That tiny glimpse of her usual salty self eased some of his tension. Her lashes lowered as she stared at his name and credentials stamped in gold foil on the dark card. But then he noticed her shoot him another glance from beneath her lashes. When her gaze lingered below his chin, and the tip of her pink tongue darted out to wet her lips, he relaxed even more.

Not afraid. *Aware.*

And, maybe afraid of what he made her feel. She'd left so fast the other night, but was it possible she still wanted him as much as he wanted her? Was once not enough for her either?

God, I hope not.

He shifted his stance, and she quickly focused her gaze on the card in her hand again. "Are you actually being serious right now?"

"I'm always serious when it comes to numbers, Roxanna."

He let his voice drop a notch lower when he said her name, and noticed her hand tremble in reaction. When she lowered her arms to clasp her hands behind her back, the move pushed her small breasts against her snug, long-sleeved, black shirt.

Loyal's breath caught in his throat as his blood rushed below his belt buckle yet again.

Holy shit. This was not normal. He was about three seconds away from vaulting over the counter to get to her.

"Have you hired anyone yet?" he asked with a hint of impatience.

She shook her head.

"Then, as my first client, I can offer you a substantial discount."

Her head tilt was laced with suspicion. "What's the catch?"

I want you to be mine.

His Adam's apple bobbed with a hard swallow. *Whoa. Easy there.*

"Why would there be a catch?"

She stared at him intently, as if trying to get a read on him. He gulped again at the possibility she was using her psychic wiles to see into his head.

You don't believe in that shit, remember?

Taking a deep breath to steady his nerves, he insisted, "There is no catch. If you're happy with my work, give me a good recommendation should anyone ever ask."

Her gaze slid down again and his blood heated. Then she looked to the side and shrugged her slim shoulders. "I'll think about it."

What?

"What's to think about?" Exasperation sharpened his voice.

Desperation was more like it. He wanted a *yes*, right now. He wanted her to take him in the back. Right. Now. So he could work on her numbers.

One orgasm, then two.

Her chin rose at his tone and she shot back, "Whether or not I want to deal with you being an ass on a regular basis, for one."

The sudden urge to grin took him by surprise. He barely contained it as he asked, "And two?"

She hesitated. "What exactly do you mean by *substantial discount?*"

This time, he couldn't contain a small smirk of victory. "Whatever you think is fair. Maybe throw in a dinner or something."

"Or something." Her voice had now gone hard. She rocked back on her heels and folded her arms in front of her. "*There* it is."

"What?"

"I'm not going to pay you with sex, Loyal."

He'd wanted her to say his name, but not in that pissed-off, offended tone. Heat climbed the back of his neck even as his dick got stuck on the word *sex*. "That is *not* what I was suggesting at all."

"No? So, if I said let's go in the back right now, you'd say no?"

His heart nearly stopped in his chest. *Holy fucking shit.* She *had* read his mind.

Seriously freaked out, he took a step back.

Her eyebrows rose in challenge. "Yes or no, Loyal? What's your answer?"

This time her voice went the slightest bit husky when she said his name, and with the way his pulse reacted, he couldn't have lied if his life depended on it. "Yes. But it wouldn't have a damn thing to do with accounting."

137

The words sat between them, and in the silence that fell, the wanting between them became a tangible thing. Her face flushed, and her breathing turned as shallow as his. He waited for her to invite him to the back.

Begged her with his mind to invite him to the back.

She uncrossed her arms, looked at his card again, and then brushed the edge over her palm as she stepped around to his side of the counter. Anticipation slammed his heart against his ribs, but she bypassed him without a glance and strode toward the front door.

As she walked, she said over her shoulder, "Like I said, I'll think about it. Come back tomorrow and I'll let you know."

He trailed behind her like a damn dog panting after a bone. "Tomorrow's the election."

"Right." She unlocked the door and held it open for him to leave. "Wednesday night, then."

Night. She's already said yes. She's just making me sweat.

All right, fine, he'd play the game. He could wait two more nights.

Fuck. Two more nights.

"Wednesday night," he agreed.

Knowledge shimmered in their shared smile, and then she dropped her gaze and practically hugged the edge of the door, his card still clutched in her fingers. "Goodnight, Loyal."

Holy mother, he *loved* his name in her voice. He had to shove his hands into his pockets to keep from reaching for her. He wanted to kiss her, just a taste to tide him over, but one touch, and he'd bet a million dollars he wouldn't be going anywhere.

Instead, he asked, "Do you like snakes?"

Her head jerked up and a confused smile tugged at her mouth. "Does that question have some sort of hidden meaning?"

Loyal laughed. "No. It's completely innocent and serious. I swear."

"O-kay." She eyed him for one more moment before answering, "Yes. I like snakes. Why?"

"No reason in particular. How about rats?"

That one drew a frown. "Now I'm scared."

"Of rats?"

"Of *you,* and your questions. Why are you asking me about rats and snakes?"

"Just curious." He smiled at her perplexed expression and stepped out into the light cast by the overhead streetlamps. "Good night, Roxanna."

CHAPTER 17

$\mathcal{R}$oxanna locked the door after Loyal, flipped her sign to *Closed*, realized it had already been flipped, and flipped it back again. Worried he'd see her acting like a befuddled idiot, she hurried to the register counter to turn off the lights for the front of the store, then turned around to lean against it as she pressed her hands to her hot cheeks.

What the hell had just happened?

And what the hell did I just agree to?

Sex with Loyal is what she'd agreed to. Again.

Oh, he could pretend he was offering his accounting skills all he wanted, but they both knew what services he was really coming back for. So much for *one night*. Her heart raced, and her body tingled in places he'd pleasured so exceptionally two nights ago.

She'd thought he might kiss her at the door—wanted him to—but thank the Lord he hadn't. One touch of his lips and she'd have said the hell with waiting until Wednesday. She'd have hauled him in the back to the over-sized lounge chair in her reading room and had her way with him right there.

Her core muscles clenched with longing.

Thank God he hadn't called her bluff. By respecting her request, he'd saved her without even knowing it. He'd given her time to think things through with a rational mind instead of a wanton heart.

So the real question was, could she do it? After all these years of fantasizing about him while also hating him and now liking him, could she sleep with him for as long as it took for him to get tired of her and still escape with her heart unscathed?

The swift, painful squeeze in her chest confirmed her worst fears.

No, she couldn't.

Somehow, between now and Wednesday, she had to figure out a way to make herself immune to Loyal.

Yeah. Somehow, between now and Wednesday, she had to figure out how to do the impossible. Unfortunately, she was more likely to get the numbers in her accounting program to add up.

Numbers.

Roxanna straightened as her brain started working again. That was the key. She'd make it all about business. Call *his* bluff and actually have him balance her books—and *pay him money* to do it.

She blew out a shaky sigh and brushed her hair back from her face before finishing up her closing procedures.

Tuesday morning, she made it out to vote and back again before opening the shop at nine. It was a busy day of stocking new inventory with Tessa and Darcy in between scheduled readings, and as soon as she locked the door at six, she went upstairs to change and get ready for the Governor's election night party. Early exit polling put the race closer than expected after the opposition party had done everything they could to spin the hell out of the now-old secret love child story and discredit the Governor.

After checking her coat a little after eight, Roxanna made her way through the crowd into the ballroom at the hotel, her fingers clutched nervously in the skirt of her blue bohemian maxi dress. Another one of her clearance items she'd always liked, but hadn't needed until after the fire. It was a bit summery with the off-the-shoulder neckline, but she left her hair down to mostly cover her shoulders and help keep her warm. She wore her black combat boots again, and the entire time she'd laced them up, she'd pictured Loyal taking them off.

She only had one more day to somehow become immune to him. As often as he popped into her mind, it wasn't looking good. As keyed up as she was about seeing him tonight, it definitely wasn't looking good.

Spotting his youngest sister's long, dark ponytail not far from the doors by the campaign swag table, she went over to say hi as upbeat music pulsed through the ballroom speakers. Shelby gave her a warm smile and wave as a tall, chestnut-haired guy beside her leaned down to say something in her ear. She smiled at him even as her shoulder and lower body seemed to instinctively arch away. It was a minuscule movement, she probably wasn't even aware of the reaction, but Roxanna's radar kicked on immediately.

She shifted her gaze to the guy for a quick assessment. Probably mid-twenties—close to Bells' age, wiry, but good-looking in an unassuming way. He seemed familiar, and when she joined the two, Shelby introduced him as Chad Mayer, one of the campaign workers.

She guessed she'd seen him at another event, but didn't recall meeting him directly. He didn't offer a hand to shake, so Roxanna extended hers to get a read. His grip was deferential, and he pulled away quickly. He didn't strike her as negative or positive.

It wasn't that she couldn't read him like Loyal, or her mother, but more so the guy was neutral. His aura was a dull gray, indicating blocked energy fields. Not much emotion to work with, not even in the pale blue eyes that kept straying to Shelby, and that made her stomach flip uneasily.

"How's the night going?" she asked. "Have they started reporting yet?"

Bell's sleek hair swished with her headshake. "Not just yet. Should be soon though. You got any predictions?"

"No psychic ones," she said with a laugh. "All I can say is he got my vote."

At the word *psychic*, Chad's blue gaze landed on Roxanna. When his aura took on a cloudy, grayish, blue-green tint, an icy shiver worked down her spine. She met his gaze but he quickly shifted his attention to Shelby while reaching to put a hand at the small of her back.

Again, she noticed the youngest Diamond make an infinitesimal shift away from his touch.

"You want anything to drink?" he asked her. "I can go get us something from the bar."

"Um…no, thank you, I'm good. I think I'm going to find the rest of my family."

"I'll come with you." Roxanna quickly hooked arms with the younger girl who was like the little sister she'd never had. "I want to thank your mom for the gift basket she sent over."

"Have a good night, Chad," Shelby said over her shoulder as they left. "Thanks again for all your help."

Roxanna glanced back and caught a dark frown before his expression went blank. She waited until they were out of earshot by the buffet tables to bend her head and ask, "What's the deal with him?"

Shelby grimaced. "We've been working together the last

couple of months for the campaign. I know he's interested, but there's nothing there for me. It's been a little awkward trying to discourage him."

She frowned with concern. "Has he been pushy?"

"Oh, no," Shelby assured her. "He's harmless. Nice enough, and even kinda cute, but I just felt bad I'm not attracted to him when he's made it clear he likes me."

"You have nothing to feel bad about. We can't help who we're attracted to." As she knew all too well.

"Yeah, I know. And I guess it really doesn't matter, since I won't even see him anymore now that the campaign is over."

"Good."

Shelby glanced up at her with a questioning smile as a voice called out behind them.

"Rox—wait up!"

They both turned to see Mae threading her way through the crowd.

"Nice turnout," she exclaimed.

"My mom knows how to draw them in," Shelby boasted. "Free food and drinks."

"You don't think your dad has a little something to do with it?" Roxanna teased.

"Eh." She shrugged her shoulders with a sassy grin and they all laughed as they reached the private meeting room reserved for family adjacent to the stage area. Asher and Honor stood just outside the room with Merit and Robert.

Roxanna's pulse sped up as she cast a glance around, but she didn't spot Loyal's dark head anywhere. Asher pulled her into a side hug as Celia joined the group, and the noise level rose with everyone's greetings.

"I don't think he's here yet," her best friend whispered.

"Who's not here yet?"

He gave a soft snort of disbelief, and she allowed a slight smile. He knew her too well. Plus, she'd talked to him and

Honor the Sunday after Halloween. He'd been upset, but it seemed more so out of concern for her getting hurt than her having slept with his older brother. It was a relief he wasn't mad at her, and yet his worry was another reminder that there was no future with Loyal.

"You good?" he asked quietly.

"I'm good." She shot Honor a quick smile and raised her voice to address the rest of the group. "How's everyone holding up here? Excitement is super high, I see."

"Numbers are just starting to come in." Celia pointed to a TV beside the stage with reporting data scrolling along the bottom of the screen. "So far, they look promising despite the exit polls."

"It's still early," Asher cautioned.

They'd all shifted to form a circle, with Celia and her husband opposite Roxanna; Asher, Honor, and Mae to her left; and Merit and Shelby to her right. A little tingle of energy from the youngest Diamond brother drew her glance to see his gaze on Mae as Honor formally introduced her workaholic best friend to everyone. His aura sparkled bright red, though that was nothing new with the playboy brother. A fleeting tinge of pink, however, piqued her interest.

"And this is Asher's youngest brother, Merit," Honor finished.

When Mae's gaze met his, her eyebrows flashed upward.

He offered his trademark sexy grin to the pretty blond. "Yes, my name is Merit. But you can call me Handsome."

Sexual energy arched between the two like an invisible lightning bolt. There was an answering surge of red in Mae's aura, but to her credit, she rolled her eyes with a laugh. "How much use does that line get?"

Yep. The savvy single mother wasn't about to get snowed by a cute come-on, no matter how smoothly delivered.

"Too much," Asher answered for him.

145

Merit let it slide off his back with a smirk, completely unapologetic of his philandering ways.

"Does it actually work?" Mae asked him directly.

"Every time."

"Well, sorry to break your record, but I've heard all about you, Merit." She put the slightest flirtatious emphasis on his name.

"That's not fair. I haven't heard much about you at all." He flicked an accusing gaze toward his older brother and Honor, then shifted his attention back to Mae, his charm at full throttle. "But I'd like to, gorgeous."

"You have no shame," Celia declared.

"Leave Mae alone, Merit," Asher warned. "She's already got a man in her life."

His crestfallen expression sparked a round of laughs.

"Where is Ian tonight?" Honor asked.

Roxanna only half-heard the blond's cryptic answer as she spotted Janine Diamond in the private reserved room with Estefan and Elena Torrez.

"I have to talk to your mom for a moment," she told Asher quietly. "I'll be back."

Inside the room, the low rumble of voices through the open back doors drew her gaze. Her heart skipped at the sight of Loyal talking with the governor. Just then, the Torrezes walked past on their way to the ballroom, and his mother gave her a wide smile.

"Roxanna, I'm so glad you came."

"I wouldn't miss it," she said as the woman who was more like a mother to her than her own pulled her into a warm hug. Roxanna squeezed her eyes shut as her chest tightened. She really had found family when she found Asher.

"How are you doing after the fire?" She ran a soothing hand down Roxanna's hair before stepping back. "Do you need anything?"

"No, thank you, I'm fine. You've already done more than enough with that amazing gift basket. It's been a huge help with just the right things. I loved everything."

The gift cards had been exceedingly generous and helped her fill in her new clearance wardrobe with clothes from places she wouldn't normally have been able to afford.

"I'm glad. I felt so bad I couldn't bring it over myself, what with the campaign being so busy." She stuck one hand on her slim hip. "I trust Loyal behaved himself? He had strict orders to be nice."

"He was fine." *More than fine.* Heat climbed her neck as she shot a pointed glance toward the door, where things looked to be getting heated between him and his father. "Is everything okay out there?"

Janine frowned in their direction before turning away with a sigh and shake of her head. "Mark has offered Grayson money for a veteran's foundation, but only if Loyal steps in as the CFO."

"Ah." And given the way Loyal felt about his surprise brother, clearly, it wasn't going over well.

"My husband seems to think forcing the two of them to work together will help them get over their animosity toward each other," Janine continued. "But they're both so darn stubborn. In truth, all *three* of them are stubborn."

"You'd almost think they were related or something," Roxanna joked.

"Right?" His mother smiled, but it fell away when a loud bang revealed Loyal shoving through an outside exit, and Mark turned toward them with his jaw clenched as tight as his fists. He gave a quick head shake as he returned to the room.

His expression cleared to a subdued smile as Roxanna stepped forward to give him a hug hello. The energy around him revealed his frustration with his son tangled with a deep fear of losing him. She wished she could reassure him it would be okay, but without knowing what had just transpired between the two, she had to focus on the reason they were all there in the first place.

"I'm looking forward to your victory speech later." As she said the words, she couldn't help a glance toward the door Loyal had left through.

"Do you know something we don't?" the governor asked.

"No, no. I'm simply being optimistic."

"Well then, let's hope we get enough votes that you get to hear the speech."

Roxanna smiled her agreement, but noticing Janine and Mark exchange a long glance, she took her cue. "I'll leave you two be. Again, thank you so much for the basket, and good luck tonight."

When she exited the room, she saw the gathering near the doors had somewhat dispersed, so she gave Honor a smile and wave and continued to the bar for a glass of wine. While she waited, she couldn't help but think of Loyal outside.

Upset. Alone.

When the bartender set her Riesling in front of her, she ordered a double Black Maple Hill whiskey, then took both glasses out the back where Loyal had disappeared. Of course, she knew full well seeking him out was not the way to build up immunity to the man, but she couldn't seem to stop her feet from moving.

He'd slept on the couch to make sure she was okay the night she'd been drunk. The least she could do now as return the favor.

She'd simply check to see if he was okay, give him the drink, and leave.

CHAPTER 18

$\mathcal{L}$oyal wished he smoked so he'd have something to dull the edge of his anger. Better yet, he was going to start keeping a bottle in his truck. A couple of shots of whiskey would be welcome right now. Smashing the empty bottle against the brick wall would be even better.

The sound of the door had him whirling around for round two with his dad. The sight of Roxanna in a blue hippie dress and her combat boots stopped his heart for a few seconds before jolting it back to life at breakneck speed. Her creamy shoulders were bare, that long glorious hair loose, and though the overhead light cast her face in shadow, he could feel her gaze trained directly on him.

"Hey," she greeted casually. Then she lifted her hand, and the light above the door revealed a glass three-quarters full of amber liquid. "I thought you might need this."

Holy fuck, that was creepy as hell.

In the next second, he decided he didn't give a shit. "You read my mind."

A smile ghosted over her glossed lips as she stepped

forward to hand him the drink. "Not really. I saw you with your dad."

"Oh." He leaned his butt back against the front bumper of his Range Rover, lifted the glass, and downed half the contents in one gulp. As the whiskey burned down his throat, he blinked in surprise at what was left, then looked at her. "Black Maple Hill?"

"It's what you drink, right?"

"Yeah." But how did she know that? Was it more of the mind reading, or was she that observant?

"Observant."

The single word answer to his silent question sent a shiver down his spine as she took a sip from the wine glass she'd been holding in her other hand.

Shockingly, he felt a smile tug at his mouth as he asked, "How many of those have you had?"

Her soft laugh in the cool night air gave him a shiver of a whole different kind. "This is my one and only. No more wine drunk for me."

"I'm happy to take you home if you need me to."

Her lips crooked up as she planted her butt on the bumper next to him. "I'll be fine."

She sat close enough for her shoulder to brush against his while she crossed her feet at the ankles. Thinking of her ass against the bumper, he longed to feel her bare cheeks in his palms again.

Tomorrow.

Or, if he played this right—*tonight.*

She shot him an indecipherable look and slid her delectable ass six inches *away* from him.

Loyal grinned to himself, and this time he took only a sip of his favorite drink. Let her read his mind. She was still out here, right?

Yes. And the crazy thing was, he hadn't thought of his dad

or Grayson or the foundation since she stepped through the door. And even though he just had, he didn't want to punch anything.

In the middle of him marveling how less than two minutes with her had taken the edge off his anger when a couple weeks ago she would've triggered it, she asked, "Want to talk about it?"

"Not really."

"It could help."

"What are you, a psychic *and* a psychologist?"

She lifted her shoulders while taking another sip of wine. She didn't say anything, but instead of her silence taking the pressure off, he felt compelled to speak. The mental mind voodoo tightened his shoulders while his fingers clenched his glass.

"My dad wants me to work with my half-brother." Just saying the words left a bitter taste in his mouth.

"Your mom mentioned starting a veteran's foundation?"

"Yes. And my father—grand charitable bastard that he is —won't give him the money if I don't agree to be the CFO."

The hell of it was, his dad was extremely generous, but in this case, for some reason, he was being bull-headed.

"And you don't want to be CFO."

"Hell no."

"Is it that you don't want the job?"

"It's not the job."

"Do you not want Grayson to have any money?"

Loyal frowned. "The money's for charity, not for him."

"So, you don't want the veterans to have it."

"No, of course not. I don't give a f—" He broke off and drew in a controlled breath. "I don't care about the money."

"Which means Grayson is the only problem."

"Brilliant deduction, psychic." He downed the rest of his

drink and wished for another. Damn Roxanna wasn't so relaxing anymore.

She turned her head and glared at him.

Guilt slammed forward. "Sorry. That was me being an ass again."

"Yes. Kind of like you refusing to help veterans because you don't want to work with your brother."

Well, fuck—she sounded like Grayson now. And he really hated that the guy had kind of sort of extended an olive branch the other night at the Halloween party. If anyone was going to do that, *he* would.

Out of sheer peevishness, he corrected, "*Half*-brother."

"You don't have to call him that. I know who you're talking about."

"I call him that because that's what he is."

She sipped her wine, her expression contemplative as she eyed him over the rim. "Does it make you feel better that he's half and you're whole?"

"What kind of question is that?" he snapped with annoyance.

"When you insist on making the distinction he's only a *half*-brother, you're elevating yourself over him. And you're closing yourself off to acceptance."

Holy shit, she really was psycho-analyzing him—and fuck, she was good, too.

"Why do *I* have to accept him?" he groused. Then he cringed inwardly. He sounded like a five year-old, not a gown-ass, thirty-year-old man.

Roxanna held her glass in front of her as she twisted slightly toward him. "Like it or not, Loyal, Grayson isn't going away. And since you can't change that he's a part of your family, you have to figure out a way to move past it. Because if everyone else accepts him and you don't, you'll be the outsider, not him."

That bald truth hit him harder than if she'd full-out swung a two-by-four upside his head.

He shoved away from the Range Rover and paced a few feet away, the empty glass in his hand hard against his thigh. How did she know that he feared being pushed aside and replaced when he hadn't even wanted to fully acknowledge it himself? It was downright stupid and childish and fucking insecure, which is why he keep shoving it aside. Which only made him angrier whenever he had to face the guy and acknowledge he existed.

But could she be right? Was he doing it to himself?

"Can I ask you another question?"

He snorted and swung around. "You haven't asked for permission so far, why start now?"

She smiled briefly. "How rich are you?"

He lifted his shoulders uncomfortably, not wanting to brag when he knew she wasn't so well off.

"You're worth millions, right?" she pried. "Is it all your money, or is it tied up in a trust fund?"

"We each assume full control of our trust funds at thirty." He tapped the glass against the side of his leg as he stared at her boots peeking out from beneath the hem of her blue dress. "And I've done well enough on my own, through hard work and investments."

"Then why don't *you* give Grayson the money? No strings attached."

Loyal's hand stilled as he lifted his head in surprise.

Huh. Now that *was an idea.*

He hadn't even thought of that angle. Dad couldn't insist on him being CFO if he used his own money. He also wouldn't look like such a selfish bastard for saying no, and best of all, he wouldn't have to work with his *half*-brother.

"You know, I like that," he said, warming up to the idea fast. "I *really* like that."

153

Roxanna smiled, and he was hit with a sudden urge to haul her into his arms and kiss her. Then he noticed a shiver shake her bare shoulders, and saw the goose bumps on her pale skin. Here he was all warm in his shirt, vest, and suit coat, while she was freezing in the November night air.

He set his glass on the hood of his vehicle, then shrugged out of his coat and moved in to sling it around her shoulders. Her startled gaze rose, but got caught up on his mouth. He gathered her long hair back to pull it free, loving the cool silkiness of it against his skin. His breath hitched as her lips parted the tiniest bit and her tongue darted out for a quick sweep. The moisture left behind glinted in the light from over the door behind him.

Releasing her hair, he gave a quick rub up and down her arms over his coat. "That better?"

"Yes, thank you," she breathed. Then she blinked and stiffened as her gaze met his for a split second before bouncing away. "We should get back inside."

Loyal inched closer. "I don't want to go back inside."

He heard her hard swallow, heard the shallow rasp of her breath to match his, but when he tightened his grip on her arms and leaned forward, the hand not holding her wine glass flattened against his chest to hold him back.

"Loyal, I can't. *We* can't."

He chose in that moment to believe she was only talking about them kissing outside the ballroom while his whole family waited inside for the election results. It wasn't any worse than them having mind-blowing sex in the stables while his whole family was up at the house for the Halloween party, but he listened to his gut and didn't push her.

He reached for his empty glass, then stepped back to give her some space. She gulped down the rest of her wine while she straightened from the bumper.

As soon as they stepped back inside, she started to slip his coat from her shoulders.

"You can keep it until you're warm."

She cast a furtive glance around and handed it over. "I'm good. And...um...about tomorrow—"

"Yeah, about that," he interrupted as he took the suit coat. "You close at six, so I was thinking I'd pick up takeout on the way over. Any preference?"

"No. Loyal, I don't—"

"I'll get Italian then. There's a great place near my hotel."

Right outside the doors to the family suite, she swung around to face him. "You can't come over."

"Why not?"

"Because, you can't."

He did an eyebrow raise and head tilt to let her know *because* wasn't going to cut it.

"I hired someone else."

He wasn't coming over for the accounting and they both knew it. She wanted him, but like last night in her shop, she was running scared. So he called her bluff. "Liar."

Her gaze narrowed and her chin lifted as she insisted, "I did."

"Who'd you get?"

"You wouldn't know them."

"Gimmie a name."

Her gaze flicked toward the ceiling for a second. "Sheldon Cooper."

He snorted. "You do know they run *The Big Bang Theory* reruns all the time, right?"

She gave a frustrated little growl that was surprisingly sexy, then her expression set with determination. "We can't do this."

"Yes we can." He'd go crazy if they didn't.

155

She shook her head, a hint of desperation in the movement. "I'm serious. Do *not* come over."

He leaned forward. She leaned back, eyes wide, pupils dilated. It took every ounce of will power he had not to touch her as he reached past to wrap his hand around the door handle behind her.

"Like it or not, Roxanna, I'm coming." A little thrill shot through him when her breath hitched, and arousal turned his voice husky and rough. "And I'm going to add up your numbers so perfectly, you're going to beg me to do it again and again."

Then he lost his will power and pressed a hard kiss to her parted lips. When he opened the door, it nudged against her back, and she looked a bit dazed as she stepped aside.

Good. Let her think about that *until tomorrow.*

CHAPTER 19

$\mathcal{F}$inished with her final reading for the day, Roxanna said goodbye to Tessa at four, and went to pour herself a fresh cup of coffee as a new customer browsed the gemstone section. The Governor had won his senate bid last night, and the victory celebration had gone past midnight. She'd been exhausted when she got home, but the moments out back with Loyal replayed in her head and made sure she still didn't get much sleep.

Coffee was her last resort to keep her alert in case her unwanted self-appointed accountant showed up.

Unwanted? Biggest lie you've told yourself yet.

She stirred a dash of cream and sugar into her cup, and even the noise of the construction between her shop and Honor's new next-door bakery faded away as Loyal's sexy voice filled her head.

"I'm going to add up your numbers so perfectly, you're going to beg me to do it again and again."

Never in her life would she have imagined an accounting reference could sound so dirty and sexy. Last night, those words had made her weak in the knees and her panties

157

damp. Thankfully, he'd opened the door and nudged her aside, because two more seconds, and she'd have grabbed his vest to drag him back out to his Land Rover with its huge back seat, tinted windows, and condoms in the glove box.

She'd spent the rest of the evening subtly using Honor and Mae as shields, because every time Loyal's dark gaze caught hers, she instantly remembered how amazing he felt inside her. How the heck was she supposed to combat that—especially when she couldn't drink any more wine?

All day today, every time she'd caught a glimpse of Asher next door, or when he'd come over into the shop to bug her, his dark hair had made her do a double-take. Even worse, every damn time the door chime sounded, Roxanna's pulse leapt, and her gaze shot to the front of the store. The closer it got to closing time, the harder her heart thumped.

"You're going to beg me to do it again and again."

Damn him.

Damn yourself. You're the one who had to go after him outside.

Yeah, she did only have herself to blame for that one. She should've left it alone—left *him* alone.

She took her coffee back to the register to ring up her customer's purchases, then tidied up the counter and carried a stack of mail back to her desk. Her messy desk that was re-growing uneven piles of crap. She should clean it again, but figured it was a good deterrent should Loyal actually show up.

Rigid, buttoned up Loyal would hate her disorganized mess.

But no—if she ended up putting him to work, the room would be much too small with him watching while she cleared him a spot, so she was better off doing it now.

Forty-five minutes later, in between two more customers, she had the desk all ready to go. She opened all the relevant files on her computer, left her password by the keyboard, and spun her chair to go finish out the end of her day up front.

"Wow, look how—"

Roxanna exclaimed and jumped as Asher spoke from the doorway. "Geez, you scared the crap out of me."

"You've been jumpy all day."

She avoided his gaze and rose from the chair to walk toward him with her empty cup. "Too much caffeine trying to recover from the late night. And I keep forgetting you can walk through the opening in the wall now and sneak up on me."

They were connecting the bakery and Lift Your Spirit to share café tables as well as cross-promote to customers. Until the glass doors were installed between the two shops, all Asher had to do was slip around the plastic sheeting over the huge-ass hole in the wall.

He shrugged and grinned as he glanced behind her. "You cleaned the desk again. What are you looking for this time?"

"Nothing, smartass. I am turning a corner and keeping up with things."

"Yeah, right," he scoffed.

She brushed past him. "I am." From this moment forward. "What's up, anyway? How's everything going next door?"

"Good. Mae's crew is packing up for the day, and Honor and I are heading out, too. We're going to grab drinks at Nick's and thought we'd see if you wanted to meet us for dinner after you close. Mae and Ian are coming, too."

Roxanna glanced toward the front of her shop, half-expecting Loyal to walk in at any moment. She should go. It would serve him right if she wasn't here when he showed up —then he'd know she was serious that nothing more could happen between them. But part of her didn't want to be serious. Part of her wanted him to play with *all* her numbers tonight. Again and again.

Her cheeks burned hot at the wanton thought. "Thanks, but I have a lot to get done here."

Asher joined her over by the tidy register counter and crossed his arms. "Like what?"

"I'm switching out some inventory," she said vaguely.

"You did that yesterday."

"I have more to do." She had a few items she could switch around to make it so she wasn't lying. "And I'm going to work on my books again."

"You should've hired someone to do those by now."

She shrugged. His scrutinizing gaze made her nerves twitch.

"You're avoiding me because of Loyal," he accused.

Her stomach pitched as she shot him a frown. "I am not."

"Are, too. Last night you barely even talked to me."

She hadn't talked to him because Loyal had been hanging out with him much of the time. But she'd been avoiding his brother, not him. "It was a busy night. You guys all had a lot going on."

The shake of his head said he didn't buy it. "Listen, I know it's been hard adding Honor into the mix, and I—"

"I love Honor," she insisted. "I am nothing but thrilled you found your special someone."

"I know, and she loves you now, too." They shared a brief grin over that. "The thing is, I know it's been different, and I just don't want what happened between you and Loyal to make things weird. You mean too much to me for him to get in the way of our friendship."

Heaviness settled in her chest. She did her best to hold her smile as she reached out to grasp his forearm. "Same here, Ace. But we're good. I promise."

And for her to keep that promise, she had to get over Loyal and move on.

"Okay." Asher pulled her in for a quick, tight hug, then

backed toward the plastic sheeting covering the opening between the two shops. "You're sure about tonight?"

"I'm sure." She forced a smile. "Lots to do."

"You know where we are if you change your mind."

"Have fun."

Honor called goodbye through the opening as they left, and everything got quiet once they locked up. She filled her last hour cleaning the coffee area, vacuuming the carpet, and switching a few things in her front displays to keep from lying to her best friend. She might have also been keeping an eye out for Loyal.

Six o'clock came.

Then five after.

And ten after.

Finally, she locked the front door, flipped her sign, and headed to the back to shut off the lights. All the while, she told herself she was happy he'd listened to her. Thrilled. It made her life so much easier.

Twenty minutes past six, she turned off the light for the storage room and office, and yanked open the door to go upstairs. She was not disappointed in the least that he hadn't showed. She wasn't angry either—she was *relieved*.

Except, suddenly there he was, coming through the outside door from the back parking lot, carry-out bags in each hand. She pulled up short, her heart lodged high in her throat as excitement woke up her whole body with an electrifying shot of adrenalin.

Loyal smiled when he saw her. "Hi."

She still wasn't used to smiles instead of scowls. The flash of his white teeth through his dark stubble, and the way his eyes crinkled as if he was genuinely happy to see her made it hard to catch her breath. His dark gaze took stock of her black pencil skirt and form-fitting charcoal cashmere sweater. The heat in his gaze telegraphed to her body and spiraled down to settle low in her belly.

He wore business casual, as usual. Slim khakis, light blue shirt tucked, pants belted, with a dark brown vest. His usually styled hair was mussed, as if he'd run a hand through it a time or two. He should look nerdy, or stuffy, or *some*thing other than deliciously sexy.

"I didn't think you were coming," she said, striving for indifference.

"Yeah. Sorry I'm late. Josephine's was swamped." He let the door shut behind him and lifted the bags in his hands. "You want to take this upstairs, or sit at one of your shop tables?"

If she took him upstairs, she might as well take him straight to the bedroom. She absolutely could not do that. Not after her conversation with Asher. In fact, if she had any smarts at all, she'd tell him he was too late and she leaving to meet his brother and Honor at the pub.

Instead, she stepped back and held the door open for him to enter the shop.

She'd have to make do with half-smarts tonight.

As he passed by, the delicious smell of Italian spices almost covered up that faint scent of his cologne she loved so much. Almost. She took a discrete inhale and savored all the aromas in the air.

Loyal glanced right, into her dark office-storage area, then paused for a longer look to the left through the hanging beads leading into her reading room. Like in the store, she kept a Himalayan salt lamp lit twenty-four seven, and the orange glow was bright enough to make out her table and chairs, plus the large chaise lounge against the far wall.

But he didn't stay there long enough for her to feel the need to explain, and as he moved on to set the bags on one of the tables, she followed to flick on the bright lights over the coffee station. There would be no leaving it to ambient lighting to give a romantic feel.

"You didn't have to do this," she told him.

"This is just one of many apologies I owe you from the past six years."

Her heart warmed at those words, but she said, "The other night was apology enough."

Loyal started taking containers from the bags. "If *that* was an apology, then it definitely wasn't enough."

Heat flamed through her when she realized he thought she'd been referring to their time in the stables. "I meant on the bench," she clarified. "You apologized on the bench."

"I'll apologize anywhere you want, Roxanna."

How about right here?

But when he lifted his gaze with the husky statement, she swallowed hard and shook her head as much for herself as for him. "You have to stop that."

He stared at her for a moment, then set down the container in his hands and stepped around the table. "Why? There's no use denying the chemistry between us. Lord knows I've tried from the day we met."

The words shocked her enough that a few seconds later, she found herself backed up against the coffee station. He trapped her with a hand braced on each side of her against the counter. Then he dipped his head until his stubble-rough cheek rasped against her smooth one.

All rational thought scattered as his warm breath fanned her ear.

"We're both consenting adults here. What's the harm in indulging?"

His lips brushed her ear before sliding across her neck, to the underside of her jaw. Roxanna started to tilt her head to give him better access, then she desperately latched on to one last shred of common sense.

Leaning back, she drew her hands up to push against his chest. The urge to let her fingers explore the hard planes beneath his shirt and vest had her clenching them into fists.

"The harm would be to me," she said softly, eyes closed as she wrestled between pulsing desire and self-preservation. "You have nothing to lose, Loyal, but I could lose everything."

He went still, and she opened her eyes when he eased back a few inches to see her face.

"Tell me what that means."

She searched his expression to see he genuinely didn't understand. Taking a deep breath, she lowered her gaze and admitted, "You have the power to break my heart—in more ways than one. If we do this and it goes bad—*when* it goes bad, because you don't do relationships—I will lose not only my best friend, but the family I've come to love as my own."

His Adam's apple bobbed hard with his swallow.

"I never knew what a family was until I met Asher and he took me home to meet all of you." Tears stung her eyes, and she tried to blink them away. "Your parents, your brothers and sisters...I don't know what I'd do if I lost them. They're the only true family I've ever known."

CHAPTER 20

*L*oyal lifted a hand to swipe his thumb over one of the tears that escaped down Roxanna's cheek. That sharp ache settled in his chest again, making it hurt with each breath he took. He wanted her more than he'd ever wanted any woman before, and yet what he wanted would hurt her.

Because he couldn't promise forever. Not again.

Why not?

He hesitated for a brief second, but quickly retreated from that thought. "So, what does that leave us with? Friends?"

"I hope so," she whispered.

"I don't know if I can be friends with you," he admitted. When her dark brows drew together, he added, "I mean, I won't go back to being a jackass, but, my problem is, I can't be in the same room with you without wanting to touch you and kiss you. I get hard just looking at you. Especially after the stables."

As he spoke, her fists had smoothed out against his chest, no longer pushing, more like caressing—and suddenly, he couldn't resist. He tipped her chin up and covered her mouth with his.

The electric spark was an instantaneous jolt, fizzing through his veins and hardening his body in seconds. Her soft gasp allowed him access inside her mouth, and he stroked his tongue deep. She slid her hands up to thread through his hair as she kissed him back with equal hunger. Closing the space between them, he gathered her into his arms.

He was fast losing his mind when her words echoed in the deep, dark recesses of his mind.

"The harm would be to me."

Loyal tore his mouth from hers and buried his face in the crook of her neck. There was that scent again. Sweet. Sexy. Tempting as all hell.

He lifted his hands to cup her face as he leaned his forehead against hers. "I'm sorry. I keep doing that when I shouldn't."

"I know," she agreed. But she didn't push him away, even though his erection pressed against the juncture of her thighs. The thought of lifting her skirt made his fingers flex ever so slightly against her scalp.

"Where do we go from here?" he asked.

"I don't know, exactly."

Longing edged her voice, and he had to fight with everything he had not to kiss her again.

"Maybe we should start with dinner?" she suggested, her voice high and breathy.

"Good idea." He moved his body back from hers, started to dip for that one last kiss, but then forced himself to completely step away. Turning his back to her, he discretely adjusted himself as he surveyed the small table. "I, ah, brought a bottle of wine, but given the circumstances, maybe alcohol isn't such a good idea."

"Probably not." She cleared the roughness from her voice and asked, "Water or coffee?"

"Water."

When she sat down with two glasses a minute later, he'd opened the containers and set out thick, wax-coated paper plates, napkins, and heavy duty plastic utensils. "Take your pick. Shrimp scampi with linguini, tagliolini with truffles, chicken alfredo, or baked ziti."

"Nothing with rats or snakes?"

He glanced up to see her smiling and chuckled. "No. No rats or snakes."

"What was the deal with that anyway?"

"I was curious about things you like or don't like."

Her eyebrows rose as she picked up her fork. "And *that's* what you started with?"

He shrugged. "For me, it fit at the time."

"O-kay." Their gazes connected and held for a long moment before she dropped her attention back to the pasta. "Well, here's one for you, I love Italian, and it all smells amazing. Do I have to pick one, or can I try some of each?"

"Go for it."

He did the same as her, scooping a little of each pasta onto his plate. As they began eating, he found himself thinking not only of what she'd said about his family, but a comment she'd made about her mother rose in his memory.

"Would you be willing to tell me about your family? Or lack thereof, it seems."

Dismay flickered in her eyes as she reached for her water. She seemed to debate in her mind as she chewed, then she swallowed her food and sipped from her glass. "It's lack thereof, definitely, so I'll give you the Cliff Notes version. I grew up in Wisconsin. My mom left us when I was nine, my dad buried himself in his work and traveling, and I was left with my super religious grandparents who never liked my mother and pointed out every day how I was just like her."

She'd started out as if recounting simple facts, but at the end, her voice dripped with hurt and resentment.

"Sounds shitty."

"It was. They didn't understand me or what I do—never even tried. Who I was, who I *am*, was never acceptable to them."

Her words sparked his guilt once more. For six years, he'd done the same thing as her grandparents.

"The day after I graduated high school, I packed everything I owned in my Jeep and moved here."

"The same Jeep you drive now?" he asked with surprise. "That was what, ten years ago?"

"Yep. It was ten years old when I bought it, I've had it for ten years, and I'll drive it another ten if I can."

He'd seen her Jeep. He was shocked it was *still* running, but that was neither here nor there. "Why Colorado?"

"I visited once as a kid and loved the mountains."

Something in her voice had him shaking his head. "I don't buy that. What's the real reason?"

Surprise flashed in her eyes that he didn't accept her pat answer, but she looked down at her plate to stab a shrimp with her fork. "You wouldn't believe me, so let's just leave it."

"Your reason is not for me to judge."

Her lips twisted wryly. "Well that's a new one."

"I'll keep my word, Rox," he promised.

Her head lifted at his shortened version of her name. He'd never used it before. Never felt comfortable enough to use it before.

His heart pounded hard as her gaze met his. It felt like he'd suddenly crossed a line and there was no going back. Not that he had any idea what the line was or what it meant.

After a charged moment, she simply said, "Colorado felt

right. When I left Wisconsin, I had no clue where I was going, I was just getting away. Getting out. I drove west because it's more miles to the ocean, but once I saw the mountains, I knew fate had brought me home, and I stopped driving."

She *knew* fate had brought her home. He was starting to feel that way himself. "That's not so crazy."

"I didn't say it was crazy, I just didn't think *you'd* believe it."

"I have family in Texas, my uncle and aunt and my cousins, but all the years I was there, it never felt right until I came back home." After a couple more bites, he said, "So, you moved here and the rest is history. Do you still talk to your family?"

She shrugged slightly. "My dad, two times a year. He calls on my birthday, I call on his. Not my grandparents though. My leaving only proved to them I was exactly like my mom, and I have figured out life's too short for their negative judgment."

Cue another wave of guilt to crash at his feet. He vowed right then to make up for being a judgmental ass if it took him the rest of his life.

Whoa. That's a little far out into the future.

In his head, he turned around and spotted that line he'd crossed earlier about a mile behind him. Desperate for a distraction, he asked, "And you haven't seen your mom since you were nine?"

"Oh, no, I've seen her."

He raised his eyebrows, and her indecision was evident as she chewed, swallowed, and sipped. Then resignation settled in.

"I was in the middle of my first year of college when my mom tracked me down. We reconnected, and things were great at first. I thought I'd finally gotten my mother back, but she only stayed four years this time." Her jaw clenched for a moment. "Just long enough to use me, clean out my bank accounts, and skip town again."

His hand stilled as he stared at her in shock. "Your *mother* stole money from you?"

"Over ten thousand dollars."

"Wow. That's...unbelievably...*low*. I can't even imagine."

"Because no one in your family would ever do something like that."

"We have our issues, but yeah, underneath everything, I'd trust any one of them implicitly.

"I will never trust her again," she vowed.

Hurt was back in her voice, and he wanted to get up and pull her into his arms for a hug. But touching her even in comfort wasn't a good idea. "I'm sorry you had to go through that."

She shrugged. "I don't care to ever see her again, but on the other hand, I don't regret that she found me."

"How do you not?"

"Because I found myself again. It probably sounds strange, but it was like she gave me permission to be *me* again." She rested her fork on her plate while skimming her gaze over the shop spread out behind him. "Ultimately, she is the reason I have all this."

"How so?"

"For years, my grandparents told me my abilities were nonsense. My dad didn't want to hear about them either, so I stopped talking about the things I saw and felt, and eventually, I stopped listening, too."

"Listening?" To her grandparents?

"To my intuition."

Had he asked that out loud?

"To the little flashes that would come to me when I touched someone," she continued, "or when I read their aura.

All the emotions people wrap around themselves like an invisible blanket. I shut it all down and pushed it away and tried to be normal...tried to be someone they could love."

Loyal had a hard time swallowing past the lump that lodged in his throat with those last whispered words. If she was trying to make him pay for his years of being an ass, it was totally working.

"Not that it mattered." Another shrug underscored her words. "I guess I look too much like my mom, and every day they saw her instead of me. My grandma told me that's why Dad stayed away so much. She blamed me for that, too, though it probably didn't help that he and my mom named me after her as well."

The hurt in her voice had him wanting to scream at her family for being so horrible to her even though he'd done the same damn thing. But he hadn't known what they'd done. He hadn't wanted to know anything about her at all. Now he wanted to know everything.

"They made that big of a deal of your middle name?"

She shook her head. "First name, not middle. My mother is Roxanna Kent, too. I'm the female equivalent of a male junior."

"That's unusual."

"My mother is unusual."

So was she. Unusual and unique in a way he'd never allowed himself to notice before. Never allowed himself to appreciate before.

Now that he wasn't looking at her with his preconceived notion that all psychics were frauds, he could see an individual person with feelings and emotions and a life he would have never imagined. And he was shocked to realize all the feelings swirling around in his head and heart right now had nothing to do with wanting her so bad he was still semi-hard.

Desire still simmered on the back burner—it always had with her—but now he was finally getting a glimpse of the woman his brother and family loved so much, and he genuinely liked her. The more time he spent with her, the more he wanted to spend with her so he could learn as much as possible.

"How did your mother help you start your shop?" he asked.

"She didn't directly help—that would involve being in my life. No, her help came in the form of encouraging me to open myself up again. Stop suppressing who I am, listen to my spirit guides, and channel the energy that flows around me, and through me. Reconnecting with my abilities led me here."

A couple of weeks ago, those words would've sounded so hokey. They still sounded odd, but he no longer felt the need to cut her off at the knees because of his self-righteous anger over her belief.

"Is your mother a psychic, too?"

She set her fork down and wiped her mouth before setting her napkin on her empty plate while pushing it aside. "Honestly, I don't know for sure. She's one of the few people I can't read."

The last time she'd said that had been about him. He'd assumed it was an excuse because she was afraid he'd be able to spot her scam, or that maybe she wasn't talking straight because she was drunk. But now he recalled her saying the same about her mother that night, too.

So, did that make him special, or not special enough?

Whichever it was, being in the same category as the thieving mother she despised turned his stomach. Until a couple weeks ago, he'd put himself in that group. Now he wanted out.

Done with his meal, Loyal took his plate and hers and rose to toss them in the garbage. "Have you ever asked her?"

He caught her shrug when he turned back to the table.

"Well, she acts like she is, so I've always assumed so."

"Acts?"

As if realizing how that had sounded, she grimaced. "Like I said, I can't really read her. But, she has to be, otherwise where else would I have gotten it from?"

"Is being psychic hereditary?"

"It can be. Anyways, it wouldn't matter if I asked her or not, because I wouldn't believe a word that came out of her mouth."

He had a gut feeling the woman was just really good at being an evil bitch who took advantage of her daughter who only wanted someone in her family to love and accept her. No wonder she'd fallen for his. Oddly enough, Merit flashed in his mind, and how just once, he wanted their dad to ask him for something—anything it had sounded like.

But then Roxanna stood up and leaned over the table to put covers on the leftovers. The second his gaze traced the curve of her hips, his younger brother was instantly forgotten.

She stacked the four containers on top of one another then set them back in the bag. "You're going to be eating Italian for a week."

Normally, he didn't eat leftovers. He never ordered so much that he *had* leftovers. "You got a fridge in the back?"

"Yes."

"Then we'll have lunch tomorrow."

She swiveled around on her boot heel. "We?"

"I'm a genius when it comes to numbers, Rox, but something tells me I'm going to need more than one night to straighten out your books."

The moment the words were out of his mouth, his mind

went straight to his warning—or promise?—in the hall outside the ballroom the night before. Judging by the fiery blush on her cheeks, her mind went to the same exact place.

You're going to beg me to do it again and again.

Lord help him, he might be the one who ended up begging—even knowing full well how much he could hurt her.

"So, let's get to it, shall we? Show me where I'm working," he said a little too brightly. Because somehow they had to be only friends.

He wasn't sure how the fuck that was going to work, but for her sake, he'd try.

"The computer is all ready in the back room," she said as she moved past him, food in hand.

He followed her, his gaze locked on the sexy roll of her hips and the back and forth swish of her shiny brunette curls. He already knew they were long enough to wrap around his wrist. One little tug would give him full access to the smooth line of her throat, and then he could skim his lips lower.

Just thinking about it took him from half to full mast by the time she reached the back room. In an attempt to buy some time to talk himself down, he paused at the beaded doorway of the gypsy-looking room on the right.

CHAPTER 21

*R*oxanna closed the fridge as the sound of the beads hanging in front of her reading room clinked together in that musical harmony she loved so much. She went to the doorway in time to see Loyal step inside.

Her stomach got all fluttery as she crossed the floor and passed through the beads. With only the salt lamp and the tiny star-lights on the ceiling, it was too dark. Too intimate. Too seductive. She flipped on the lights, but they were muted by design, so it didn't help as much as she'd hoped.

"So, this is where the magic happens?" he asked without looking at her.

"It's not magic," she bristled automatically. "I'm not a witch."

"I don't know." He lightly trailed his fingertips over the top of her satin covered table. "It feels like I've been under your spell since the night of the fire."

She didn't respond to that. What could she say after their earlier conversation?

Likewise. And by the way, I've changed my mind. I don't care if you can't do forever, I'll take now.

She could say all those things, but she wouldn't. If she wanted to ensure she didn't lose the rest of his family, she couldn't.

Then why did she still want to so damn bad? Why had she been thinking about taking back her 'just friends' decree from the moment they sat across from each other at the table?

Loyal's gaze travelled slowly around the room, taking stock of her space. The decorating had been specifically designed for comfort, relaxation, and to facilitate a positive energy flow. One of the walls was painted to appear as if there was a huge bay window overlooking the Rockies. As much time as she spent in the room, that gorgeous view was for her own benefit as much as for clients.

She wondered what he saw as he looked around. Did he like the warm colors and soft light? Could he feel the affirmative energy, or would he only look at her crystal ball and tarot cards on the side table and consider the cliché psychic trappings as another layer of her fraudulent enterprise? They had been given to her as a gift from clients and were for decoration only; hence their placement on the side table near her chaise lounge. But he wouldn't know that, and she didn't feel the need to explain.

She swallowed hard when he turned around to face her, his brown eyes serious. She wished she could read him, and at the same time was relieved she couldn't. Some things she shouldn't know—didn't want to know.

"Do you talk to dead people?"

"No." She frowned. "That would be a medium."

"Can you read minds?"

"No."

His gaze flicked up past her shoulder as he asked, "How does it work? What exactly is it that you do?"

"Why are you asking about all this now? I know you don't believe, so what's the point?"

"I've never let myself get to know who you really are. Now that I have, I'd like to know more." He squinted and stepped toward her, but he still wasn't looking at her.

She moved aside to put distance between them again, and that's when she saw he was reading the diploma for her bachelor's degree from CSU. She'd earned every credit through hard work, so yes, she displayed it—but on the darkest wall, where most people didn't even notice. Of course, *Loyal* would notice.

"You have a psychology degree?"

There was a hint of surprise and respect in his voice. She wasn't sure if she should be offended or proud.

"It compliments what I do. Gives me a deeper understanding of human behavior," she explained briefly.

In truth, suppressing her abilities in high school had left her frustrated with no outlet. She'd chosen psychology so she could help people. After her mother coaxed her into using her gift again, after she then stole the money that was supposed to help pay for her master's so she could become a licensed counselor, Roxanna had put her degree to use by guiding customers in positive life affirmations.

Loyal pivoted back to face her. "Maybe your...abilities, are really you applying what you learned to make educated guesses."

She shook her head at his typical skeptic attempt to give a logical explanation to what he refused to believe in. "You're walking a thin line."

"I'm trying to understand so it makes sense."

"I've done what I do since I was a little girl, Loyal, and I knew nothing about psychology and human behavior back then. Listen, I'm not going to stand here and try to convince you when you obviously don't have an open mind about what I do."

"I'm used to dealing in numbers. They're concrete," he said. "I can see them and touch them. It's hard for me to wrap my head around something I can't prove."

She crossed her arms and tried a new angle. "Do you believe in God?"

He looked surprised by the question. "Yes."

"Have you ever seen him?"

"No."

His smile told her he knew where she was going, but she continued anyway. "Touched him?"

"Of course not."

"So, you have no *concrete* proof of his existence, yet you still believe he exists?"

"Do you?"

"I do, but we're not talking about me."

"Okay, yeah, I get what you're saying." He glanced toward the table and then back to her. "Show me."

"Show you what?"

He pulled out one of her two chairs and sat down. "Give me a reading."

She didn't move. "I already told you I can't read you."

"Are you sure? Because you frickin' nailed it the other night about Grayson."

"That was more psychology than psychic," she admitted. "Besides, even if I could, I don't feel like I have to prove anything to you."

"You don't want to make me believe?"

"I can't make you do anything, Loyal, nor would I want to. It's your choice to make, not mine."

He nodded. "Fair enough. Which puts us back at you telling me what you do and how you do it. Open my mind to the possibilities."

She eyed him with annoyance, wondering why he was so hell bent on getting her to talk about it right now. "I kind of already explained it earlier."

"You feel things and see things." He sat back, palms and eyebrows lifted in exasperation. "That really clears it up."

Fine. That *was* somewhat vague. As he rested his palms on his legs and watched her expectantly, she huffed out a breath and stalked over to where he sat. "That's my chair."

"Does it matter?"

She stared him down to let him know it did, but that ended up being a huge mistake when all her frustration was swept away by an intense wave of awareness. Her heart rate sped up as heat flooded her body before pooling low in her belly.

The bob of his Adam's apple told her he felt the energy shift, too. So did the obvious bulge behind his zipper.

All her arguments from earlier were incinerated, carried up and away on a wisp of imaginary ash. She wanted to see and feel things with *him* again. Denying what was in her heart and soul, suppressing her true essence...she didn't want to become that person again.

Your true love will be loyal and true.

Maybe her true love literally was Loyal...maybe he wasn't. But whichever it was, she'd never know if she didn't take the risk to find out, would she?

CHAPTER 22

$\mathcal{H}$e wasn't budging from her chair, so Roxanna stepped in close and hitched up her skirt far enough to place one knee on the little section of fabric visible between his spread legs. His eyes widened, and he audibly gulped when she rested her hands on his shoulders and leaned forward.

"What are you doing?" he asked.

"Changing my mind."

"Okay."

She smiled and lifted one hand to run her fingers through his hair. "Is it really okay?"

"You won't hear any argument from me." Then his eyebrows dipped. "Although, what about your books?"

"You can play with all the numbers tomorrow."

"You're sure?"

"You're not?"

He smiled, but it didn't last. "Another thing—"

"It sounds like you're arguing."

"I just wanted to say, when it comes to the whole relationship thing—"

Roxanna pressed her finger to his lips with a shake of her head. "We don't need to go over that again. I know the score, Loyal. I know what you're willing to offer—or not willing to. I'm okay with it."

His gaze met hers, and he looked sad for a moment. She felt a pulse of that sadness pass from his lips to her finger and wanted to make it go away. Needed it to go away.

She dragged her finger across his full bottom lip, then reveled in the scrape of his stubble against the palm she placed along his jaw. "When I say that I feel things, it means I can intuit things without trying."

"How do you do that?" he asked, his voice low and rough.

"Information comes to me when I touch people." Her lips quirked as she gazed down at him. "Most people, anyway. What they're feeling, what they believe. I build on that by reading their aura, which is like an energy field around their body, and then I offer guidance and suggestions for positive improvement in their lives."

"Sounds like you're counseling them."

She was impressed he was still listening with her knee pressed up against his crotch. She reached down to undo the three buttons on his vest. "Guiding only. I'm not licensed, so there's a big difference. People come to me with questions, sometimes vague, sometimes specific, and I try to guide them toward what will make their spirit joyful."

His hands rose to her hips, and he slipped the tips of his fingers beneath the hem of her sweater. "Can you intuit what would make my spirit joyful right now?"

She gave a soft laugh and started working on the buttons of his light blue shirt. "I don't have to be psychic to figure that out."

"No, probably not," he muttered as he pushed his hands up, lifting the cashmere to expose her stomach, then her lacy, black bra.

Roxanna stopped what she was doing long enough for him to drag her sweater over her head, then finished with the buttons and parted the material over his chest. He smoothed her static-charged hair back from her face, his gaze shifting down to focus on her breasts. She ran her hands over the hard planes of muscle she'd uncovered, then up over his shoulders to push the shirt back, and down his arms.

Loyal sat forward, but when he became distracted placing kisses along the edge of her bra, his sleeves got caught up at his wrists, down around his waist. A useless tug had him letting loose a frustrated growl.

Inspiration struck, and Roxanna grinned as she pushed him back in the chair to effectively bind his arms at his sides.

"Hey—"

She cut off his protest with a hard kiss. His lips parted beneath hers, and she slid her tongue inside to explore while skimming her hands down over his tight abs until she reached his belt buckle.

"If my hands were free, I could help you with that," he said against her mouth.

"I got it," she assured him while dragging his zipper down.

She urged him to lift his hips so she could tug his pants down. His briefs followed, and then she wrapped her hand around his full-blown erection. His breath hitched a second before his primal, guttural groan filled her mouth.

Sensual details imprinted on her senses as his tongue continued its tango with hers.

Velvet over steel. Hot. Pulsing.

She gave a soft stroke up and down his rigid length, exploring, testing. He pulled unsuccessfully against his shirt again, and she felt a little thrill at having control as to where this was going. Last time he'd given her pleasure first. Now it was his turn.

Softening her kiss with a final suck on his bottom lip, she

then skimmed her lips down his throat and chest. She had never done this before, so she copied what he'd done the night in the stables. If it felt good for her, it stood to reason it went both ways, right?

Another low groan confirmed he liked the tip of her tongue teasing his nipples, but she didn't stay there long. When she reached her end goal by kneeling between his legs and took him in her mouth, he shifted, sliding his hips farther forward on the chair. His breath was a rough rasp in and out as she circled his tip with her tongue, learning the shape, his taste, and exactly where to press to elicit another growl from deep in his chest.

She gripped his base with one hand and leaned to take him in farther, sliding her lips down the length of him until his tip nudged the back of her throat. Amazed she wasn't gagging at that point, she pulled back and did it again, only this time she sucked on the way back up.

"*Holy fucking shit, Rox,*" he rasped.

Safe to assume he liked that.

She smiled slightly before repeating the movement. He shifted beneath her, his body moving in frenetic little jerks in the chair as he struggled against the shirt binding his wrists.

Next thing she knew, his fingers speared into her hair. For a brief second, his hands clenched as he pushed her head down. In the next moment, he reversed direction and pulled her up until he popped out of her mouth.

He leaned forward in the chair, his mouth crashing down on hers. As he nipped and licked and explored with deep, hungry strokes, he urged her to her feet with him. She tried to get lost in the passion, but a niggling little worry took root in her mind.

"Was that not good?" she asked between kisses.

"It was fucking awesome."

"Then why did you stop me?"

He unhooked her bra and tossed it aside. "Because I can't have one orgasm after another like you can, and I want to be inside you when I come."

"Oh." Her worry subsided.

"You can finish that some other night. Promise."

Some other night.

Her heart leapt in her chest at the weight of those three little words.

He kept the kisses coming, his mouth urgent on hers while his hands sought the zipper of her slim skirt. When it slid down to pool around her feet, his hands palmed her ass, and he made another one of those sexy, deep throated sounds against her lips.

She was down to her thong and her boots. He'd managed to divest himself of his shirt and vest earlier, and now toed off his shoes and socks before kicking aside his pants and briefs. He held her against him, skin to skin as he kissed her neck and backed her around the chair to the oversized chaise lounge against the wall.

"Gimmie one sec," he murmured before leaving her.

She took the first second to admire his gorgeous, naked body as he swiped up his pants to dig in the pocket. Realizing he was getting a condom, she sat down to start untying her boot laces.

"Leave them."

She glanced up in surprise, and then he was in front of her, dropping to his knees. Expecting him to undo her laces himself, she was surprised when he reached for her thong instead. As he wrestled her panties over her clunky boots, she understood he'd literally meant to leave them on, not for her to leave them for him to take off.

Once her thong was gone, his mouth was back on hers, his hands gripping her shoulders to ease her onto her back.

He followed her down, his weight settling between her thighs.

"Loyal, I'm not leaving my boots on," she muttered against his lips.

He lifted his head enough for her to see his grin. "They're sexy as hell."

"I thought it was high heels guys liked?"

"Heels don't hold a candle to those boots, Roxanna."

"Really?" she asked skeptically.

"Scout's honor."

It felt kinda weird, but when he pushed inside her with one smooth stroke, she quickly forgot about everything but the feel of him filling her completely. She drew her knees up high and planted her heels on the lounge. He didn't move his hips right away. Instead, he bent his head to tease the tip of her left breast. She arched up into his mouth, gripping his biceps as he sucked hard, nipped, then soothed with his tongue.

Sensation flooded her core, making her muscles clench hard around him.

"Again," she breathed, her eyes fluttering closed.

He complied, lavishing attention on one side, then the other, drawing it out until she rocked her hips against his in a desperate plea to get him moving. He pulled almost all the way out before thrusting deep again. She gave a low moan of approval, and he continued with slow, deep strokes while kissing and biting his way up her throat, to her mouth.

She wrapped her arms around him, gripping his back, then his buttocks, needing him deeper each time. His rhythm increased, and soon a tingle began to build deep inside.

Roxanna tipped her head back, pulling away from his kiss as she filled her tight lungs with needed oxygen. Loyal's head rested next to hers, his hot breath rasping against her ear as he moved faster.

He reached back to grasp her hand and raised her arm over her head, then did the same for the other. His fingers wrapped around her wrists as he held them there while his movements grew hard enough to rock the lounge beneath them, driving her closer and closer to the edge.

His guttural groan vibrated against her ear. "It's never been like this for me," he whispered roughly.

Her racing pulse skipped a beat. "Me neither."

Although, considering he'd given her her first real orgasm only four nights earlier, he should already know that.

"You're beautiful, and amazing, and we're not even done and already I want more."

She nearly stopped breathing as she felt his head lift at the same time her body coiled tight in a flood of sensation. Barely able to comprehend what he was saying, she opened her eyes to find his dark, intense gaze on her face as he continued to move inside her with increasing urgency.

"Loyal." His name came out as a plea.

To take her with him over the cliff.

To never let her fall alone.

To love her as she loved him.

"I want more than two nights, Roxanna. I want to see where this goes."

His voice was rough and raw and full of his own plea as his next deep stroke sent her flying. He followed moments later, and then the delicious weight of him collapsed on top of her. As their breathing calmed, she pulled free of his slack grip on her wrists and threaded her hands through his thick, soft hair.

He made a low humming sound of contentment while shifting so he could leverage himself to lay beside her, his head pillowed on his bicep. She rolled to her side, one leg thrown over his hip as she palmed the side of his face. His thick lashes lifted, revealing his beautiful, gold-flecked brown eyes.

A dizzying combination of hope and fear tightened her chest. "Was that a heat of the moment thing?" she asked softly.

He shook his head, his mouth curving into an intimate smile as he smoothed her hair away from her face. "I meant every word. I truly am under your spell."

A tiny niggle of discontent caught her off guard. "I am not a witch."

When she moved to get up, Loyal's hand on her arm kept her from going anywhere. His raised eyebrow paired with the smirk on his lips. "Touchy about that, are we?"

She glanced down as she shrugged her shoulder. "Instinctive defensiveness."

"That's understandable. But you don't have to be with me anymore, Roxanna."

A soft sigh escaped. "I'm still getting used to that."

His hand slid up her arm until he cupped the nape of her neck. He used his thumb to tip her face up so he could lean in to caress her lips with his. "I guess I need to apologize again."

"No," she assured him. "That's not what—"

He rose up over her, the increased pressure of his kiss rolling her onto her back again. He kissed her until she was breathless and aching for him to be inside her once more. She didn't have enough experience to know if that was normal or not, and for once she didn't care.

Loyal was braced on one elbow, and his other hand cupped her breast, kneading and fondling until he dragged his mouth from hers and leaned down to suck the tip into his mouth. She whimpered her approval as she clenched her fingers in his hair.

"I've decided to work on numbers tonight after all."

Her brain scrambled to catch up. "What?"

"I'll be up for apology number two in about ten minutes."

Heat pulsed through her when she figured out his meaning.

"And in the meantime..." His hand took up where his words trailed off, his fingers skimming down her belly, tickling her navel, then sliding lower.

Orgasm number two was tallied in the reading room, and a third in the bedroom up in the second floor apartment where she'd accidentally climbed into bed with him a few short weeks ago.

Minus the boots this time.

CHAPTER 23

$\mathcal{W}$aking up with Roxanna Kent in his arms was something Loyal had never even considered to be a possibility. But for the first time in six years, he wanted more than one night of release. Specifically, he discovered, he wanted a hell of a lot more than one morning of her in his arms.

She apparently didn't sleep with the light cancelling shades drawn, and he found himself squinting against the first rays of sunrise while she still slept. Her long, glorious hair spilled across the pillow as her sooty lashes rested against her cheeks. He had to fight the urge to tug her closer so he could suck on that full bottom lip of hers.

A deliberate shift of his shoulder moved the sheet enough to expose her breast closest to him, and he drank in the sight. Small and pert, they were the perfect size to fit in his hands. When she was aroused, her hard nipples pressed into his palms, turning him on even more.

Hell, simply looking at her right now had his morning erection throbbing with need.

He warred with that need versus the consideration of letting her sleep after how late they'd stayed up last night.

The decision was taken out of his hands when she shifted, and the arm she rested over his across her stomach tightened. A smile curved her lips, and her eyes opened as she turned her head toward him on the pillow.

"You're up," she murmured.

Wry humor twisted his lips. "Yeah, I'm up."

Her gaze sharpened, the languid sleepiness giving way for heated awareness. "What time is it?"

"A little after six-thirty."

She gave a soft groan of protest and closed her eyes. However, at the same time, she rolled onto her side away from him, then scooted back to spoon against him. "Why are you awake so early?"

"The shades are open," he complained.

"I like to see the morning when I wake up," she explained. "Not darkness."

Of course she did. With the dawn light illuminating her beautiful face, he shouldn't complain. He wouldn't ever again.

Seeing her cheek crease from her smile, he lifted his hand to cup her breast and lightly pinched her nipple. "It also doesn't help that there's a naked witch beside me."

She wiggled her backside against his full-blown erection. "Take that back."

"No." He gave a gentle tweak of her other nipple, and his scruff scraped her shoulder as he leaned in to nip her earlobe.

Her sharp intake of breath had him pushing his hips forward. He loved teasing her like this—and he loved that she had relaxed her defenses enough to tease back.

But things got serious when he couldn't help but reach down and discovered she was wet and ready. He slipped a finger between her folds and massaged until she was writhing against him. She reached up and back to twine her fingers in his hair, and the pull on his scalp sent a tingle down his spine. Her ass pushed against his front, but when she shifted for him to enter her, he had to pull back with a rough sound of regret.

"No more condoms."

He increased the pressure of his finger strokes until she gasped his name and came apart in his arms. As she came down, he lightly nipped her shoulder, then soothed with his tongue.

Roxanna hummed as she turned over to face him, her hand moving over his chest, his abs, then lower. He hissed in a deep breath when her hand closed around his rigid length.

"I've got two options for you," she murmured in a husky voice.

"I'm all ears."

"I can finish what I started last night, or—"

"Yes." The thought of her lips around him again had his blood pumping extra hard.

Her fingers squeezed. "Let me finish."

"Roxanna, it doesn't matter what the other option is. I'm good with either one." When she released him and rolled away onto her back, his heart leapt in ridiculous alarm. "I'm sorry. Please—what's the other one?"

"I thought it didn't matter?"

When she simply arched her eyebrows in mutiny, he huffed out a breath and flopped back to grin at the ceiling. "You are definitely a witch."

Suddenly she loomed over him, her hair falling forward to caress his chest. "I'm on birth control."

His pulse skipped. Her cheeks flushed as she traced a circle around his nipple with her fingertip. "I told you there was only one other person besides you, and that was years ago in college, which means I'm clean." Her gaze rose to his. "So, if you are..."

The thought of sliding into her heat with nothing between them had him breathing like he'd just run a hundred yard dash—and he hadn't done that since high school. Not used protection or run the hundred yard dash. He worked out, but there was no need to sprint when you weren't on the track team.

"I haven't been with anyone in a while," he got out. "And I had my yearly physical before I left Texas, so...yeah, I'm good, too."

A soft smile curved her mouth. "What will it be then, Mr. Numbers? Option one or option two?"

Blowjob or bareback?

"Two," he replied without hesitation.

Her smile widened, and she braced both hands on his chest while swinging her leg over to straddle him.

Holy shit.

He'd had her multiple times last night, and yet here he was, certain if his pulse raced any faster, he'd pass out before they got to the good stuff. His hands instinctively rose to grasp her hips, and her long curls flowed around her shoulders, trailing down to tickle his chest as she lowered herself onto his shaft until he was fully sheathed in her heat.

His fingers clenched as he let out a low growl. The feel of being inside her with nothing between them was fan-fucking-tastic. Her inarticulate response drew his gaze from the erotic view where they were joined as one, up to her face. The corner of her bottom lip was caught between her teeth, and she looked unsure. He reached one hand up to cup her cheek.

"What?" he asked.

Her tongue darted out to wet her lips, but she wouldn't look him in the eye. "I haven't done this before."

He was surprised at her sudden shyness, yet royally turned on by the fact she was brave enough to tell him. And even more ridiculously thrilled it was another first he got to claim.

"I'm not sure what will feel good for you," she added quietly.

"All of it."

Her quick smile gave way for uncertainty again. He gave a little thrust with his hips and was rewarded by her soft intake of breath.

"All you gotta do is move," he encouraged. "Up and down, back and forth, side to side. Whatever feels good for you will feel good for me."

With her cheeks endearingly rosy, she tried each suggestion, and it didn't take long for her to figure out what she liked. And what she liked, he *loved*. Every move she made sent white hot sensation rippling through his body.

When she found her rhythm, he reached up to play with her breasts, then snuck a hand between them to ensure she finished before or with him. Her speed increased, and he began moving with her, his breath rasping in and out as her muscles tightened around him.

"Holy shit, Rox...oh, God...that's so damn fucking good."

Her head tipped back as she gasped her release, and he gripped her hips as his own release built. At his urging, she continued to ride him until he nearly blacked out from the force of his climax.

As the morning filtered through the sheer drapes to bathe the dark-haired goddess sprawled out on top of him in golden sunlight, he thought he just might fucking love this woman.

CHAPTER 24

*R*oxanna sent Mae a smile through the gaping hole between Lift Your Spirit and Honor's soon-to-be bakery before carrying a mug into the back room. While the construction crew was making headway framing up the connecting arch with sliding glass doors, she'd been readying the shop to open in ten minutes, and Loyal had started reviewing her accounts in the back.

She slowed her steps as she ran her gaze over his body in her desk chair. He'd left to shower and change at his hotel, and returned in a black button up shirt, medium gray dress pants, and black leather boots. Without a vest, his hotness was on display in a whole different way. He'd left the top two buttons of his shirt unfastened, and with his shirtsleeves rolled halfway to his elbows, his muscled forearms looked yummy as all hell.

"Coffee's done."

He glanced up as she approached, and the beauty of his smiling eyes got her right in the heart. Emotion swelled in her chest as he took the cup with its splash of cream and sugar. She wanted to step up between his knees, grasp his stubble-covered jaw, and kiss him with all the love in her heart. But, she also didn't want to smother the guy and chase him away.

She loved him, and yet she was still falling for him, too. If she fell too far, and he left her like her mother had, she wasn't sure how the hell she'd handle that.

When she started to turn back to the shop, he set the cup down and caught her by the waist. "Roxanna..."

She ended up on his lap, one arm draped over his shoulders, the other braced on his chest. With his cologne enveloping her in its familiar, delicious scent, and the heat of him warming her butt and thighs, it was a good place to be.

"You can't leave before I get a chance to properly thank you."

He captured her lips in a slow, thorough, bone-melting kiss. At some point, he slipped a hand under the hem of her long-sleeved, lavender sweater.

With his palm sliding up past her ribcage toward where her heart beat an unsteady rhythm, she murmured, "That's the best thank you I have ever received." *May I bring you coffee for the rest of our lives?*

Hmm. Not falling too far might not even be an option any longer.

"Told you I was exceptional."

She gave a soft shove against his chest. "You should've warned me you were egotistical, too."

His hand reached her breast, and he thumbed her nipple through her bra. Desire twinged in her core as he asked, "Did you really need a warning for that?"

"No," she confirmed with a soft laugh. "Definitely not."

She leaned in to press her lips to his once more.

"Rox? Are you back—*whoa*."

Asher's voice in the doorway shot Roxanna off Loyal's lap at the same time he yanked his hand out from under her sweater. She hastily straightened her top as her best friend's gaze bounced from her to his brother.

"Morning, Ace." Her face felt unnaturally warm, and her voice was an octave higher than normal. "I didn't realize you and Honor were here yet."

"Obviously." He leaned his back against the doorjamb and crossed his arms. "So, this is an ongoing thing now?"

She met his gaze as the question made her heart go haywire. Loyal had said he wanted to see where things went between them, but between last night and this morning, they hadn't specifically defined what that meant. Was this a fling for him to test the waters and see how long it lasted? Or were they boyfriend and girlfriend now?

Soulmates 'til death do us part?

She didn't want to presume anything—least of all that last bit.

When she heard Loyal rise from the chair behind her, her heart raced faster. She glanced back at him as his firm hand on her hip drew her to his side.

"Yes, it's ongoing," he said to his brother. "Is that a problem for you?"

Her pulse skipped a few beats as she fought to not grin like a love-struck idiot.

"Not for me," Asher replied, his gaze locked with Roxanna's. "So long as you both know what you're signing up for. Because as I recall, only a few weeks ago you two couldn't stand the sight of each other."

"We've worked things out," Loyal said in a tight voice. "We're good now. Really."

She gave a short nod of confirmation, and finally, Asher said, "If you say so."

Hating the distance between them, she lifted her eyebrows and forced what she hoped passed for a carefree grin. "So, what's up?"

"Nothing. I'll talk to you later."

She frowned as he left abruptly, and then slowly turned to look at Loyal. "What exactly are we signing up for here?"

Before he could answer, Asher returned to the doorway, startling her yet again. "How about we have dinner Saturday night?"

"You and me?" Roxanna asked for clarification.

"You guys, and me and Honor."

Loyal's hand flexed on her hip. "If it's okay with Roxanna, I'm game for the inquisition."

She shot him a glance, and he shrugged his shoulder. She turned back to Asher. "I'm good with dinner, but not an inquisition."

He didn't even smile. "My house at seven?"

They both agreed, and he was gone again.

Suddenly, her stomach was flopping around like a fish out of water. Dinner with her best friend and his new fiancé was something she'd done a half-dozen times over the past four months, but this would be different. She and Loyal would be there together. As a couple.

And he hadn't answered her question from before yet. What exactly was their status? Was he going to love her and leave her, or had he truly meant to go against his own rule of no relationships?

When she lifted her gaze, she found his gold-flecked one on her. He looked like he was about to say something, but instead his gaze rose to the clock hanging above the door, and his hand fell away from her hip.

"It's nine o'clock."

"Yeah. I better get out there and unlock the front door."

197

She did her best to squash her disappointment as she turned to leave. Then she decided the door could wait another minute or two and swung back.

"I thought I knew the score here, and I was ready to accept it, but then you said you wanted to see where this"—she gestured between the two of them—"goes. I know this is crazy early to push, but I need to know if this is still just sex, or if it's more to you?"

"*Just* sex?" he asked with a little smirk.

She wasn't in the mood to tease no matter how cute the damn man was. "You know what I mean. What are we doing? What do *you* want out of this? If it's just going to be a fun fling, fine. But I need to know so I can—"

His finger pressed against her lips to stop her from talking. Then he stared at her for a long moment, his gaze moving over her face as if he were committing it to memory.

"It hasn't been *just sex* since the stables, Roxanna."

"It hasn't?" she barely managed to ask past the lump in her throat.

"No. As to what I want? The simple answer is *you.* I want to spend time with you. Most especially if we're having sex, but also, even when we're not. I want to know the things you like, the things you don't like, what makes you laugh, and what makes you cry."

Him. He was going to make her cry any second now.

"I want us to be together. As a couple."

She swallowed hard. "Exclusively?"

"One hundred percent exclusively." His tone dropped considerably. "I do not share."

The rough possessiveness in his voice sent a little thrill down her spine. The thought of him wanting her to be his—and only his—spoke to her heart on a soul-deep level.

"What do you want?" he suddenly asked.

She tilted her head the slightest bit and saw a hint of

uncertainty in his eyes. Knowing he wasn't so cocksure about her reply brought a happy smile to her lips. It meant her answer mattered to him.

"I want the same."

After a split-second flash of relief, he grinned back. "Good." He grasped her shoulders for a quick kiss, then set her back a step. "Now, go open your damn door, witch, and let me get back to work."

She narrowed her eyes and shook her head at the *witch* part. If she hadn't still been smiling when she left, she might have convinced him she was annoyed. But the truth was, she kind of enjoyed the teasing, especially since it was their own secret joke.

Darcy arrived to start her shift at ten, and the blond part-timer wholeheartedly approved of the new accountant in the back room. "Holy hotness," she whispered as she joined Roxanna over at the coffee station with Honor and Mae.

Mae pointed her stir-stick at Roxanna. "I told you it was Loyal."

I know! her heart squealed with joy.

"It's way too early to even say that," she warned them *and* her already lost-cause heart.

They all chatted a few more minutes, and with a promise to bring wine at dinner on Saturday, Roxanna went back to work as a customer stepped up to the register.

Her first reading in the afternoon went from bad to worse when she couldn't shake memories of her and Loyal horizontal on the chaise lounge the night before. She fibbed she wasn't feeling well, and sent the woman away with apologies and a free booking for the next week.

She managed to get through the rest of the afternoon by putting her chair on the side of the table where her back faced the chaise lounge. Even then, concentrating was exhausting, and when Darcy clocked out after her final reading, she leaned against the register counter, wishing it was six o'clock instead of five. Thinking of another whole hour before she could go take a bath and then a nap, she uttered a soft groan.

"What's the matter?"

She jumped slightly, then gave her dark, tall-drink-of-water accountant the side-eye. "Someone kept me up late last night. And after last night in my reading room, it's been a little hard to concentrate on work in there today."

"I'd say I'm sorry, but I'm not." True to his word, his grin held not one smidgeon of remorse.

"Me neither," she agreed with a reluctant smile as she noticed he held papers in his hand at his side. She hadn't had a chance to check in with him since they'd come back from lunch. She was kind of afraid to ask, but did anyway. "How's it going back there?"

His grin morphed into a grimace as he lifted the papers. "I have questions."

"Okay."

"I've come across a number of withdrawals and a few deposits I don't see any paperwork for."

"I might not have any, but let's see if I can figure them out."

He gave her a funny look as he stepped up to the counter to spread the papers out. Most of them she was able to tell him right off the top of her head what they were. He made notes, but his frown deepened with each figure they reviewed.

"How come you have invoices for some of these but not others?" He indicated a supplier she'd been using for the past four years, who sent regular shipments every month.

"I should have them all. They're probably filed already."

"And receipts for stuff like this?" This time he pointed to a number of small withdrawals from local gas stations, restaurants, and her favorite grocery store.

"I told you, those are all personal."

"Then they shouldn't be on your business credit card."

"I only have the one credit card. I mean, other than a few store cards, but I only use them at those stores."

"You don't have a separate card for your shop?"

The note of censure in his tone sparked her defenses. "No. I've never needed to. It's not that big a deal."

"It is when you can't balance your accounts."

"I've told you what everything is for," she countered. "My other accountant never had an issue with it."

"What about this? You've got a twelve-hundred dollar deposit, but again, no invoice to go with it. Where'd that come from? What's it for? You need a paper trail to back this stuff up or you'll be screwed if you ever get audited."

Roxanna leaned down to look at the bank statement as the dollar amount tripped her memory. She'd forgotten all about that, and hadn't even known it had been deposited.

"That one I'm not sure on," she admitted reluctantly. "It was a personal check that came in, and Darcy was supposed to follow up on it."

"It's your business. *You* should follow up on it."

She straightened, shifting back on her heels as annoyance surged forward. When the door chimes rang for incoming customers, she shot a glance at a hipster guy and two girls who entered, and lowered her voice. "Normally I would, but the past few weeks have been a little crazier than usual. I forgot about it because I was dealing with the fire—replacing my driver's license and social security card, and credit cards and clothes. Then there was the election—and then *you*."

His expression seemed to say none of those were a good enough excuse. Heat rose in her face, leaving her feeling inadequate and irresponsible.

"Just like your mother," Gram's voice echoed.

Roxanna set her jaw as she scraped the papers together in an uneven stack and thrust them against Loyal's chest. He grabbed for them as she said, "I'll ask Darcy about the check again tomorrow, and I've answered you about the rest, so is everything set back there now?"

"Not even close."

"What?" His somber tone dropped her stomach straight down to her feet. "Why not?"

"Because there's a reason things haven't been adding up for you, but I haven't figured it out yet. I want to go through your profit and loss statements from the past few years. Maybe even from the time you opened."

"Why? My old accountant did all those."

"Exactly why I want to go through them." His gaze narrowed as he tilted his head. "You never noticed anything weird on them?"

"No—not that I really understand them. Besides, I've known Mirela for years. We worked together at a previous job, so as long as the numbers balanced out the way they should, I trusted it was right."

"You're too trusting, then. And if you're going to run a business, you should know how to read your own P&Ls."

His judgmental tone was starting to piss her off. "Not all of us like numbers, Loyal. I thought that's what accountants are for."

"And clients like you are the reason some accountants are richer than they should be."

His criticism struck a deep nerve. "Speaking from experience are you?"

"Don't turn this around on me. You know where my money comes from. I'm just trying to figure out where yours is coming from—and going to."

She got stuck on the first part of his last sentence. There it was. He still didn't trust what she did.

Noticing the hipster guy was heading their way, she pushed Loyal toward the back, along with her hurt and disappointment. "It's coming from customers and clients. How about you do your job, and I'll do mine."

CHAPTER 25

*L*oyal's heart thumped heavy in his chest as he made his way up to the second floor. The only thing Roxanna had said to him between their financial discussion and closing time had been a terse, "Good night," before turning away from him to head up to the apartment alone.

That had been almost two hours ago. First he'd been pissed off she wouldn't even listen to his sound advice. Then he replayed the conversation in his head a few times—or a dozen—and realized he could've been more tactful. And he should've backed off the moment her defenses shot up.

Now he'd be lucky if she opened the door.

After a deep breath, he knocked and waited, and when he saw a flicker of movement in the peep hole, he stood a little straighter while lifting a large bouquet of red, orange, and yellow roses from his side. It was an additional agonizing twenty-seven seconds before the door swung open.

Her flinty gaze went straight to the flowers. He swept his over her pinned up hair that was slightly damp at her nape, the plush white bath robe from his mom, and the rainbow-striped, fuzzy socks on her feet. When he looked up again, he saw her expression had softened some and the tightness in his chest eased—a little bit anyway.

"I'm sorry." He got right to the point. "I get tunnel vision when I'm working, and obsessed with fixing the problem to the point where I'm so focused on the end goal I miss everything else. I didn't mean to be a jerk, I was only thinking of the people I've seen go out of business for stuff like that, and I don't want to see that happen to you."

She'd gone back to staring at the roses as he spoke, absorbing his words before releasing a soft sigh. "I'm sorry, too. I got defensive because it made me feel stupid for not knowing more about business stuff. The possibility that my previous accountant who is also a friend I trust may have taken advantage of me makes me feel like even more of an idiot."

"Anyone can get taken advantage of. It doesn't make you an idiot, it means you maybe trusted a little too much."

"Great. I'm a gullible idiot."

"You have a good heart."

"I still feel like an idiot. I feel like people will look at me and think, *'If you're really psychic, shouldn't you be able to spot something like this a mile away?'*"

"Sounds like that's what you think *I* think."

"Don't you?" she challenged. When he shook his head, she retorted, "Well, I do. Kind of. I mean, I should be able to sense a person's intentions. And a lot of times I can, but sometimes…"

"Sometimes you can't. And that's okay. No one is perfect."

"I should be able to tell these things when it matters," she insisted a bit morosely.

Seeing as he was still standing in the hallway holding the roses, he extended them toward her. "Can you sense my intentions right now?"

She rolled her eyes and reached for the flowers. "Anyone could guess your intentions right now, Loyal."

"But I'm not asking to stay."

"You're not?"

He liked being able to surprise her. "No. I just wanted to let you know I'm sorry, and I'll see you in the morning. That is, if you still want me to work on your stuff?"

"I do."

Relief flowed through him. He smiled and stepped back before the desire to find out what she was or wasn't wearing under her robe ruined all his noble intentions. He'd bet a million dollars it was nothing. "Then I'll be here by nine. Good night."

He made it down the stairs, outside, and was opening the door of his Land Rover when his phone vibrated in his pocket. He pulled it out to read the text.

Roxanna: *Did you ask Asher what my favorite flowers were?*

He slid into the driver's seat as he replied: *Yes. He immediately asked what I did to screw up already and wouldn't answer me until I told him. I didn't think that one through.*

Roxanna: *Of course he did, and no, you didn't.*

He closed his door as another one came through.

Roxanna: *I didn't say thank you. They're beautiful.*

He typed his reply, hesitated over the corny, cliché line, then hit send anyway: *Not as beautiful as you.*

Cliché it may be, but it was also true.

Roxanna: *Would you like a proper thank you for the flowers?*

His heart rate sped up as he recalled their kiss in her back room after she brought him coffee that morning.

Loyal: *I would not presume to ask for one, but if you're offering...*

Roxanna: *How long will it take to get your number-loving ass back up here?*

He was out of his vehicle and back at her door in record

time—and discovered he'd have won his bet about what she wasn't wearing under her robe.

Saturday night, Loyal pulled into his brother's driveway as big, fat snowflakes drifted down to dot the windshield. They were supposed to get up to three inches, though it was sure to all melt by the next day.

"Asher seemed better about everything today," Roxanna said as he turned off the engine and reached for the bottle of wine down at her feet. "Less...protective."

He understood the hope in her voice. She wanted this to go as smoothly as he did. "Maybe me asking about the flowers helped."

"Or he's going to use it against you."

"Against me, or us?"

She grinned as he hurried around to open her door. "You," she confirmed. "I'm like a sister to him, so he's gonna stand up for me."

He shuddered, his hand at the small of her back on their way to the door. "Don't ever say that again."

"What?"

"That you're like a sister. I *am* his brother, and the last thing I want to do is think of you like a sister. That's just..." He gave an emphatic shake of his head on their way to the door. "Ew."

She laughed as the front door opened to reveal Honor slipping on her winter coat. The cake baker stepped out onto the porch and took hold of Roxanna's arm to steer her back down to the sidewalk. "You have to come across the street with me."

Roxanna frowned back at Loyal as she asked, "Now? Why?"

"My wedding dress came in, and I'm dying to show someone. Asher is on the back patio grilling steaks, Loyal."

"It's snowing."

"Relax. We're not going to eat outside," she said.

He glanced at the door, then back at Honor urging Roxanna toward the driveway.

His future sister-in-law caught his look. "We won't be long. Promise."

"Divide and conquer," Roxanna warned him. "Be prepared."

Honor jerked her hand away from her. "Damn it. I always forget you can do that."

She smiled before arching her eyebrows at Loyal.

"Oh, go ahead." He forced a laugh past the tightness in his gut. "I can handle my own brother."

He watched them cross the street through the falling snow, short and tall, redhead and brunette, then turned back to make a face at the door. Blowing out a heavy sigh, he went inside, but kept his jacket on as he set the wine on the counter, grabbed a beer from the fridge, and made his way out to the back patio.

"Hey," he greeted when his younger brother turned at the sound of the sliding glass door.

Asher shot him a quick glance from the grill. "I wasn't sure you guys would show."

"We said we would." He twisted his cap off the bottle and tucked it into his pants pocket. After a long pull, he asked, "What's for dinner?"

"Steak."

He waited a few moments. "Just steak?"

"Of course not just steak," Asher groused. "Honor's got potatoes and some vegetable in the oven."

Silence fell again, and after Loyal downed about half his

beer in a couple swallows, he lowered his hand and said, "Can we just get this the fuck over with?"

His brother looked up from the grill, his dark hair dotted with snowflakes and drops of water from what had already melted. "You better not just be screwing around with her."

"I'm not."

"You sure about that?"

Loyal narrowed his gaze as annoyance surged through him. "You sure *you're* not jealous?"

"I'm sure," Asher replied calmly. "Maybe you're not nearly as bad as Merit, but I also know you're not looking for anything serious."

"Wasn't looking."

His brother's head jerked up, surprise evident on his face. "And now you are?"

He shrugged. He and his brothers were close, but they didn't usually talk about feelings. And while he thought he could be falling for Roxanna, he wasn't about to spill his guts to Asher two seconds before they all sat down to dinner.

"Rox has been through an awful lot with her family. I don't want you to hurt her if you suddenly decide this isn't for you."

"What if she hurts me?" he asked indignantly. "I take it you got no problem with that side of it?"

"She wouldn't hurt you intentionally."

"Neither would I her. Give me some fucking credit, man."

"You used to."

Sonofabitch, he had him there. He downed the rest of his beer. "I didn't understand I was hurting her at the time."

Asher gave a soft snort of disbelief.

"You know what, she and I have talked about all that already." Loyal blew out a silent sigh. On the one hand, he was pissed Asher was making such a big deal about him and Roxanna together. On the other, he had to admit he liked knowing someone had her back. Someone like his brother, who he knew was a hell of a good guy, and a good friend to her. And his family, who he did not doubt would be there for her no matter what.

"Listen, I know she's been through a lot. She told me all about her mother and family issues."

Asher's surprise was evident once again. "She did?"

"Yes. And I know we've done an about face these past few weeks, but I never really let myself see *her* these past six years. The situation with Lisa tainted everything."

"But suddenly you're just over it?"

"Basically, yeah." He reached up to rub the back of his neck, then brushed the snow from his hair. "I swear to you, Ash, I'm not just messing around with her. First of all, I wouldn't do that knowing she's your best friend, and second...well, now that I know her better, I can see she's pretty great, and I think I might be—"

The sound of the sliding glass door cut him off, and they both jerked around to see the women in the doorway.

"How are the steaks coming?" Honor asked in a cheerful voice.

"Almost done." Asher gave him an assessing look before turning back to the grill.

Loyal breathed a silent sigh of relief. He'd almost spilled his guts anyway. When his future sister-in-law stepped outside, he quickly traded places with her to join Roxanna inside.

"How'd you fare?" he asked in a low voice as he set his empty on the table and shrugged out of his jacket. When he went to hang it on the hooks by the front door, she trailed after him.

"Not too bad. She wanted to know if it was just fun or more serious."

That seemed to be the question of the week. Odd how

they'd had the exact conversation the previous morning, and yet he still found himself nervous as to her answer. "What'd you say?"

Roxanna shrugged when he faced her. "That we were seeing where things went."

He frowned slightly. In his mind they'd moved past that.

"What about you?"

He swiped his hand through his hair to disperse the melted snow, then shot a glance toward the kitchen where he could hear hushed voices. "Asher is worried I'm going to hurt you."

Her head tilted toward the right. "Are you?"

He hadn't expected that question. Although he didn't know why. It was a perfectly logical follow-up. "I will do everything in my power not to," he vowed quietly.

She smiled and stepped close to flatten her hand on his chest. "Then we're good. I don't care what Asher, or Honor, or anyone else thinks right now. We've been upfront with each other, so that's all that matters."

He caught her around the waist to tug her against him. "You're not only beautiful, you're pretty damn smart, too."

She smiled as he bent his head to capture her lips with his.

"Dinner's done," Asher bellowed.

Their mouths smiled against each other before they separated, and Loyal rested his hand at her back on their way to the table. He loved touching her any chance he got.

The meal was delicious, and after a couple of awkward moments when they first sat down, the tension eased. They didn't lack for lively conversation, and there was a lot of laughter to go along with a fair amount of ribbing. Honor particularly seemed to enjoy any embarrassing story he or Roxanna offered of Asher, even though his brother promised he'd make her pay for egging them on later.

When they were done, Loyal helped to clear the empty dinner plates, and then they all sipped on a second glass of wine while Honor dished up slices of her triple layer salted caramel chocolate cake.

It was absolute heaven, until about two seconds after his first bite when Asher asked, "So, Loyal, has Rox told you how many kids she wants?"

He nearly choked on his cake as Honor gave an indignant gasp and backhanded the jerk on the arm at the same time. "Asher! Seriously?"

"What?" he asked with fake innocence.

"You don't ask a question like that."

"Why not? You and I have had the conversation."

"Yeah—in *private*."

Loyal shot a glance at Roxanna to find her watching him, her cheeks stained red. Of course the kid conversation hadn't come up yet. And the best thing to do right now would be laugh it off, but as he ran his gaze over her features, he realized the idea of kids with her wasn't so alarming. The out-of-the-blue question had caught him off guard because he'd put thoughts of a family out of his mind after his last failed relationship, but a dark-haired, brown-eyed little mini-Roxanna could be totally doable.

With the other two still arguing why you shouldn't ask that question of couples who were newly dating, he asked in a low tone, "How many?"

Of course, his brother and fiancé would choose that moment to shut up.

Roxanna darted a look across the table, then her gaze met his and held. "Being an only child was lonely."

"So, at least two."

"I was thinking more like six."

Six?

212

One little number and he suddenly found it hard to draw in a breath.

Then again, six was not a little number when talking about kids. Being one of six siblings, he knew.

Hold up—six siblings?

His body flashed hot, then cold.

Because Grayson made number six. When had he started counting that guy in the mix?

He swallowed hard, scrambling to come up with a reply as a myriad of emotions whirled in his head and heart.

Then he noticed a slow smile curve Roxanna's mouth, and he suddenly saw the mischief lighting her eyes as a snort of laughter came from across the table. He shot Asher a glare and found him grinning like an idiot.

Loyal dropped his fork on the side of his plate and sat back in his chair as he looked from one to the other. "Oh, I see. That's how it's going to be?"

Asher lifted a shoulder as Roxanna reached over to teasingly nudge his thigh. Honor just shook her head, though he'd bet she was trying to hide a smile so she didn't encourage the two.

He shook his head as he scooped up his fork for a big bite of cake. Seeing the two best friends share a grin as he chewed, he pointed his fork at his future sister-in-law. "I think you and I need to form an alliance."

"Oh, hell yes, count me in. I've seen these two in action too many times now."

CHAPTER 26

$\mathcal{L}$oyal set one file aside on Roxanna's desk and picked up another. Over the past two weeks, he'd gone through most of her past accounting, and was now finishing up with the first year she'd opened the shop. He'd started to form a solid theory, but didn't want to say anything to her about it yet. He could still be wrong.

He hoped he was wrong—though it wasn't looking to go that way.

Yesterday, the whole situation had gotten him thinking about that psychic hotline scam from six years ago. He'd been able to deal with the financial loss, but that wasn't the point, and worse, he knew there were others who weren't so lucky. He'd filed a complaint against Spirit Guides Now, and the owner, Leander Tanner, with the better business bureau and law enforcement, but the guy had cleared out the offices and skipped town before any formal charges had been brought by the district attorney.

Curious to discover if anything had ever come of the situation, he'd looked up his past contact at the police department and called to see if Tanner had ever been caught and charged.

Detective Kushner had laughed when Loyal reminded him who he was and why he was calling. "This is a hell of a coincidence. Something came across my desk last week that brought that case back up. I can't give you any details, but I'm following a lead that might make the case. I'm waiting on a search warrant as we speak."

After giving his cell number for updates, Loyal had gone back to work on Roxanna's books. In the afternoon, he sent an email with the name of her former accountant to the P.I. he'd hired to check into Grayson back in May. He needed to know more about Mirela Rose before he could voice his suspicions.

More than once throughout the evening and again this morning, his mind returned to what the detective had said about following a new lead. Roxanna couldn't read him, but maybe she'd be able to intuit something if he told her about the case and gave her the guy's name?

All of a sudden, the idea that he fully accepted her abilities registered on his consciousness.

Whoa. When had that happened?

He sat back in the chair as he brushed his knuckles along the underside of his chin. Probably about the same time he couldn't keep his eyes off her each day and saw for himself the honest goodness in her heart as she interacted with her clients, customers, and friends. And even him.

She was so far from the person he'd thought all those years, he was ashamed to fully realize how closed minded he'd been. The other night, they'd rehashed everything one last time. After a back and forth forgiveness session, both agreed it was over and done, water under the bridge.

They'd settled into a routine, work during the day, dinners in or out, and spend the night either at the apartment upstairs, or occasionally, his hotel. Brunch at his parents' house the previous weekend had his mother beaming, and Merit making off-color remarks about their years of verbal foreplay. Roxanna didn't take his shit any more than Loyal did. He loved that she fit right in with his family—as she always had—and he began to envision a future with her.

With six little rugrats hanging all over both of them.

He smiled at the mental image and shook his head in wonder at the difference moving back to Colorado had made in his life. He'd gone from simply going through the motions, to being happy and looking forward to each day. The only source of discontent in his life now was Grayson, and even that had softened as he'd considered Roxanna's suggestion from a few weeks ago.

He was giving serious thought to offering the guy his own money for the foundation, but was waiting for some information from his lawyer as to how to set things up. After that, he'd see about meeting with his...brother to propose the idea.

Roxanna breezed into the room, her long hair loose over the pink sweater she'd paired with a floor-length, gauzy gray skirt and new suede ankle boots. The feminine combat boots would always be his favorite, but these were damn sexy, too. As always when she was near, his body went on alert.

"How's it going back here?" she asked.

"Slow."

She stepped behind the chair to massage his shoulders. "Are you sure you have to do all this?"

"I am."

He hung his head with a low groan as her magic fingers worked to release the tension in his neck. After longer than he would've asked for but wasn't about to tell her to stop, she smoothed her hands over his shoulders and leaned forward to slide them down the front of his chest while her breasts pressed against his back. Peppermint teased his senses as her warm lips caressed his neck just below his ear, sending a shiver down his spine and a surge of blood to his groin.

"I'm leaving for lunch with Mae and Honor in a few minutes. Are you sure you don't want me to bring you anything back?"

He reached up to grasp her hands with his. "Thank you, but I need a break soon anyway. A walk down to the coffee shop will be good."

"It's freezing out there."

"Good. I need to cool off now that you're getting me all hot and bothered with no hope of relief until later."

She nipped his earlobe. "I'd say I'm sorry, but I'm not."

"Witch."

Her husky laugh made his dick harden even more behind his zipper. Then he heard her inhale, and a soft hum vibrated against his skin. "God, I just love the way you smell."

"Roxanna," he groaned in warning.

Pulling one hand free, she turned his head enough to cover his mouth with hers, her tongue hot and sensual as it slid past his teeth to explore and seduce. He tried to spin the chair around so he could pull her onto his lap, but she stepped back out of reach with a knowing smile.

Tease.

"Tessa's got the front. I'll be back in an hour," she said over her shoulder while grabbing her coat on her way out.

"Have fun," he called just as her sexy ass sashayed out of sight.

He looked at the computer screen, then decided to take that walk to get a sandwich. Too bad Asher was away on a photo shoot for the morning, or he'd have asked him to join him.

A half-hour later, he walked back to Lift Your Spirit, keyed in the code for the rear entrance lockbox, and opened the door to find a uniformed officer standing in the open doorway leading into the shop.

Alarm sent his heart up into his throat. "What's going on? Is Roxanna okay?"

"Who are you?" the short, brunette woman asked.

"Loyal Diamond." He stepped forward to see past her, but she lifted a hand to keep him back. "What the hell is going on?"

"Kushner," the woman hollered over her shoulder. "Didn't you say you talked to a Diamond yesterday?"

Kushner? What the fuck?

Confusion laced with inexplicable dread as Detective Kushner stuck his bald head out of the back room of Lift Your Spirit and frowned at Loyal. "Let him through."

When he stepped past the woman officer, Loyal spotted Tessa sitting on the chair outside of Roxanna's reading room. The pregnant employee's green eyes were wide, and she lifted her hands and shoulders in an *I have no clue* gesture.

"Did you call Rox?" he asked in a low tone.

She shook her head. "They wouldn't let me."

"Mr. Diamond," the detective greeted, suspicion in his voice and expression. "What brings you here?"

"I'm doing some accounting work for the owner."

"Roxanna Kent?"

The disapproval in the man's tone when he said her name raised the hair on the back of Loyal's neck. "Yeah. Can someone please tell me what the hell is going on?"

Someone better answer soon. He sounded like a fucking broken record.

The detective thrust a slip of paper his way, and when he took it, the words *Search Warrant* flashed like a neon sign. As he skimmed the document, *Roxanna Kent*, *Lift Your Spirit*, and *Spirit Guides Now* all jumped out at him.

That dread in his stomach solidified into a heavy ball.

"I told you yesterday I was following a new lead. How long have you known Ms. Kent?"

He jerked his head up to stare at the guy. "She and my brother have been friends for the past six years. She and I have, ah, recently started dating."

Kushner's eyebrows rose. "Interesting."

"Not really." He glanced down at the wedding ring on the guy's finger, then looked at the search warrant again as he muttered, "It happens."

"She really lets you see her books?"

"Yeah. Why?"

"You come across anything out of the ordinary?"

Fuck. What was he supposed to say to that?

I'm not talking until my lawyer is present.

Only he wasn't the one being investigated.

"I only started helping her out a couple of weeks ago. Her previous accountant was a woman by the name of Mirela Rose."

A blond woman in plain clothes searching through one of Roxanna's file cabinets looked up at that name, and Loyal's neck tingled. She met his gaze for a brief second, shifted her pointed look to the detective beside him, then went back to searching.

"May I ask what exactly you're looking for?"

"You going to help us find it?"

Loyal fought to not clench his jaw in irritation and waited.

"Do you know when Ms. Kent will be back?"

"She's at lunch, so maybe a half-hour or so?"

"That's what I told them," Tessa chimed in from behind them.

The detective's lips thinned with his glance in her direction, then he returned his attention to Loyal. "Did you know your girlfriend used to operate Spirit Guides Now with Leander Tanner?"

His eyebrows rose in disbelief. "What? No way."

For good measure, he repeated the detective's words in his head, and again, had the same immediate reaction.

No fucking way she worked for that scammer—or with him for that matter.

Kushner gave him a grim smile. As the light from overhead glinted off his shiny scalp, Loyal read the pity in his eyes.

"They ran the hotline for a little over three years," the detective revealed. "She didn't open this shop until after the guy skipped town."

He frowned. "How come you didn't go after her then?"

"We didn't know who she was until last week. We got a complaint from a woman she defrauded for twelve-hundred dollars."

When he heard that number, that fucking dread ball in his stomach grew spikes. "How?"

"The woman who came to us said she paid her for a"—Kushner did air quotes—"séance, but when she arrived at her house, Ms. Kent told her she never received the check, and requested cash instead. Then a month later, the original check was cashed, and when she called to complain, Ms. Kent's phone number was disconnected."

"Roxanna doesn't do séances," Tessa said.

Took the words right out of his mouth. But the twelve-hundred dollars...

"That's just the tip of the iceberg," the detective warned. "All we need is one thing to connect her to the hotline, and we've got her."

Now Loyal's jaw clenched hard as he shook his head in denial. Two months ago, he might have believed this. Now? Nope. No fucking way.

He paced toward the register. Kushner barked at him not to touch anything, so he swung back around and leaned against the wall next to Tessa. The clock dragged on as they watched the search.

"Rox didn't do anything," Tessa muttered after a bit. "This is bullshit."

"I agree." In fact—he pulled his phone from his pocket.

Kushner immediately turned from the door. "Sorry, but no phone calls."

"Not even to my lawyer?"

The detective's eyes narrowed. "Why would you need a lawyer?"

"It's not for me. You've got the wrong person," he told the guy just as a loud exclamation came from out in the back hall. Roxanna was back.

"Oh my God." Fear rang in her voice. "What happened?"

"Which one of you is Roxanna Kent?" the officer outside asked.

"I am. Is everyone okay? Loyal? Tessa? Did something happen at the bakery?"

Honor and Mae's alarmed voices joined in until the officer spoke over all of them.

"No one is injured. Settle down. Ma'am, we need you to step inside. No, not you two. Stay out here."

Loyal caught a glimpse of Honor and Mae's confused expressions, but the moment Roxanna passed through the door, everything else faded.

Her frantic gaze met his, darted toward Tessa, then back to him. "Are you guys okay?"

See? This woman couldn't be who they thought she was. She cared too much about other people.

He loved her too much.

"We're fine," he assured her.

When they moved toward each other, the detective

stepped between them. Finally, Roxanna seemed to see the other people in her shop. Her dark eyebrows dipped down in a fierce frown as she leaned past Kushner to look into the back room. "What are they doing?"

"Remember that hotline that scammed my ex?" Loyal asked.

Her head whipped around and all the color drained from her face. Her wide eyes met his, full of fear. In that instant, he knew that she knew he'd found out. Exactly what, he didn't know, but the detective did, didn't he?

Seeing the guilt in her face...

His chest constricted so tight it hurt to breathe. He hadn't thought anything could be worse than being left at the altar, but he'd been wrong. He hadn't been in love with Lisa like he was with Roxanna. Lisa had left him, but she'd never really lied to him about who she was.

"Loyal," Roxanna said, her voice vibrating with remorse. "It's not what you think. I—"

He shook his head as even with his heart shattering into a million pieces, his first instinct was to protect her. "Shut up."

She reached her hand toward him. "Let me explain."

He gave another emphatic shake of his head.

"Got something," the blond in the back room called out. They all turned to see her holding a handful of papers in the air as she slammed the file cabinet shut.

"What is that?" Roxanna asked.

"The evidence we're looking for." The woman handed her find to Kushner, who scanned the top page, then flipped through the others. Loyal saw the Spirit Guides Now logo on the top of the front page, and what looked like a list of names, addresses, and phone numbers.

"What exactly is this?" Kushner asked Roxanna.

"It's an old client list."

The confirmation of her deceit in her own voice twisted Loyal's insides.

"It's yours?"

"Yes, but it's not what it looks like. I only have it because I offered them free readings when I first opened. All of them."

She looked at Loyal as she explained, her voice pleading for him to believe her. He was still trying to process the fact she'd run the scam hotline with Tanner. So much for being upfront with each other.

The detective handed off the papers while pulling his handcuffs from his utility belt. "Roxanna Kent, you are under arrest for fraud, and conspiracy to commit fraud."

Son-of-a-fucking-bitch.

CHAPTER 27

*O*h my God. What the hell is happening?

Roxanna's purse was taken from her, and a not so gentle hand grasped her shoulder to turn her around. While the officer instructed her to put her hands behind her back and shackled her wrists with cold, steel handcuffs, all she could think was, *I should've told him.*

Why had she never told him?

Because you were afraid he'd look at you exactly as he's looking at you right now.

The set of his jaw and betrayal in his eyes broke her heart. He hated her, and what he thought she'd done. She understood how he could think that, and yet anguish tore through her. "Loyal, please, if you would just listen to—"

"I said *shut up*, Roxanna," he snapped. "Don't say another fucking word."

The cold, brutal words were like a slap in the face, stunning her into silence. Tears burned her eyes as the bald officer instructed the others to finish the search, then steered her through her shop and out through the front doors to a waiting squad car.

The vehicle was half-way down the street before her brain shifted past the shock and fear of losing the man she loved to what the hell was going on. She hadn't done anything wrong. She tried to ask the officer exactly what fraud he thought she'd committed, but he only offered his actual title of detective, and nothing more.

Anxiety rose up, and she couldn't get the chaos in her mind to settle down so she could think straight. When they pulled into the station, the detective parked, then escorted her up the front steps and into the building. Men and women in uniform and suits gave cursory glances during her march of shame through the main area of the police station. They were used to this.

Civilians were easy to spot as they stared at her, their auras sparking with curiosity as they wondered what she'd done. She forced her chin up and stiffened her spine. She hadn't done anything wrong.

Except lie to Loyal.

That took a little wind out of her indignant sails as Detective Kushner took her into a stark room with a table, three basic metal chairs, and a mirror on one wall. She'd watched enough TV to assume it was two-way, and there were likely people watching her on the other side. The detective instructed her to sit on the side with the single chair, then he removed one cuff, threaded it through a bar on the table, and reattached it to her wrist.

She had a fleeting thought that he hadn't said anything about her right to remain silent, but before she could ask, he left her in the room.

Alone.

Feeling like a criminal.

The minutes ticked by one by one. First five, then fifteen, then half an hour, all as she vacillated between anger, confusion, and despair. At the hour mark, helpless tears welled up

225

and it took everything she had not to let them fall. She reined in her emotions and sat with her spine ramrod straight while she waited.

The room looked cold, felt cold, and yet they'd left her winter jacket on, so she was sweating. Probably more from fear of the unknown than being hot. Because she wasn't hot.

All it had taken was one glacial look from Loyal, and she'd been frozen from the inside out. He would never forgive her for this. He would hate her for life, and now she would not only lose him, but Asher and the rest of the family.

Her family. She'd begun to consider all the Diamonds hers after years with Asher, and even more so as she and Loyal grew close—as she fell in love with him for real, not just because of some childhood vision.

But should she really be surprised that he'd turn on her? If her own mother, father, and grandparents couldn't love her, why would she think anyone else would?

Another layer of ice encased her heart, and she was help-less to stop the hot tears that streaked down her cheeks.

CHAPTER 28

*L*oyal scrubbed his hands over his face, trying to make sense of everything as Mae, Honor, and Tessa talked over each other while discussing what they thought was going on and what they could do to help. Their voices kept derailing his thoughts, and finally he dropped his arms to his sides, fists clenched in frustration.

"I swear to God, you all need to just *shut up* so I can figure this out," he ground out.

Silence fell as they turned wide eyes to him.

"This isn't right. Something isn't adding up."

The moment the detective had taken Roxanna away in handcuffs, the moment he'd seen her being marched out of his life, Loyal knew she was innocent. He felt it deep in his soul that she was not the person the police thought she was. Shame mushroomed that he could've gone back to believing the worst about her even for a second.

But he didn't have time for that. His feelings didn't matter right now. He had to figure out what the fuck was up so he could help Roxanna.

"She didn't do it." Honor wore a ferocious frown as she glared at him as if daring him to argue.

"I know."

"Yeah, you better know." Her eyes widened for a brief moment, and she reached for her pocket. "I have to call Asher."

"Do that." He turned to the blond construction worker standing beside her. "Mae, I need you to call the law offices of Striker and Stowe. Tell them Loyal Diamond needs someone to meet me down at the police station ASAP. Tessa, you need to stay here and take care of whatever needs to be done for the shop when the police are finished."

They were still in the back, and Loyal fought his impatience as he paced to the door. "Is it possible for me to look at something on the computer?" he asked.

The officer seated in the desk chair shook his head. "Sorry man, it's evidence."

"Can you at least look up a file for me?" He lifted his hands in supplication. "I won't touch anything."

The officer looked askance at the blond woman who'd seemed so excited about finding the client list. The blond gave a slight shoulder shrug and nod, but she walked over to watch exactly what Loyal wanted the other officer bring up on the computer.

He gave the sign-in information and navigated the guy into the accounting program.

"What are we looking at?" the blond asked as she leaned closer to view the screen.

"Bookings and corresponding payments for the first year Ms. Kent was in business here at Lift Your Spirit."

"There are no payments for more than half of them."

"Exactly."

"Then she took cash."

He shook his head. "Cash, check, or credit is clearly indicated. She has no reason to mark some and not others. She said she had the list to offer them comp readings. Why would she do that if she was one of the scammers?"

The blond woman glanced at him, her gaze narrowed with speculation. "Why are you advocating *for* her. Weren't you one of the original complainants from six years ago?"

"Yes. But you guys have the wrong person. Roxanna wouldn't scam people."

The moment the words were out of his mouth, something in his brain clicked. Dread washed over him with sickening clarity, and he had to consciously fight to keep his expression impassive.

He summoned a polite smile and softened his tone as he indicated the screen. "Is it possible for me to get a printed copy of that? You're going to have the computer, and now you have the sign-in information, so it's not like I'm taking anything you won't still have."

She hesitated, but then relented with another terse nod.

Loyal grabbed the papers hot off the printer and met Honor in front of the reading room beads. "I'm going to the police station."

"I'm coming with you," she said. "Asher's going to meet us there."

"Gavin Stowe said he's on the way, too," Mae advised.

"Thank you." He thrust the printout in his hand at Tessa. "Look at these names. Do you recognize any of them?"

Her gaze skimmed the top page. "This is from six years ago. I didn't work here then."

"I just need to know if any of those people still come to Roxanna for readings?"

She looked a little closer. "Yeah. There's a handful of people here that are regulars."

"Mark them for me. Hurry. We need to get going."

Two minutes later, he and Honor were out the door. He drove his Land Rover while she perused the list.

"What are you thinking?" she asked.

He didn't want to say it out loud, but there was no way to avoid it. "It's her mother."

"What?"

Honor's confusion told him Roxanna probably didn't talk about the woman to many people. He didn't blame her. The bitch wasn't worth a second of her daughter's time or consideration.

Only now, Roxanna was going to be forced to deal with her again, however indirectly. He hated what it might do to her.

"Roxanna's parents named her after her mother. They share the same exact name."

Honor's eyebrows rose in surprise.

"And she said they look very much alike. I would imagine the woman has used that to her advantage over the years. Plus, as her mother, she probably knows Rox's social, and other information that would let her gain access to stuff she shouldn't."

"Her own *mom*?" Incredulity dripped from the words.

"The woman abandoned the family when she was nine, but showed back up in her life when she was in college. Rox had suppressed who she was for years, trying to make her family happy, but when she reconnected with her mother, the woman helped her to accept who she was and got her to start using her psychic abilities again."

"Ah—for the hotline," Honor guessed.

"Yeah, I think so." Loyal made a left turn and the station was right ahead. "But she was just using her. She said her mom left town abruptly after clearing out her savings of over ten thousand dollars."

"Holy shit. What a bitch."

"Yeah. I think *she's* the one who worked with Tanner. And I think all the free readings when Rox opened the shop was her way of trying to make up for what her mother did. I was going to call some of her clients from back then that still go to her now, and see what their stories are for the hotline, and now Roxanna."

"That could help. Not to mention, common sense says if she'd been the one running the hotline scam, the last thing she'd do is stay in town and open a shop under her own name."

"Exactly."

Loyal made the final turn into the station lot to park, and took the papers from Honor as they headed inside. At the door, he stepped aside for her and an older lady who'd walked up behind them to enter first.

"Hey man, wait up."

Loyal turned and saw Asher jogging across the lot. Honor moved back outside meet his brother on the sidewalk, so he continued inside in time to hear the lady ahead of them ask the front desk officer for Detective Kushner.

"He asked me to come down and identify the woman who stole from me."

Loyal's pulse skipped before racing at warp-speed. That was too much of a coincidence.

He moved closer as the officer requested her name, then instructed her to wait right there. Martha Rowen looked to be about in her mid-sixties, her clothes likely designer to go with her Coach handbag, her rich auburn hair stylish and obviously—though expertly—colored.

Hearing Honor and Asher behind them, he discreetly motioned them to stay back. Asher frowned and took another step. Loyal gave a fierce head shake, then smiled with sympathy when the woman at the counter glanced his way.

"Hi. Sorry, I couldn't help but overhear. Hope you get your money back."

"It's not the money." She sniffed with disdain. "She preyed on my grief, promising me she'd be able to talk to my Jack one last time."

The séance woman.

"I'm sorry," he said again. "Was Jack your husband?"

"My son. Not only did I not get to talk to him, but she charged me twice."

He shook his head. "That's terrible. Why would she charge you twice?"

"I sent her a check, but when she showed up at my house for the…ah, ceremony…" She paused, shooting him a quick glance as if afraid he'd judge. He offered an encouraging smile and she continued. "She said she didn't receive the check and insisted I pay her cash right there before Jack's spirit crossed over. Weeks later, she cashed the check she said had been lost. I had forgotten to cancel it."

"How much was it?"

The woman looked away with a grimace. "Twelve hundred dollars."

Roxanna's mysterious check. Had her mother instructed the woman to send it to the shop, or had it been a mix-up?

Detective Kushner approached the counter, giving Loyal a hard look before turning to the lady. "Mrs. Rowen, thank you for coming in. If you will please come with me?"

"I'd like to come with as well," Loyal said.

The bald detective gave him a stern look while holding open the half-door for the woman to pass through. "There's no need."

"Please." He lifted the papers. "I have information you'll find enlightening, and after Mrs. Rowen says her piece, I think we can clear some things up."

He drew in a deep breath, then blew it out in a huff. "Fine.

But you will keep your mouth shut until I say you can speak, understand? Do *not* interfere or you'll be out so fast your head will spin."

Loyal nodded solemnly, before turning to his brother and Honor as he followed Mrs. Rowen. "Both of you fill Gavin in when he gets here, please."

"Will do," Asher promised as Honor nodded.

When they reached the room where Roxanna was being held, one look at her through the shaded glass and Loyal's chest constricted in pain. Her loneliness was palpable. He wanted to rip the door off the hinges and pull her into his arms and tell her she'd never be alone again. Seeing the cuffs still on her slender wrists made his fists clench with anger.

All of a sudden, she stiffened and swiveled her face toward the glass. Beside him, Mrs. Rowen sucked in a soft breath.

"Is that her?" Detective Kushner asked.

Loyal held his breath as he waited for her answer.

CHAPTER 29

*R*oxanna's breath shallowed out when a prickle along the nape of her neck told her she was no longer alone. No one had entered the room, so she stiffened her spine and turned her head toward the mirror.

A long minute later, the door opened and her heart lurched hard when she saw Loyal with Detective Kushner and an older lady.

He's here! her heart sang.

But he wasn't smiling. In fact, his eyes were dark and deadly serious, almost pitying, and she couldn't get a read on what that meant. Gulping against a surge of anxiety, she did her best to keep breathing so she wouldn't pass out while they filed into the room.

"Ms. Kent," Detective Kushner barked. "Do you know this woman?"

She looked from him, to the well-dressed, auburn-haired woman, to Loyal. His *"Don't say another fucking word,"* echoed in her head. Except when her eyes met his, he gave her a brief nod as if to say it was okay to answer.

Looking back at the lady, she studied her features care-

234

fully, noting a sad tinge of grief clouding her aura. "I don't recall ever meeting you. I'm sorry if we've met and I've forgotten."

"You have nothing to be sorry for, dear." The lady turned back to the detective. "I told you it's not her. They look alike, but the woman who performed my séance was much older."

The words sank in, and the resulting flash of heat left Roxanna sick to her stomach.

Her mother. Oh my God, how had she not put it together before?

Because I never expected to hear from Mom again.

Well, wasn't this just the shittiest way to reconnect? Loyal's sympathetic expression told her he'd come to the same conclusion. Her heart warmed with a tiny spark of hope, but she squashed it down.

"I don't do séances," she said quietly.

"I told you," Loyal said.

"Zip it, or you're out of here." The detective shot him a glare, then turned back to Roxanna. "Did you cash her check for twelve-hundred dollars?"

Another wave of nausea hit, and she felt herself blanch as her gaze bounced from Loyal to the woman. Shame bubbled up as she met her light blue eyes. All she could do was be honest. "What's your name?"

"Martha Rowen."

She nodded with recognition. Meeting the detective's gaze, she said, "Yes, the check was deposited in my account. It shouldn't have been, because I wasn't sure what it was for when it arrived in the mail. I'd intended to follow up on it, but I was dealing with an apartment fire and it slipped through the cracks." She met Mrs. Rowen's gaze once more. "The money is set aside until I knew what it was for. I will return it to you, and I apologize you've had to deal with this."

The woman nodded, no malice in her eyes. "These things happen. I understand."

Detective Kushner gaped at her, then blew out a rough sigh. Loyal lifted the papers he'd been holding at his side, his eyebrows raised in question. Before the man could respond, an officer and a blond man in a sharp, navy blue suit and red tie filled the doorway.

"Ms. Kent's lawyer is here."

The guy in the suit shook hands with Loyal, and then said, "I'd like a moment alone with my client, please."

Mrs. Rowen turned to leave, but quickly spun back and leaned over the table to grasp Roxanna's hand. "She's your mother, isn't she?" she asked softly. Sympathetically.

The sting of tears was almost instantaneous. She nodded as she bit her bottom lip to stop it from quivering.

"I'm so sorry, dear. I know I don't know you, but I can't believe you would deserve that."

A bright, glowing light suddenly appeared out of nowhere to surround the woman. Roxanna stiffened slightly, her hand instinctively grasping for Martha's. She'd never seen anything like it before in her life.

No one else gave any indication of seeing anything unusual, not even when a second light joined the first. The wedding ring on the woman's left hand warmed against Roxanna's skin. When Martha shifted to leave, Roxanna held firm to her hand. The older woman's blue eyes narrowed in question.

Achingly aware of the others in the room, she leaned forward to speak softly. "You've lost two people very close to you. Who else has passed besides your husband?"

The woman's eyes widened, then flooded with tears. "My son," she choked out. "Jack."

The lights around her pulsed, and Roxanna received a

soft, electric jolt through her body. Martha's sharp gasp said she'd felt it, too.

Giving the older woman's hand a reassuring squeeze, she said, "They're together. They're here to let you know they're okay, and they love you."

She didn't know how she knew it, but she did.

The lights pulsed again, undulating, creating ripples of energy that washed over her in the most amazing sensations.

The woman's free hand rose to her trembling lips as tears spilled over her lashes. "Oh my Lord, I can feel them." The handcuffs rattled against the metal bar as she jiggled Roxanna's hand with excitement. "I can feel them. Thank you. Thank you so very much."

As the energy waves eased, Roxanna gave her a tremulous smile, and they each let go. When the narrow-eyed detective extended a hand for her to precede him from the room, Mrs. Rowan's aura was a clear, beautiful pink. A tiny measure of peace nestled in Roxanna's heart. While she absolutely hated what her mother had done, in this moment, she was grateful to have been able to release the grief of the woman her mother had swindled.

Loyal stayed behind with the lawyer, but she was having a hard time finding the courage to look at him. She had her hope of why he was here, at the police station, in this room, with a lawyer he'd clearly gotten for her. But she was terrified of allowing that hope to blossom. She'd worked for the very people who'd scammed him and gotten him dumped at the altar. Cost him thousands of dollars. Left him humiliated. How could he ever forgive her?

"Roxanna."

His low voice compelled her to lift her head, and the look in his eyes nearly stopped her heart.

"It's going to be okay."

CHAPTER 30

*A*little over three hours later, Loyal walked Roxanna out to the waiting area a free woman. The moment she thanked Gavin Stowe and the lawyer left, Asher and Honor smothered her with hugs right there in the police station.

He was dying to hold her in his arms, but once she was there, he wasn't going to want to let go for a long time, so he was biding his time until they got home.

"It's over. For me at least," she was saying. "Between what Loyal brought, and everything I told them from when I worked at the hotline, they've cleared me with the condition I testify when my mom and Leander Tanner are caught."

"You going to be okay with that?" Asher voiced the concern Loyal himself had.

"I am. Or I will be." Roxanna lifted her hands up in a helpless gesture. "She can't keep doing what she's doing. If she hasn't already, she could ruin someone's life. Messing with their emotions when they're grieving and vulnerable so she can scam them out of money is wrong. I have to do what I can to stop her."

238

Loyal's chest swelled with pride. If her ungrateful grand-parents could see her now. She was nothing like her selfish, self-centered mother. She was kind and honest, gentle and compassionate, *good* and beautiful.

"And you know how I could never get my accounts to balance out?" she asked Asher. "Loyal figured out Mirela was skimming, and come to find out, she's a distant cousin of my mother's."

"You think your mom was part of that, too?"

"I don't doubt it for one second." She frowned, then quickly glanced around the station. It was busy and loud, and dingier than before now that darkness had fallen outside. "Anyway, do you guys mind if we get out of here? I've had enough of this place to last me a lifetime."

"Do you need anything?" Honor asked.

"I just want to go home and go to bed."

Loyal didn't even think of sex as he caught Asher's glance and stepped up to rest his hand at the small of her back with a nod to his brother, indicating he'd take her home. She thanked them for being there, and then they said their goodbyes and parted ways in the brightly lit parking lot.

She was quiet as he held the passenger door of his Land Rover open for her. She slipped inside, but he paused before closing it.

"Roxanna." His voice graveled out, and he had to clear his throat to start again. "Back at the shop...I'm sorry I doubted you."

"Loyal, don't. I don't blame you," she said softly, still not looking at him. "How could I? It looked bad, especially since I hadn't told you. I hadn't even told Asher."

"It was only for a moment, and then I knew as soon as you were gone you couldn't do what they were accusing you of, but I am still so damn sorry. And telling you to shut-up—I didn't want you to say anything they could twist and use against you."

She stared straight ahead, her gaze on the police station through the windshield. "I don't really want to talk about this here. Please."

He frowned at the dejection in her voice, but decided not to push it. She was exhausted and emotionally drained, and the least he could do was get her home so she could recover and regroup.

Once out of the lot, she remained quiet, and his gut clenched at the gaping hole that seemed to be widening between them. He needed to fix this, but didn't know what else to say to make it better.

"What is it about me that my own mother can't love me?"

At her soft, anguished whisper, he glanced over to see her staring out the passenger side window. The light from the dashboard glinted off the wetness on her face, and a golf-ball sized lump lodged in his throat.

Her fucking mother. No, make that her whole fucking *family.*

Loyal swerved over to the side of the road and threw the Rover in park. Roxanna's head swung toward him in surprise as he unlatched his seatbelt to face her. His heart cracked at the sight of her tear-streaked cheeks.

"Shit." Her head ducked as she reached up with trembling hands to wipe at the moisture. "I didn't mean to say that out loud."

"I love you."

She jerked her head back up, her eyes wide.

"Even when I didn't want to like you, I was drawn to you from the second we met. At first I fought it because I was engaged, after that, I fought it for all the wrong reasons, until the night of the fire. Maybe even for a little bit after, but the truth of it is, as soon as I caught one glimpse of the woman you are instead of who I *thought* you were, I was done for. I couldn't *not* love you."

Her cheeks were wet again, and he unfastened and got her seatbelt out of the way before cupping her face with both hands. He intended to swipe the new tears from her cheeks with his thumbs, but as her luminous gaze stayed with his, he instead leaned down to kiss them away while his own eyes stung.

"Listen to me, Roxanna, and believe every word I say. *You* are not the problem. Your mother is. She's the selfish one who can't love anyone but herself. She doesn't deserve someone as wonderful as you in her life." He moved his lips to her other cheek. "Hell, I probably don't, either, but I'm going to do my best to earn the privilege of having you in my life every day."

Realizing she'd been dead silent since he said, *"I love you,"* he experienced a moment of panic.

"If you'll have me, that is."

Her head ducked again, and the next thing he knew, she burst into loud, gasping sobs and sagged into his arms. He held her tight against his chest, rocking slightly as he smoothed her hair, until the sobs became sniffles, then hiccups, and finally there was silence in the dark cab.

She flattened one hand on his chest, sliding it until her palm covered where his heart thumped in his chest.

"I love you, too."

The whispered words made his heartbeat speed up, and her fingers flexed lightly against his wet shirt. He wanted to tilt her head up to his, but she was still tucked in pretty tight and not moving.

"When I was younger, I had a vision that the true love of my life would be Loyal and true."

He gave a tiny, involuntary head-jerk. "Seriously?"

"I don't joke about visions, Loyal."

He grinned as he recalled saying something similar to her about numbers. His grin widened when he realized she was teasing him. The tightness in his chest shifted, and he suddenly knew they were going to be okay.

"When we were first introduced and I heard your name, I thought it was fate," she continued. "I was also young, and foolish, and you were—"

"An ass."

"Engaged. And then you weren't, but yes, you were an ass, too. As time went on and things didn't change, I knew I needed to get over you and move on, but my heart never quite got on board with my head."

"I love your heart," he murmured. He didn't apologize for being a jerk again. They'd agreed that was in the past.

She finally pushed away from his chest far enough to see his face in the dim light of the dash. "And then you moved home. The morning after the fire is when I truly got my first glimpse of you. Not the wounded man afraid to believe, but the loyal and true man you are in here." Her palm moved over his heart. "You are beautiful and amazing, and I do love you with all my heart."

The sting in his eyes returned, and he blinked hard while giving a self-conscious sniff. "Well, now you know what can make me cry."

"I'd much rather make you laugh."

She reached up to wipe his tears, then leaned in to give him the sweetest, most wonderful kiss he'd ever experienced. Nothing but goodness and love.

"Thank you," she murmured against his mouth. "For coming for me. For believing in me. For...loving me."

He cupped the back of her head and whispered, "Always," before sealing his vow for all three with his own kiss of pure love.

EPILOGUE

On a bright, sunny Saturday in mid-January, Roxanna and Honor held a joint grand re-opening/opening for Lift Your Spirit and Honor's new specialty cake shop, Must Love Frosting. The morning was a smashing success, crazy busy, but filled with the love and laughter of family and friends, and a whole lot of customers.

Senator Diamond and Janine flew back from Washington D.C. to attend the event, and at one point, Roxanna found herself surrounded by almost the entire Diamond family —*her* family.

With Loyal's help, she'd come to accept not only would she never receive what she'd always wanted from her mother, but the fact she no longer *needed* anything from her to feel worthy of love. Loyal, Asher, and the rest of them more than made up for her sorry-ass side, and Honor and Mae were a whole other kind of family she'd come to cherish.

Before noon, she was able to hug Martha Rowen, and buy her guardian angel driver Leonard from the night of the fire a dozen cupcakes to take home for him and his granddaugh-

243

ter. Loyal shook the man's hand and thanked him for saving her from walking in the cold that night.

There was a fun moment when Mae introduced Merit to Ian, and Merit realized the 'man' he'd been jealous of the past couple of months was her six-year-old son. Based on the guy's open *no single moms* rule, Roxanna fully expected Merit to lay off the flirting after that. The surprise came when he and Ian hit it off like best buds.

On a mid-afternoon trip through the store to offer cake and coffee samples and see if customers had questions, she spotted Loyal leaning against the wall behind the register, cell phone in hand, brow furrowed. She'd started sensing more with him the past couple of months, his moods and feelings, though she wasn't sure it was psychic reading so much as being attuned to the man she loved.

Setting her tray down on the counter, she sidled up beside him. "Everything okay?"

"Just trying to word this text to my brother."

She lifted her gaze to his. Asher and Merit were both over on the bakery side. Which meant the only brother he'd need to text was Grayson.

"What are you texting him for?"

"I'm going to offer him money for the foundation."

"Finally?" It had been almost two months since she'd first suggested he use his own money.

He blew out a breath. "Yeah. It took a little longer to sort out the details than I expected. Plus my lawyer said it was best to wait for the new year."

"Okay, but now it's all set, right?"

"Yes."

"Then why are you frowning?"

"Because it's not going to *only* be my money. I'm adding mine to Dad's."

Comprehension dawned, and she smiled. "You're taking the CFO position."

"Yeah. Grayson's going to be pissed."

"So maybe it's better you do it in person."

He made a face. "He's still going to be pissed."

"He'll get over it," she predicted with confidence. "Especially when he realizes he can help twice as many people with twice as much money."

"I hope you're right."

"Grayson might be bull-headed"—*like you can be*—"but he isn't stupid."

Loyal shrugged as his lips twisted with a slight smirk. She smacked him on the arm, leaned in for a two second kiss that may have stretched to five—okay, seven—then stepped away to pick up her tray.

"Roxanna."

She heard the need in his voice, and her panties were instantly wet. She arched him a look over her shoulder as she moved far enough away to avoid the temptation to jump him.

Chin dipped low to his chest, he gave her a devilishly sexy look through his lashes and a little jerk of his head toward her reading room.

Eyes wide, she darted a look around the busy store and shook her head.

He raised his eyebrows.

She shook her head more emphatically. No way was she going to have sex right there with people in her store. The fact that her buttoned-up accountant wanted to was almost as shocking. And a major turn on, too.

"Later," she promised huskily before walking away.

She couldn't believe he'd been serious. As she emptied her tray twice over the next thirty or so minutes, she imagined sneaking into the back room. It was way too crazy to contemplate. He definitely hadn't been serious.

Her phone buzzed in her pocket and she smiled when she saw who'd texted.

Loyal: *It's thirty-seven minutes later.*

Roxanna snuck glances around the shop as she replied: *Stop it. Where are you?*

Loyal: *Waiting.*

She frowned toward the back and saw the three lines of beads on one side of the door sway the tiniest bit. He *was* serious.

Forbidden excitement skyrocketed her pulse.

She hadn't scheduled any readings that day, so the lights were off, and there was no reason for anyone to go in the room. If they were quiet, no one would know.

Oh my God, she was considering it.

She did a quick scan of the shop and saw customers had thinned out during the past few minutes. Tessa and Darcy were both working the full day, and were currently chatting at the coffee station, taking a break while they could.

Loyal: *5 minutes. 1 orgasm for each of us. Let's do this.*

Oh my God, she was doing this.

Roxanna sucked in a shallow breath and willed her heart rate to slow down as she approached the girls. "You guys mind if I take a quick ten minute break? I just need a few minutes of quiet in the back to recharge."

"Go ahead. I got the register," Tessa agreed before they waved her along and continued their conversation. No one else paid her any mind as she slipped through the beads into the dim room.

Loyal grasped her arm, spun her around, and pressed her up against the wall in the darkest corner away from the door. He whispered a soft, *"Shh,"* to quiet her over-excited gasp, then covered her mouth with his.

As his tongue dueled with hers, she fumbled between them to undo his belt and push his pants down enough to free his erection. He lifted her long skirt, and in one swift jerk, ripped her thong right off. Her eyes went wide as her heart jolted in her chest.

"*Loyal!*" she whisper-shouted, even though it might be the hottest thing he'd ever done.

"Five minutes," he muttered nearly soundlessly against her mouth, hoisting her up to wrap her legs around his waist as he entered her in one stroke. "No time."

Her fingers clenched in his hair at the delicious sensation of him filling her up. "I told the girls I was taking ten."

He stilled for a moment. "Well, damn. Wish I'd known that."

She rolled her eyes, then had to bite back a moan when he began to thrust into her. It was quick and dirty, but he reached between them to make sure she came with him and muffled her involuntary cry of release before his spent weight pinned her to the wall.

"Love you, witch," he whispered against the side of her neck.

"Love you, too."

And in less than ten minutes, she was back out on the floor with a secret the two of them shared through hot, steamy, breath-stealing glances the rest of the day.

After a jam-packed morning and afternoon, there were still enough customers to keep busy until closing at six p.m. Employees and family on both sides helped with clean-up before kicking back with coffee or wine and slices of pizza Roxanna and Honor ordered for dinner. The whole day had been filled with sweets and caffeine, so more substantial sustenance was required.

Slowly people began trickling out, saying their goodbyes as thank you's were called back, until by nine-fifteen, it was just Honor and Asher, and Loyal and Roxanna, sipping wine at one of the café tables on Must Love Frosting's side.

When Loyal noticed Roxanna's glass was empty, he leaned back in his chair with a barely fabricated yawn. "We should probably get going." He rose and pulled out her chair. "Tomorrow morning will be here soon enough, and Rox has some numbers for me to look at yet tonight."

She grinned at him, and the way her cheeks turned pink got his blood pumping faster. From the corner of his eye, he saw Honor look up from her plate with wide eyes and a grin.

"That's your code word!"

"What?" Roxanna tried to play it off. "We don't have a code word."

"Ours is cake."

Asher shot his fiancé an all-suffering sigh. "Butter Cream, you defeat the whole purpose of a code word if you tell people."

"You guys also use frosting," Loyal said.

"Whatever," Asher groused. "Lock the damn door behind you. Your ass is as white as Robert's."

Loyal didn't feel one bit sorry for his brother for catching them in Roxanna's reading room last week. "Maybe you should stop walking in where you're not supposed to be."

"Maybe people should stop doing *number stuff* where they're not supposed to."

"Right. Because you've never had *cake* anywhere but the bedroom."

"All right, boys," Honor mediated with a laugh.

Roxanna grinned at her, then hooked her arm with Loyal's. Pressed against his side, the heat of his body had her recalling their tryst in the reading room earlier. She squeezed his bicep and pulled him toward the sliding glass pocket doors connecting the two shops. "They can have their cake wherever they want, and we'll do our numbers wherever we want."

Once on their side, she closed the doors, flipped the lock, then knocked on the glass for Asher's attention. When he glanced over, she gave him a thumbs up and a grin. He rolled his eyes, but a second later, she saw his aura flare with red sparkles as he watched his fiancé heading into the back kitchen.

"A hundred bucks says they're going to have cake in the kitchen right now," Loyal predicted from behind her.

Yep. Ace was already on his feet and chasing after her.

Roxanna let her shoulder brush against Loyal's chest as she walked past to flip off the lights over their side of the café area. A glance over her shoulder caught him watching her every move as he slowly paced after her.

As her pulse sped up, she reached to strip off her sweater on her way to the reading room. "What number are we working on tonight?"

"Five."

Oh boy.

For someone who'd never liked numbers, she positively *loved* them now. Almost as much as she loved him.

Thank you for reading!

I end up falling in love with all my characters and books, but I gotta tell you, Loyal and Roxanna's story was the most fun I've had writing in a couple of years. (Since CONNED.) Something about this couple just clicked and the words flowed so smoothly, it was amazing. I hope it came through for you as a reader, and if it did, I would be so very grateful if you'd leave a review for *Love Loyal and True* where you purchased the book, or at a favorite retailer.

How can you make sure you never miss a new book? JOIN my Newsletter and here's what you get:

*FREE bonus books
*New release announcements
*what's going on in my writer's life
*exclusive first-look bonus content
*cover reveals
*special sales

http://smarturl.it/WebSJNNewsletter

FREE reads!
Romantic suspense & Contemporary Romance
with heartwarming Happily Ever Afters
Sign up for my newsletter today!

Next up in the **Must Love Diamonds Series** is *Love You, Baby*.

"My name is Merit, but you can call me handsome."

Cocky, sexy playboy? Check
One night of hot passion? Check
Pregnancy test two months later? Positive

Single mother Mae Lockhart ghosted her best friend's new brother-in-law after the wedding, because no way in hell was she going to let herself fall for another irresponsible playboy. Thanks to her bad luck, ignoring him is no longer an option.

Merit Diamond hates that his family doesn't respect him, but it's always been easier to bolster a bad boy rep than try to measure up to his successful siblings and risk failure. Then one ordinary Sunday, his dad cuts him off without a penny and the woman who's been haunting his dreams shows up on his doorstep to tell him he's going to be a father.

Now he has seven months to get his shit together and earn Mae's respect. Somehow he must convince her he can not only be a good dad, but the one man she can trust her heart to for the rest of her life.

Chapter 1

One little decision can change your life.

A wrong decision. A stupid decision.

A definitely not little decision.

Mae Lockhart stared at the two pink lines on her home pregnancy test and couldn't believe she'd been so stupid. Again.

Her downfall this time? A guy named Merit.

Upon their introduction the night his father had been elected to the United States Senate, she'd lifted her eyebrows to help hide the fact the man had taken her breath away from the moment she'd laid eyes on him.

"Yes, my name is Merit," he confirmed with a sexy grin. *"But you can call me Handsome."*

She laughed. "How many times have you used that line?"

"Just a few."

Yeah, a few hundred, she'd guess. "And how often does it work?"

"Every time."

And what had she done? She'd proved him right the night her best friend and his brother got married two months ago. As they waved the couple off in the groom's vintage '69 Camaro with the obligatory Just Married decorations, she'd been overcome with giddiness—and maybe a tad too much champagne—and turned a sultry grin up to the tall, dark groomsman.

"So, Handsome, what are your plans for the rest of the night?"

Because she'd had a babysitter for twelve more hours and wasn't about to give up her opportunity for adult freedom only fifteen minutes after midnight. Not to mention, he wasn't merely handsome, he was hot as hell in that tuxedo, could charm the panties off a nun, and those gorgeous golden-brown eyes of his promised more fun than she'd had in seven years.

Actually, seven-plus long, celibate years.

Sober, responsible, conservative Mae blinked against the sting of tears as she looked at the pink lines again. "One night of fun," she whispered, "for nine months of pregnancy and eighteen years of—"

"Mom! Hurry up! I gotta pee."

Mae jumped as her six year old son's fist pounding on the door underscored his plea. She hurried to stuff the test and wrappers back in the box as she rose from the toilet. "One sec, Ian. I'll be right out."

She buried the pregnancy test box in the waste basket, then flushed and washed her hands so she could splash cold water on her face.

"Mooommm."

Mae took a breath and opened the door to find him dancing from foot to foot. "Morning, Scoob."

She stepped aside as he rushed past, then pulled the door mostly closed behind her when she stepped into the hall. For a moment, she leaned against the wall, heart thumping hard at the thought of adding a baby to their duo. For six years— seven in two weeks—it had just been the two of them against the world.

What would Ian say when she told him? Would he be happy he was going to become a big brother? Or would he be upset?

No. He'd be happy. That's just the kind of awesome kid he

255

was. The kind of kid she'd never once regretted a day in her life.

She tilted her head toward the cracked door to ask, "What do you think? Pancakes or eggs this morning?"

"You said we could have muffins," he called back. "Remember?"

That's right, she'd bought a pack of four at the store yesterday. "I forgot."

The toilet flushed and then he opened the door. "Geez, mom, how could you forget?"

Mae pointed toward the sink. "Wash."

He huffed out a sigh, but turned back to do as she said.

"I've got a lot on my mind," she answered his question.

"You always say that," he grumbled.

"Because I always do. You're up extra early this morning."

"It's Friday Fun Day at school today."

He had that tone again. How could she forget Friday Fun Day before the 4th of July?

Because she truly did have a lot on her mind. Monday she was starting construction on Shelby Diamond's vet clinic, between now and then she had to fix the lawn mower and cut her six-inch tall grass to avoid more dirty looks from her neighbors, and she had to make a casserole for the holiday picnic at her brother's house tomorrow. Not to mention dishes and laundry both needed to be washed, the house cleaned, bills paid, paperwork filed, and—

I am pregnant!

A rush of panic had her drawing in a steadying breath. "Brush your teeth and get dressed, bud. You can watch Scooby Doo while you eat breakfast."

"*Yes.*" He grabbed his toothbrush with a grin, always thrilled when she let him watch his favorite cartoon while she got ready.

She narrowed her eyes at his reflection in the mirror.

Come to think of it, this was the third morning in a row he'd gotten up before she'd had a chance to take her shower. Little smarty pants was working her. Being it was summer school, she decided to let it slide.

"Make sure that toilet seat goes down."

She ruffled his hair before going to her room for a clean Lockhart Construction logo T-shirt and jeans. The TV blared to life as she returned to their one bathroom in their little two bedroom home. While she showered, dressed, and applied minimal make-up, her mind whirled like crazy and her stomach balled up in a tight knot, threatening to reactivate her earlier nausea.

Now she knew it was morning sickness, not just a stomach bug. And knowing she was pregnant also explained her bouts of dizziness the past couple of weeks. She hadn't experienced either while pregnant with Ian.

Speaking of which, she couldn't help but think about the last time she'd been in this situation almost eight years ago. Things had been so different, and yet, they were so damn similar. She'd been all alone, broke, and determined to love her child even if his father wanted nothing to do with them. She might not be broke anymore, but she was still single, and she would love this baby even if its father wanted nothing to do with them.

Her pulse skipped at the thought of telling Merit Diamond she was pregnant with his baby. Hell, it skipped more than a few beats at the thought of telling her best friend she was pregnant with her new brother-in-law's baby. She hadn't told Honor about her hook-up the night of her and Asher's wedding. Hadn't planned to, either.

That night had been amazing, and yet she'd done everything possible to forget the guy's smile, his sexy, husky laugh, the fire of his touch on her skin, the feel of him over her, in her, taking her higher than she'd ever gone before. The man was dangerous to her in a way only one other man ever had been, and she refused to go down that road again.

The first week after the wedding, Merit had texted and left her a couple of messages. He said he wanted to see her again. Her heart had done a giddy little dance, but common sense reminded her she couldn't afford to let emotions overrule cold, hard facts. She had to keep a clear head for both herself and Ian.

Asher had made more than enough comments about his playboy younger brother. As the stories went, he was a one and done type of guy, and messages or not, leopards didn't change their spots. So, she'd ignored him, hoping he'd lose interest and move on to his next conquest.

The second week, he'd sent her one text and left one message. The third and fourth weeks, he was down to one text each week. Now it had been a month since the last time she'd heard from him, and with each week that had passed, she was convinced she'd been right to not respond. Clearly, one night with her hadn't magically changed the guy into someone worthy of dating and letting into her son's life.

Of course, him being the brother of her best friend's husband meant she'd run into him sometime in the future, but she'd figured she would deal with that when the time came.

Unfortunately, this morning, the future had arrived in the form of two pink lines.

You don't want to miss what happens when Mae tell's Merit he's going to be a dad, so mark your calendar now!

Love You, Baby releases Nov. 2019

About the Author

New York Times and *USA Today* bestselling author Stacey Joy Netzel always promises Happily Ever After in her books, but the journey to get there is going to one heck of an adventure! She lives in N.E. Wisconsin with her family, a horse and some cats. She writes steamy romantic suspense and small town contemporary romance with sexy, rugged heroes, and strong, resilient heroines. Colorado, Wisconsin, and Italy are favorite settings for her books, and she is a three time winner of Wisconsin Romance Writers' Write Touch Readers' Award.

Hearing from readers is a very special thing for any writer, so pop in and say "Hi!" at any of the below locations. And once again, reviews are always appreciated.

Thank you, and happy reading!
~Stacey~

www.StaceyJoyNetzel.com
http://smarturl.it/WebSJNNewsletter

facebook.com/StaceyJoyNetzel
twitter.com/StaceyJoyNetzel
bookbub.com/authors/BookBub